Captives
and Kings

Captives and Kings

CRAIG & JANET
PARSHALL

HARVEST HOUSE PUBLISHERS

EUGENE, OREGON

Unless otherwise indicated, all Scripture quotations have been taken from the Geneva Bible, originally published complete in 1560. The spelling has been modernized for inclusion in this book. An electronic transcription of the translation was used, courtesy of Jeff Garrison of StudyLight.org. Their online Bible resource site, which can be found at www.studylight.org, "is packed with the most Bibles and study resources found on the Net—everything needed to help you in your study of God's Word."

Verses marked NIV are taken from the HOLY BIBLE, NEW INTERNATIONAL VERSION®. NIV®. Copyright © 1973, 1978, 1984 by the International Bible Society. Used by permission of Zondervan. All rights reserved.

Scripture quotations not fully identified in the text are as follows:

Psalm 124:6-8	p. 26
James 4:13-15	p. 96
Psalm 84:3-4	p. 115
Psalm 23:1-3	p. 243

Cover by Left Coast Design, Portland, Oregon

Cover photo © VEER David Jordan Williams/Photonica/Getty Images

This is a work of fiction. Names, characters, places, and incidents are products of the author's imagination or are used fictitiously. Any resemblance to actual persons, living or dead, or to events or locales, is entirely coincidental.

CAPTIVES AND KINGS
Book 2 of the Thistle and the Cross series
Copyright © 2007 by Craig and Janet Parshall
Published by Harvest House Publishers
Eugene, Oregon 97402
www.harvesthousepublishers.com

Library of Congress Cataloging-in-Publication Data

Parshall, Craig, 1950-
  Captives and kings / Craig and Janet Parshall.
    p. cm. — (The thistle and the cross ; bk. 2)
  ISBN-13: 978-0-7369-1325-6 (pbk.)
  ISBN-10: 0-7369-1325-4 (pbk.)
  1. Great Britain—History—James I, 1603-1625—Fiction. 2. Scots—England—Fiction. 3. Catholics—England—Fiction. 4. Brothers—Fiction. 5. Jamestown (Va.)—Fiction. 6. Bible—Translating—Fiction. I. Parshall, Janet, 1950- II. Title.
  PS3616.A77C37 2007
  813'.54—dc22
                              2006025371

Printed in the United States of America
          07 08 09 10 11 12 13 14 15 / BC-CF / 10 9 8 7 6 5 4 3 2 1

*Even if you have been banished to the most distant
land under the heavens, from there the LORD your
God will gather you and bring you back...*

*Then the LORD your God will make you most prosperous in all the
work of your hands and in the fruit of your womb, the young of your
livestock and the crops of your land. The LORD will again delight in
you and make you prosperous, just as he delighted in your fathers.*

DEUTERONOMY 30:4,9 NIV

Chapter 1

On the night of Sunday, November 3, 1605
London, England

The fire in the fireplace of Whynniard House was burning low and collapsing into red, glowing embers. Sparks would occasionally hiss, pop, and dance up into the air. Gathered around the fire, the small band of conspirators were talking in tense, hushed voices. Each of them carefully read the faces of the others in the flickering light. Searching for signs of indecision. Or betrayal.

The rented house, situated next to the Parliament House at Westminster, was an ideal staging ground. The killing time was now only twenty-four hours away, and only a few details still remained.

Robert Catesby was taking the lead as usual. His eyes seemed to harbor some inner fire, but his voice was controlled and calm, exuding the same smooth, magnetic control that had drawn his followers to him. Though handsome, and known to be a fine soldier and horseman, his ultimate leadership quality was his willingness to risk death. And considering the task they were planning, self-sacrifice might be needed in great measure. Every one of them knew the consequences if they were caught—or if the plan failed.

"What about the powder?" Catesby asked. "Are we sure it is not spoiled again? Capable of detonating?"

"Without a doubt," Tom Wintour replied. "I checked it myself." The young man, able and of a strong inner constitution, was one whose pledge could be trusted.

"And what of the fuses? You were concerned about that." Catesby addressed the man seated across from him, leaning back in his straight-backed chair.

Guy Fawkes smiled confidently, even swaggeringly. Catesby had never liked that about him. But Fawkes's talents were unquestioned. As a mercenary soldier who had fought fiercely with the Spanish army against the English at Flanders, he had a reputation as a man of action who could carry out orders. Just as importantly, he hated the reign of the Protestants in England. He was a Catholic warrior of the faith. And Catesby knew that such a commitment of the soul was just as critical as the trained and honed abilities of the body.

"The fuses," Fawkes replied, "are at the ready."

"You said you tested the fuse lines and they didn't burn well enough…" Thomas Percy, the man responsible for renting the conspirators' house, spoke up.

"Not at first. So I nosed around for someone who might, perchance, know a good fuse from a bad one and I found such a man."

"You'd best be careful who you are dealing with," Jack Wright, Percy's brother-in-law, exclaimed in a hoarse whisper.

"Not to worry," Fawkes assured him. "I bought them through a Scotsman here in London, an adventurer and soldier. He led me to a fuse-maker."

"Name," Catesby said. "What is the Scotsman's name?"

"Philip…Mackenzie, I believe his name is. Just another ignorant Scotsman…but I do believe he knew something of fuses!"

A rude chuckle broke out among the group.

But Thomas Percy was not laughing with the rest. In the past he had been an emissary to James VI when he was King of Scotland. James had been biding his time, waiting for the aged Queen Elizabeth of England to die so he could claim the thrones in both Edinburgh in the north and London in the south.

Percy's mission to Scotland had been to garner favor with James toward the Catholic cause. The Scottish Reformation, led by men like John Knox, had effectively made Scotland a Protestant nation. But some had hoped that James, whose mother was the ill-fated but thoroughly Catholic Mary, Queen of Scots, might possess some hidden sympathies toward the Vatican.

But Percy's venture had not succeeded. James made some genteel gestures of tolerance toward Catholics, but he stopped far short of any agreement to roll back the victories won by the reformers. And he deliberately failed to put any of his pronouncements into writing. And now that he was securely seated on the throne of England, he had conveniently, so it seemed, forgotten his vague indications of friendship toward the Catholics.

"As you all know"—Percy spoke with an air of self-importance—"I know something of the Scots and of Scotland. I traveled extensively there. And grew to know the names of the most hateful of the Protestant heretics. One of them being John Knox, yes. But he had a confidant—a legal advisor—who, I believe, was named Mackenzie. Ransom Mackenzie. He is alive still, I think. Though very old by now."

"This man is not of the same family, I am sure of it," Fawkes replied. "Trust me…this filthy Scot I speak of is a brawling, cursing, drinking man. Not like those dour reformers. No—this Mackenzie seems to care little for God. He'll be no problem for us."

Catesby searched Fawkes's eyes. "Let us hope not," he added. "The future of the Holy Roman Church and the rule of the righteous here in England are at stake. We cannot—must not fail."

Suddenly there was a knock at the door.

"That must be our priest," Catesby said. "We have need to be sanctified by the Holy Church before our awesome deed. Unlock the door. Let him in."

Chapter 2

In the fashionable Blackfriars section of London, Andrew Mackenzie and his family had settled into the privileged life of those who enjoyed close contact with the Crown of England. When James was elevated to monarch of England, he brought with him to Court a parade of Scotsmen as his counselors and advisors. Andrew, no stranger to the Court in Edinburgh, was one of them. He had followed the footsteps of his father, Ransom, who had been a protégé of the reformer John Knox, then a professor of law and theology in St. Andrews, and in his later years confidant to the newly reformed Church of England.

But along with Andrew's promotion, throughout London and within certain corridors at Hampton Court where he labored as well, came a simmering distrust—even hatred—for the Scots who had come down from the north and now inhabited much of London. Thugs and bullies, the swaggerers of the East End, often targeted the unwary who were new to London as potential victims, sometimes to simply pick their pockets or rob them at knifepoint. Occasionally, though, the body of a murdered Scot would turn up on the cobblestone streets. London, though it held much promise for Andrew, was still a dangerous place.

As a member of James' religious council, Andrew was but a middle-level associate to the Crown. He hardly ever had access to even Robert Cecil, chief advisor to the king, let alone the king himself, except on ceremonial occasions—or when he and other lawyers and theologians gathered to meet at one of the palaces. Yet his move from wild Scotland to the more placid pastures of England meant significant change and opportunity for Andrew and his family.

That morning as he waited in their home's dining hall, his wife, Kate, and her cook, Bessy, were fixing a large Scottish breakfast for him: fish, buns, porridge. Working alongside the two women was Alice, the daughter of Andrew and Kate, a pretty seventeen-year-old girl with flaxen hair. But Alice stood motionless, looking out the window. Her gaze was fixed on some point far beyond the kitchen—even far away from Blackfriars, for that matter.

"Alice," Kate snapped, "ye're daydreamin' again. Will ye not help us here?"

Alice turned slowly, giving her mother a look of total bewilderment.

"Oh, for heaven's sakes, child," Kate said, "take yourself upstairs and see to the maids there. Some day for sure you'll be runnin' your own household. Let this be the practice for it."

"Perhaps," Alice gave her mother a half-glance, "the man I decide to love will not have a household like this. What of it? Perhaps we'll ride off on horses. And sleep under the moonlight together. With a life of traveling and adventure. What would be so bad about that?"

Kate walked up close and lowered her voice, so Andrew could not hear it.

"That talk is foolishness. Ye're sounding like your Uncle Philip now. May God grant you some wisdom in yer womanhood, young lady."

Then she looked deep into her daughter's eyes.

"Who is it," she asked quietly but firmly, holding Alice's arm, "that you been seein', my daughter? Who's caught yer fancy? Have you been keepin' company with a man?"

Anger flashed in Alice's eyes. She pulled away from her mother's grip and stomped up the back stairs to the upstairs rooms.

"This house is a prison!" she said tearfully, and disappeared up the staircase.

Kate sighed, and then took a steaming cup of coffee into the dining hall, where Andrew was now sitting alone at the table. At first he seemed to not even notice his wife. He was only picking at his food and gazing off into space.

On balance, Andrew was an even-natured man. But he was prone to bouts of pensiveness, even melancholy. In his intellectual prowess and moods, he was like his father, Ransom. But there was also a stubborn and resilient side too. That, undoubtedly, he had inherited from his mother, Margaret, who had grown up in the untamed regions of the northern Highlands.

"Andrew, you're not eating," Kate said, trying to broach the subject with her husband.

"What?" Andrew replied, with an air of distraction.

"Yer breakfast. Do ye not like it, my dear?"

"Oh, yes. Thought I'd be hungry...perhaps not..."

"Honestly, Andrew," Kate said. "This house has been inhabited by daydreamers. First Alice, and now you. What is it that's on your mind?"

Andrew pushed the pewter plate away from him.

"I received a letter from Jean..."

"Jean? Your father's housekeeper?"

"The same," Andrew answered. "She and her sister are concerned about father's health. His inactivity. Oh yes, he does preach once in a while there in St. Andrews. Gives a guest lecture or two at the university. But mostly he putters around the house. Sits on the stone bench in the back and stares out at the sea."

"Well, if I may say," Kate tried to be diplomatic, "your father helped spark a spiritual revolution in Scotland. He's preached the gospel over the countryside and advised the lawmakers in Edinburgh. Now he's buried a wife. Perhaps the Lord is simply giving him a rest."

Andrew was in no mood to agree. But he knew there was truth in what his wife said. He had heard all the stories about his father's work during the turbulent years leading up to the violent showdown with the French-backed armies of Queen Mother Marie de Guise. Jean Macleod, his old friend and housekeeper, always called him "the second greatest man of all Scotland"—second only to John Knox himself. His father had crammed several lifetimes into his seventy-three years. His friends would often say, "The Lord has granted him exceedingly long life—because of all his faithfulness."

"Perhaps I worry too much," Andrew said. "But I must travel north to see him soon…it's been too long."

"Aye. Too long," Kate repeated.

"But the press of business here at Court…our work on the union of the crowns…"

Kate smiled ruefully. That had been an oft-repeated phrase in their household. Andrew was part of the council assisting the great lawyer Thomas Craig of Riccarton. Craig had been brought down from Edinburgh at King James' request to study the legalities of merging the two kingdoms, England and Scotland, under one unified rule. Of course Scotland shared James as king with her richer, more powerful neighbor to the south. But the two nations still labored clumsily as separate bodies politic.

"So much to do at Court," Andrew mused absently, looking out through the windows of their estate house to the tree-lined streets beyond.

"There'll always be work, and business, and more of it than hours in the day," Kate said with a smile. "But you have only one father."

"Aye. 'Tis true…but it would help if the burden were not on me alone."

Kate rolled her eyes as she cleared the table. She knew what was coming next.

"If only my brother—"

"I don't think he's about to change natures," Kate responded quietly. "A leopard keeps its spots. And Philip will always be, I fear, a man with a wandering heart—"

"Then let his heart wander all it wants. It's his feet and hands I crave!" Andrew said with a sudden burst of anger. "He neglects his father. Shows no honor to him. And gives me no help on that account."

Kate wiped her hands on the baking towel around her waist. She walked over to her husband and put her hand gently on his shoulder.

"When did ye last talk to Philip?"

"Can't remember, it's been so long." Andrew shook his head. "But I've heard about him. In abundance. Rumors. Gossip. 'Andrew, was that your brother I heard about at the Boar's Head Tavern, fighting and brawling?' 'Andrew, what is this I hear of your brother trying to work his way into the Virginia Company and go to the New World?' I would have thought that after Philip had lost his goodwife, perhaps that would have slowed him down. That eventually he would have settled into some kind of respectability."

"Do ye know where Philip's settled now?"

"No. I think he and Peter are living in rented quarters in London somewhere."

"Peter's a good lad."

"Aye. But he'll grow to be as wild as his father I fear," Andrew snapped back.

Then his face grew exceedingly grim.

"And there have been other tales..."

Kate studied her husband's face. "Like what?"

"About some of his associates. Men of low character. Criminal types. I fear he may be frequenting very...sinister and dangerous circles."

He stopped there. Even to his own wife, he dared not speak of what he dreaded most.

So he rose abruptly, gave his wife a quick kiss, and then walked out of the house to his waiting carriage.

Chapter 3

In the crowded London tavern, a crowd of shouting men, most of them intoxicated, were gathered in a large circle. Several of them were betting on the outcome of a two-man contest in the middle of the room.

A Scotsman of medium height but muscular build, with long red hair and a short trimmed beard, was grunting as he struggled against his opponent. He was dressed well, better than most of the laborers who populated the tavern. His black, brocaded waistcoat was open at the chest.

The other man, Jacko Mundy, a huge, bald Englishman with an unshaven face and several missing teeth, wore a leather tanner's apron and a sleeveless shirt that showed his thick, hairy arms.

The two men were lined up side-by-side, each with left hand behind their back and right hand upright, locked in a grip so violent that the veins in the tops of their hands were bulging out.

"Send him over, Jacko boy!" several drunken East-Enders were yelling.

"Hold, Philip, hold fast!" a few Scots in the crowd were screaming at the smaller of the two men.

Philip Mackenzie's face was twisted in a desperate grimace. The Englishman, thinking the competition was nearly over—and was his for the winning—bared his broken, blackened teeth in a fiendish grin designed to mock his opponent.

The big Englishman began bending Philip backward in a final sweating effort. His greater bulk seemed to be winning the day. The cheers and screams from the Londoners were growing into a frenzied celebration.

But then something happened.

Philip had slightly wedged his boot behind the shoe of the other, creating a pivot. Then he ducked his head forward, then quickly to the side—the big Englishman was caught off balance as he thrust all his strength to counteract Philip's fake. Philip buckled his knees slightly, lowering himself, and flipped the huge man back over his planted boot.

The Englishman landed flat on his back with a thud so powerful that it rocked the timbers of the building. The Scotsmen in the crowd screamed and leaped up and down in the air. A few fists started flying. But before a full-scale melee could break out, the proprietor and his two barkeeps leaped into the crowd with their clubs.

"All bets settled now—good and proper!" the proprietor yelled, separating a few of the sparring men. "And hands at your sides, or we'll send you all to God's own judgment—and don't think we won't!"

There were a few threats and counterthreats. But after a few moments, money started exchanging hands. Philip offered a hand to Jacko Mundy, but the big tanner leaped to his feet and slapped it away.

"I'll not touch you again, you filthy Scot," Mundy growled. "Except to let my skinnin' knife clean you inside from out…"

"That's enough, Jacko," the proprietor snapped. "Have a pint, and then get home with you!"

Mundy was giving Philip a bone-chilling stare. But his friends pulled him away to where drinks were being poured into tankards out of a large wooden bucket.

Philip was collecting his winnings from the gamblers when his son, Peter, who had been watching from the corner, came over.

Peter, slightly taller than his father and a bit leaner, had his father's red hair.

"We'll be eatin' like kings for a while now!" Philip said, flashing the pile of pound notes he had just won.

But Peter was silent—as always slightly embarrassed at his father's wild extravagances. Just as he was, in almost equal measure, a little in awe of him as well.

At Peter's age, just twenty years old, Philip had already left England against his father's protestations and shipped out aboard the four-master of Sir Richard Granville. With the famous explorer, he landed at what would become the crude settlement called Roanoke Island in the New World. The voyage changed Philip's life, and it fueled his insatiable lust for adventure. And it planted deep within, the desire to cross the ocean again back to the New World, with its savage Indians and vast, uncharted forests and rivers.

As father and son walked through the narrow, muddy streets and dodged carriages and carts pushed by merchants, Philip was eying his son.

"I suppose," he said, breaking the silence, "you'd like to know how I beat that brute."

"I would," Philip said quietly. "He was bigger than you—"

"Aye. And stronger too."

"Then how?"

"Balance. All a matter of balance. I'll give the other man the strength and size—if I can keep the power of balance, and add to that the advantage of surprise."

"Where'd you learn that?"

"I remember your grandda Ransom telling me how he used the same thing when he was a lad. When he was staying up in the Highlands and was set on by a group of bullies—"

Peter chuckled.

"You think it's funny?"

"No. Just that I can't imagine...Grandda Ransom—"

"As a fightin' man, you mean?" Philip asked.

His son nodded.

"Then ye're not recollectin' how, once in Edinburgh he killed a French soldier of Marie de Guise, who had a sword to the throat of your Grandma Margaret."

Peter's eyes widened.

"Remember the story? Your grandda took out his sword, came up to the Frenchman from behind—and ran him clean through, from stem to stern. Left him dead there on the stones of the street. Saved my mother, he did. All that was way before I was born."

They stopped at the doorway to the staircase that led up to their rented rooms.

Philip noticed a man lurking in a dark doorway down the street. The other man gave a quick gesture with his hand. Philip turned to his son.

"Ye go up ahead. Start a meal for us. I'll be right along."

After Peter had disappeared up the stairs, Philip turned. Then he slowly approached the man who was waiting for him in the shadows.

Chapter 4

By the time Andrew's carriage had reached the Palace at White-hall, most of the Privy Council, as well as the legal and religious committees of which he was a member, were already there, murmuring in the corridors in diplomatic whispers and nods, awaiting word of the appearance of King James in the Great Hall.

Andrew considered the gathering to be mainly ceremonial. The opening of Parliament at Winchester was to take place the next day, so today the members of Court were to hear of the agenda for the opening.

Tomorrow the king would be joined by his two young sons, Henry and Charles, his daughter Elizabeth, and his wife, Queen Anne. Though fears of anti-Protestant conspiracies and plots against the rule of King James continued to be whispered around the halls of the Court, no one had raised objections to the whole royal family being so conspicuously present at such a public occasion.

As Andrew and the other members of the councils and committees were milling around in the corridors, the king was in the quiet inner chamber of the palace, leaning forward in his chair, gripping his thin hands together, and listening to the counsel of his most trusted advisor and protector—Robert Cecil, Earl of Salisbury.

Cecil was small and slightly bent. His disability caused him to walk with a limp. He had a broad forehead and piercing eyes, with an immaculately trimmed beard. He had the air of an intellectual, but he also had a ruthless sense of political survival, both for himself and for his king.

James' face was drawn and intense, his eyes wide, flitting here and there as he sat riveted to Cecil's words.

"Your Majesty," the counselor said softly but with a sense of urgency that James rarely heard from him, "there is the matter of this letter."

"Yes—the letter," James said quickly, reaching out toward the document in Cecil's hand. His advisor quickly stepped over, gave a discreet bow, and let him take it. Cecil noticed the monarch's hand was trembling.

"And this letter…was *anonymous?*" the king asked, scanning its contents.

"Indeed."

"And delivered surreptitiously to Lord Monteagle?"

"That appears to be the state of affairs."

"Is there any question of Lord Monteagle's complicity in…some manner of plot?" The King waved the letter.

"Highly doubtful, Your Majesty."

"And why do you deduce no possible taint against Monteagle?"

"Because, Your Majesty," Cecil explained calmly, "it was he who brought this letter to my attention. He rode hard all the way to my house at Whitehall. Delivered it to me personally. On the very same day his servant gave it to him…"

"And the servant had been approached by a stranger," James recounted, making sure he had possession of all the facts, "by some man walking in the shadows of the streets of London, who thrust the letter in his hand and instructed him to take it to his master?"

"Quite correct," Cecil said smiling. "Your Majesty, as always, has a quick grasp of the details at hand."

"Then," James said, handing the letter back, "there is the matter of the *interpretation* of the letter's message."

Cecil held the letter up, studied it, and then lowered it. "In my humble opinion," he said, "it clearly warns Lord Monteagle not to attend the opening of Parliament. That much is certain."

"Quite so, quite so," the king murmured.

"But why?" Cecil asked—rhetorically, for he already had an idea in his mind that could easily answer that question.

"It would appear," he continued, "that the words, 'God and man hath concurred to punish the wickedness of this time,' refer to a catastrophic event. A most horrible occurrence that is about to take place."

"Yes, indeed," James agreed quickly. "But by what device? What dark and evil artifice?"

"Let us consider these words also." Cecil pointed to a line in the letter with his finger. "*For though there be no appearance of any stir, yet I say they shall receive a terrible blow this Parliament; and they shall not see who hurts them.*"

"A most troubling...and intriguing turn of language," James said, eyeing Cecil.

"And by its meaning," Cecil said, wrinkling his brow, which brought his thin eyebrows down close to his eyes, "I gather that the attack—if an attack this be—will not be in the form of ambush, or by an assassin's knife, or gun, nor arrow—"

"For if it were," James said, interrupting, "then the victims would see 'who hurts them,' as such an attack would be from close range. Yet the letter says that such will not be."

"And further," Cecil added, his voice now in a hoarse whisper, "if that be the mode of attack, then no need for others to flee far away from the Parliament building to save themselves."

There was a silence for a few long seconds.

"Your Majesty," Cecil intoned somberly, "my mind is aflame with a single thought. That the most deadly and foretelling words in all this letter are these—"

With that he nodded his head slightly, moved delicately around next to the king, and pointed to the words, "terrible blow this Parliament."

James stared at the words just above the index finger of his chief counselor, then looked up into his eyes.

Cecil knew this was the time to act. And that the king would follow his admonitions without mental reservation.

"Your Majesty," Cecil said with steel in his voice, "we must commence a search. No stone unturned. No person beyond suspicion. A search that is relentless and complete—until the dark identity of these evil plotters is fully uncovered."

The king nodded eagerly. Then Cecil repeated his admonition.

"No one above suspicion..."

"Indeed," James said, narrowing his eyes to scan each word of the letter carefully. "No one."

Chapter 5

The meeting with King James that Andrew and the other Court officials had anticipated that day did not occur. Immediately there were whispers of some grave threat afoot.

Andrew caught sight of Thomas Craig, his senior master on the legal committee.

"Mister Craig," he called out.

Craig approached with a stern look.

"Are we dismissed today without a meeting with His Majesty?"

"Aye, 'tis true," Craig said quietly. "There appears to be some consternation…about tomorrow's opening of Parliament."

"Consternation? Of what manner?"

Craig glanced around and then took Andrew over to a corner. He placed him right up against a cold stone wall of the palace. "Ye shall not repeat this," he said under his breath. "But a grand search is under way at this very moment."

"Search for what?"

"I dunna know that. But I have the strongest belief it may involve a dastardly Papist plot against the Crown."

"And yet," Andrew said, shaking his head, "our James has been the most benevolent king toward the Catholics in this land, even though he is aligned with the Reformed religion of Christ."

"Aye, but there are those, Andrew, who have been lying in wait for years. Appeased by nothing. Willing to kill at all costs just to restore Catholic rule in the land."

The renowned lawyer glanced around one more time. Then he gave a parting warning to his protégé.

"And dinna forget this," he said in a low voice. "While it may be that it is indeed the Catholics who are in the very muscle and sweat of today's fearful plot... we—you and I, man—Scots brave and true from Scotland as we are—are still hated here in England. And if a plot against the Crown is discovered...then mind your head. And mind your family. For there's no tellin' where the blade will fall, or who the rack will twist and break."

Filled with foreboding, Andrew prepared to return home to his dear Kate and Alice as quickly as possible and there await further news. So he called for his carriage and, with the help of the palace footmen, climbed in and then began the hour-long ride back to Blackfriars. As he did, he prayed out loud for God to quash any evil plans against the king and foil any plans that would stifle the spread of the gospel throughout England. And then he spoke the words of the Psalmist:

> *Praised be the Lord,*
> *Which hath not given us as a prey unto their teeth.*
> *Our soul is escaped, even as a bird out of the snare*
> *   of the fowlers:*
> *The snare is broken, and we are delivered.*
> *Our help is in the Name of the Lord,*
> *Which hath made heaven and earth.*

Back at the palace, several advisors, including Robert Cecil, were reporting to the king.

Lord Suffolk, as acting lord chamberlain, was the first to speak.

"Your Majesty," he began with a slight hesitation. "It is my duty to report to you the fruits of our searches...the results, sire, of our preliminary search."

"Get on with it," James said sternly. "What did you find?"

"Well, we engaged a number of the palace guards and did a thorough review of the rooms of this palace, Your Majesty. And of the surrounding grounds. We sent men over to Westminster also and searched the main rooms of Parliament. We have made inquiry of all those coming and going in both places."

"And?" the king said, his voice strained with urgency.

"We found nothing."

"Nothing?" James shook his head in disbelief.

"No sign of danger or threat, Your Majesty."

There was an awkward silence. The king glanced over at Cecil. After all, it was he who had interpreted the letter to Lord Monteagle as foreboding some disaster on the opening day of Parliament.

"What say you?" James asked of Cecil, his face tightening.

"With due respect to Lord Suffolk, Your Majesty," the counselor replied calmly, "I think that a further, and more extensive, search may be in order."

"Do you doubt my competency?" Suffolk bellowed.

"No, sir," Cecil countered adroitly, "only your results. I am confident there is a murderous plot afoot. If it has not been found out, it is simply because the correct investigation has not been attempted."

Cecil turned back to the king.

"Your Majesty, may I speak to you privately?"

The king nodded and dismissed the other members of the group with a wave of his hand. When they had gone, Cecil confided his plan to the king.

"I recommend that we engage in a second search of the Parliament building."

"Well, I will tell you this," the king said with irritation in his voice, "either a full search be done, good sir, or else I will simply present myself at Parliament on the morrow—and leave my life, my reign over England, and all else to the fortunes of heaven."

"Why not both?" Cecil said. "A more thorough search—which in turn, I would wager, will fulfill the divine fortunes of God's scheme for your continued rule in England."

"How should we proceed?"

"I suggest we employ Sir Thomas Knyvett. He is a trusted member of Your Majesty's Privy Council. He is also justice of the peace for Westminster and knows the building and grounds well. He will retain some skillful investigators to help him."

"What more do you propose to investigate?"

"Suffolk mentioned a small fact to me, Your Majesty. That upon their first search of the cellar, they noticed a large supply of kindling wood."

"Why is that unusual?"

"Only in this," Cecil replied. "That the apartment adjoining that cellar—the space, by the by, that lies underneath Parliament itself—is quite small. If that is so, then why the need for such a large supply of wood?"

The king nodded. In an instant, Cecil bowed and scurried off to secure Sir Thomas Knyvett.

By the time Cecil was meeting with Knyvett, Andrew had reached home. But he had hardly dismounted from the carriage when Kate hurried out of the front door toward him.

Her face betrayed the fear only mothers can fully comprehend.

"What is it, for pity's sake?" Andrew asked, trying to calm her.

"'Tis Alice," she said, breathless and panting.

"What of her?" Andrew demanded.

"She's gone missing."

Chapter 6

In Staffordshire, a far distance from the mad scurry at Westminster, where the king's men were searching high and low, a gentleman paced about in the grand rooms of Holbeach House, his country mansion. Stephen Littleton had been a latecomer to the plans of Catesby, Wintour, Fawkes, Percy, and the others to destroy the rule of King James in one terrible explosion.

Yet the part Littleton was prepared to play was significant.

His house was capable of strong fortifications. Catesby had planned that if anything went amiss, or if, despite the destruction of Parliament, the king still managed to survive and the rebellion failed, the rebels would then retreat to Holbeach House. They could hold off the royal forces long enough then, hopefully, to rally support from local Catholics. And just as John Knox and the Protestant rebels had been successful, at least for many months, in holding the castle at St. Andrews decades before, so the Catholics would hold Holbeach House as their command post.

But the Catholics would be victorious where the Protestant rebels of St. Andrews had failed. This time, Catesby hoped, the papal supporters would hold Holbeach House long enough to summon and receive help from Spain. Surely, they surmised, Spain would then make good on her implied promises to come to the aid of the English Catholics.

But all of that was wanton speculation, and Catesby knew it. What he and the other plotters really hoped for was a detonation beneath the Parliament building that would be so cataclysmic and effective that the Protestant government of James would be crushed in one single terrifying moment. Backup plans, such as a retreat to Holbeach House, were not on their minds on November 5, 1605. Instead, most of them were in London making ready their last, fateful preparations.

But Littleton and his household staff were not. They were at Holbeach House.

In the stable, a young groom named Gideon Grove was brushing down one of Littleton's mares. But every minute or so he would stop, listen, and then survey the large area to see if anyone had arrived.

Not yet, he thought to himself. *Not yet here. Will it ever happen?*

He nervously looked down the long array of stalls again, to the opening at the other end. The sun was setting. Still, no sign of his visitor.

He poured grain into the trough, then ran his hand lovingly along the smooth neck of the mare.

Then a sound. He whirled around. He saw no one.

"Who's there?" he called out.

No answer. So he called out again.

"This is Gideon Grove...the groom of this stable...who goes there?"

For a moment there was more silence. And then a voice, light and musical, rang out.

"It is Alice Mackenzie—who is in love with the groom of this stable!"

Alice popped out of one of the empty stalls, laughing. She was dressed as a young man, her head covered in a cap and her hair pulled up under it, and she was wearing one of her father's cast-off coats.

"Would you take me for a man?" she said, running up to Gideon.

"I would take you as a lovely woman," he said, gathering her up in his arms, "trying to play the man—and not very convincing at that."

Alice laughed and pushed him back. "I will have you know that my grandma Margaret Mackenzie escaped detection from the French soldiers in Edinburgh by this very device!" she said proudly.

Gideon motioned for her to come to him. He kissed her hard on the lips, stroked her face, and then asked her to sit on a large bucket that had been turned upside-down.

"I have something to tell you." Suddenly his voice was somber.

He knelt in front of Alice and reached out and held both of her hands.

"There are plans now being made," he said, "that will change much in England. My employer, Master Littleton, has no small part in that."

"What do I care for England," Alice said playfully, "when I have you? You, dear Gideon, shall be my nation and my home. My family and my everything—"

"No, Alice," the groom replied intensely. "You don't understand. These things that will soon take place will change things for *us*…for everyone. It may not be safe for you to stay here."

"I don't understand."

"And I, too, do not fully understand all that is being planned," he said with passion in his voice. "But this much I know, that your life may be endangered if you tarry with me too long. I have overheard bits and pieces…Alice, there may be a revolution in the making. Even as we speak."

"I've run away from my home. My family," Alice said, suddenly tearing up as she began to understand the grave stakes. "All for you. For us. Why don't we both leave this place? Now. Leave together."

"That I cannot do," Gideon said, shaking his head.

"But why not?" Alice pleaded.

"Because Master Littleton has taken me in for these last four years, since my parents died. Without his help, I do not know how I would have survived. I have pledged my loyalty to him. I care not for this religious war. Or for matters of faith that are lighting a fire of revolution in this land. But I do care for my honor."

"Gideon…you speak as if you take no care whatever for God. I thought you told me," Alice said, stunned, "you would join the reformed church of England once we were married."

Gideon was looking around nervously.

"This is not the time to debate religion. Or anything else. Night will soon be falling, dear Alice. There is a spare room on the first floor of the main house next to the cook's quarters. You can sleep there tonight. But *on the morrow,* you must leave this place."

"On the morrow," Alice said, taking his hands and kissing them, "we shall see…"

Chapter 7

It was early evening, and Guy Fawkes was meeting with Robert Keyes, a member of the outer ring of the conspirators—those who had joined the plot later than most. They huddled together in the rented house of Thomas Percy. It was situated next to Westminster, and possessed critical access to the cellar that ran beneath Parliament house.

The two men had received word from their spies that the entourage from Lord Suffolk had walked through the cellar earlier that day. The group had stopped only momentarily before the large pile of wood closing off the opening of one of the larger cellar vaults. That vault lay directly beneath the House of Lords, where the king, and his family, and members of Parliament were to gather at noon on the following day.

None of Suffolk's men had bothered to peer behind the woodpile. The plot was still on schedule. And the plotters, and their deadly scheme, were still undetected.

The room was dark, except for a single candle on the floor. And as the men spoke in tense, muffled voices, they spoke to each other mostly in shadows—one dark figure speaking plans of murder and mayhem to another dark figure.

"Here's yer watch," Keyes said as he handed a timepiece to

Fawkes. "It's been set to the exact time as the pieces of all of us. When the time strikes the top of the hour at the opening of Parliament, you'll light your fuses. How much time will you have?"

"Ten minutes," Fawkes said. "I've timed the fuses thrice. Measured the lengths. They should give me goodly time to get out and down the street."

"It'll be a bloody terror," Keyes said. "Flesh blown to the sky. Showers of stone. Smoke, fire, and horror. God's judgment for sure. Doubtful that anyone will notice you running away."

Fawkes nodded. As a mercenary soldier who had fought under several different flags, he knew well that once the battle began, confusion would reign. Nothing was fully predictable. All of the well-honed military strategies would have to make way for improvisation and quick thinking—and most of all, cold-blooded singleness of purpose.

"And the little princess?" he asked.

Keyes knew what he meant.

"Yes," he replied. "Our maiden in the palace is prepared. She'll make up a convenient reason for the princess to stay behind—saying that she is flush with a fever, perhaps, and cannot attend the opening. When the explosion occurs, the princess Elizabeth will be taken to a safe house in the country. We'll make her our puppet queen, with the full power of the papacy and Spain behind her. With us pulling the strings, of course."

Fawkes stood up and donned a long, dark riding coat and wide brimmed hat. He pocketed the watch.

"We are soldiers of God," he announced. "We destroy for His glory."

"For His glory," Keyes repeated.

"The next time you see me," Fawkes said, "the revolution will have begun."

The two men clasped hands. Fawkes turned and quickly disappeared through the unlighted doorway.

He made his way down the steps to the ground floor and then opened the cellar door after lighting a small candle lamp and carrying with him an oil lamp as well.

He walked slowly down the black, open throat of the cavernous cellar. He peered into each vault, left and right, left and right, lifting his candle to check for unwelcome visitors.

But he found none. And he smiled at that.

Confident he was alone, he approached the vault blocked by the woodpile and started to stack the wood off to the side. After about thirty minutes, the wood was cleared and the contents of the vault were revealed.

There before him were twenty-six barrels of gunpowder, all stacked together. Fawkes uncoiled the ropes of fuse from inside his long coat—lengths of fuse purchased from the most skilled fuse-maker in London—and began to cut them into twenty-six short lengths. These he attached to a small hole in the side of each of the barrels. Then he spliced the fuses together, connecting them to a longer fuse, which he laid along the length of the cellar.

About fourteen hours from now, according to the plan, he would check the time on his watch. Then he would walk to the end of the fuse…twenty feet from the door to the cellar. He would set his slow-burning oil lamp on the floor and would lower the fuse end to the flame.

And he would see the fuse begin to spark and spit and burn, run out of the cellar and up the stairs, and reach the outside, where the city of London would be going about its daily business.

All but Fawkes and the others in the handful of collaborators would be unaware that death and destruction were about to be visited upon the Crown of England.

So simple, Fawkes mused to himself as he settled down against the barrels and prepared for the long night. *Just a matter of black powder...and a few lengths of the right quality of fuse.*

Fuse that had been carefully purchased by the conspirators—selected on the advice given to them by Philip Mackenzie.

Chapter 8

Andrew and Kate Mackenzie had frantically searched their lavish home, but they could not find Alice. They were certain she had left. None of the servants had seen her go. But Kate found some of her clothes missing, along with her travel bag, the one brocaded in gold, black, and red. And her spotted pony was also gone from the stable.

That night, each member of the household staff was separately paraded into the oak-paneled library. They knew that whenever they were spoken to by the master of the house in the library, that sober matters were afoot. On this occasion, the matters at hand were exceptionally serious.

Each of the servants was individually interrogated by Andrew.

Finally, Andrew uncovered the truth from one of the servant girls.

"What about the trips to Staffordshire?" Andrew asked in a stern voice.

"It's just that when the mistress asked that Miss Alice come along with me—"

"Yes? What about it?"

"Well," the girl stammered, "it's that...please excuse my manner of addressing such a delicate matter, sir—"

"Out with it!" Andrew bellowed.

"Mistress Alice...she went on the trips to oversee my buying of the household linens...she carrying the household purse and all because Mrs. Mackenzie wasn't able to attend to it herself...and on each trip she excused herself and left me alone in the town for hours on end..."

Andrew sensed he was getting to the truth. So, in lawyerly fashion, he lowered his voice, smiled, and spoke in a reassuring way.

"And what did she do, my dear? Where did she go on those occasions when she excused herself?"

"Where she went, I am not sure," the girl said, "but I do know she met a man..."

"A man?"

"Yes, a young man. Handsome he was. Looked a wee mite older than Miss Alice."

"The same man," Andrew asked, "on each occasion?"

"Yes, sir. It's the truth, sure as I'm standing here."

"Did they appear to be...familiar?" Andrew asked quietly.

"Pardon my sayin' so, sir, but they did seem most familiar—"

"When they were together, did it seem they were...cavorting... frolicking...together?"

"In a manner of speaking," she said, lowering her head and staring at the Persian rug on the floor, "that is what they were doing...most familiar indeed..."

Andrew probed more, asking whether she knew where the young man worked. Who his family might be. What household he was attached to. But she couldn't venture a guess at any of his final questions.

"Thank you," Andrew said, reaching out to shake the girl's hand.

The servant girl was taken aback by the master's unusually informal gesture.

She quickly shook his hand, curtsied, adjusted her bonnet, and then scurried out of the library.

Kate had buried herself in the master suite on the top level of the house. She was sitting in a soft chair in an unlighted corner of the bedroom. A fire, the only light in the room, crackled in the fireplace, casting flickering images on the walls. Andrew entered the room, searching for a few seconds before he could locate his wife. He approached her, took her hands, and kissed them.

He softly explained what he had learned from the servants.

"She's left for a man," Kate said in a voice filled with misery. "I knew it. I had the feeling all along…"

"How could you have known?" Andrew said, trying to assuage her guilt and remorse.

"I knew it in my heart…and so did you," she said weeping. "She was wandering off from us…finding a man…with no thought of propriety or respect to her mother and father…heaven only knows who this man might be. What dangers he may expose her to. What ruin he might bring to her life—"

"I must assure you, dear," Andrew said a little defensively, "there was not a thought in my mind that she had been bewitched. Lovestruck by some stranger…And the fact that this mysterious man would not have come to me as her father first…to present himself. For permission to call on my daughter.…"

But Kate was mired in her brokenheartedness. In her pain, she cared little for her husband's focus on how his fatherly authority had been bruised.

"You should have known, Andrew. It is your duty...as it was mine." She covered her forehead with her hand. "And I knew it in my bones—the Lord was whispering to me to mind my baby chick..."

But now Andrew's desire to comfort his wife was displaced by a rising anger.

"If you had such a feeling, then why didn't you stop her?" he demanded. "Good heavens, woman—she is your daughter!"

"As you are her father!" Kate said through her weeping. "Forever spoiling the child. Always doting on her...Oh, Andrew...what has she done? And what will we do now?"

But Andrew had been unable to determine the identity of the young man or his household. And Staffordshire was a wide area. He was at a loss to promise his wife very much.

"I will have to wait till dawn tomorrow." The night by then was inching toward midnight.

Andrew put on his nightshirt silently. Kate put on her nightgown in the dressing room. Both of them sank into the canopy bed.

"And then tomorrow," Andrew said, struggling for a sense of confidence, "I shall ride to Staffordshire and make inquires."

He knew he was to be at Westminster the following day for the opening of the Parliament, though the exact time of the ceremony was now being kept a secret by King James' advisors and would be revealed only at the last minute. But he had no intention of attending. He would set out to find his daughter. And bring her home. And bring her to her senses.

"Please find her," Kate said tearfully. "Find her no matter what."

"I pledge you my life and my soul," Andrew said, reaching out to hold her hand, "that I shall find her."

Chapter 9

Peter Mackenzie was waiting outside of the tavern on the street. It was nearly midnight. Inside, his father, Philip, was finishing what he had only described to his son as his "delicate business" which was being conducted after hours in the closed tavern.

But the young man had overheard his father's "business" conversations recently. He guessed, with some measure of confidence, that his father was collecting money owed him by a local merchant who had lost several bear-bating and gambling bets.

But Peter's mind was off from his father's shadowy enterprises. In his memory he was rehearsing the first of his several encounters with a young woman named Rose Heatherton. The dark-haired beauty had been wearing a gold-braided headpiece and a burgundy velvet dress and had been with her older brother. Peter first saw her in the London mapping and survey office where he and his father had been employed. Where he was apprenticed in the mapmaking craft with his father.

The owner of the establishment had been impressed by Philip's range of experience in mapping uncharted land—first on his voyage to the New World at Roanoke Island with the Granville expedition—and then after his return, the more civilized and pedestrian work in the English countryside. So he took on both Philip and his son, Peter.

But Philip was visibly bored with surveying and mapping land charters for rich English gentry. So, as soon as Peter was ably trained, Philip turned most of the mundane work of the shop over to his son while he slipped away to the less genteel corners of London for gambling, bartering, and conversing with rough adventurers who spoke Philip's language—that of shipping out to uncharted places, and of explorations, and the pursuit of gold and fame.

So Rose Heatherton had first strolled into the shop looking lovely and bright, walking behind her brother. He was there to inquire about the mapping of some family lands. Peter was alone in the office.

"We wish to speak to the proprietor," the brother, William, announced boldy, "about the surveying of some of our estate. Is he in?"

"He is not," Peter answered. "But I am in charge of the office in his absence."

"You?" William said in a mocking voice. "You hardly look old enough to manage the important affairs that I bring here."

"I am old enough," Peter replied confidently, "to have been apprenticed by my father, who is a world traveler and explorer. He has mapped lands that most folk have barely heard of. Lands of roaring rivers and deadly savages. And mysterious forests. And to me he has passed on his knowledge of surveys and maps. And the proprietor has placed his confidence in me also. I'm sure I can meet your needs."

"Well," William said—Rose was by then straining around his shoulders to get a peek at Peter—"we shall see. The lands of my family, our estate, that we need to have resurveyed and mapped—

sufficient for a sale in fee simple—they do not lie hereabouts. They are a far distance away from London."

With the last comment he hoped to show this young mapmaker that he, too, was acquainted with remote lands and romantic locales.

"And where are these lands?" Peter asked.

"Far to the north. In Scotland."

"My people come from there. And I have traveled extensively in Scotland myself. Where is the estate?"

"Eyemouth," William said. "Outside of Edinburgh."

"To the east?"

"Yes, seaward."

"Near the house of the Douglas clan and their lands, by any chance?"

William blushed. He struggled not to be impressed.

"Yes. That is the area," he said reluctantly.

"I know it well," Peter said smiling.

Then he hid his grin and added a coup de grâce.

"We can do this for you," he said. He threw a clever look to Rose, who tried not to smile back but failed. "However," he added with a smirk, "there may be an extra charge involved if we encounter any deadly savages in such a distant land."

Rose put a white-gloved hand over her mouth as she laughed.

"Indeed!" William blustered. "Do not try to jest with me, sir. Will your office do this for my family or not?"

After a pause, Peter nodded.

"We will," he said. "In truth, we have mapped and surveyed estates not too far away from where you speak. I will consult with my father and our proprietor. When we have estimated the price, where shall I send the proposal?"

"To this address in London," William said, and handed him a calling card. It read, *Heatherton Estates—Roger Heatherton—Riverdale House,* and then listed the street.

"And you are Roger Heatherton?" Peter asked.

"No. He was my father, who is recently deceased. I am William, his eldest son. I am managing affairs for my mother now."

"I see," Peter said, suddenly ashamed at his brash humor. "Please forgive my jesting, sir. I am sorry for your loss. I give you my word that this job shall be accomplished in such a manner as to not add to the burden of your recent sorrow."

Then he added, with a look that gave away a small bit of calculation of his own, "And we shall complete this, sir, to ease at least some of these mundane concerns your dear mother must now bear."

Rose was looking around her brother's shoulder to Peter's face, staring at him.

But there was a different look now on her pretty face. A wide-eyed look with a tender smile that seemed to be taking in all of Peter as he stood before her, as if she was beholding a long-lost friend. Or someone she should know intimately from some other place but could not remember where.

Peter reached out and shook William's hand.

"We will come again, my sister Rose and I," William said. "And will fetch with us the necessary papers next time for you to consider the mapping and surveying that must be done."

"I look forward to that, sir, very much," Peter replied with a smile. And then he added with a brighter smile as he glanced over at Rose, "and to seeing you both. It shall be my great pleasure."

Rose stepped out fully from behind her brother. "Until then," she said sweetly, "a good day to you, good sir."

As they left, William gave a little disapproving nudge to Rose.

As he held the door open, she walked through slowly, but not until she had first thrown a quick glance backward to Peter.

"Lad, are ye daydreamin' again?" Philip Mackenzie bellowed with a guffaw as he strolled out of the tavern. His voice startled Peter, whose thoughts of Rose had been abruptly interrupted, and who smiled but did not answer. Philip was carrying a leather bag that jangled with coins. He seemed pleased with himself.

As the two walked together down the dark street—only a few streetlamps were burning in the late evening hour—Peter spoke up.

"Father," he said. "What was Mother like? I remember so little..."

Philip nodded and put his arm around his son's shoulder.

"Aye. I will tell you all about your dear mother."

"And after that, I would like to talk to you...about someone..."

"Someone? Does this person have a name?"

"Yes. Her name is Rose."

Philip chuckled.

"Well," he said with a hearty laugh, "I will be sure and screw my ears on tight for that discussion!"

Chapter 10

It was an hour past midnight. Down in the cellar, Guy Fawkes was dozing as he sat with his back against the barrels of gunpowder. His candle had burnt down to half of its length. In a few hours, he would use it to light the oil lamp, which would have to burn for some eight hours or so in order to ensure a ready flame for the fuses.

He visualized, as his eyes grew heavy and he fought against slumber, what would be happening directly above him at midday. When the king and his family, the Lord Mayor of London, the Privy Council, and the bishops of that "hated and apostate Protestant Church of England" as he called it, would be triumphantly parading down the aisles of the chambers of the House of Lords.

From time to time Fawkes forced himself to rise, and stretch, and then fetch his candle, and inspect, once again, each of the joints where he had spliced together the fabric lengths of fuse.

He was as sure as any human being could be that the dry, expertly constructed fuses would serve their purpose well. There would be no delay in their burning, he figured, as the burn would be in a straight line of sparking fire along the fuse line for fifty yards or so, up to the junction of the twenty-six fuses that led to each separate barrel of explosives.

The night was cold, and the cellar was damp. Fawkes arched his back and stretched out his arms to shake off the stiffness. His body was strong and athletic, but that would not be enough. He knew that he had to be prepared to respond in an instant if the unexpected occurred. That is what his years in mercenary armies had taught him.

When you are prepared to kill, he thought to himself, *you must be prepared for the sudden counterthrust from those who would be your victims.*

Fawkes thought of the men he had killed on the battlefields of Flanders. He prided himself on striking first, and hitting hard against his victims. Young men, hardly capable of growing a full beard, with smooth faces and pink cheeks. Their eyes flashing wide open with the horror of surprise as he thrust his fire-tempered sword into their midsections. Sometimes so hard and sure and deep, that he had to lay his boot on their chests as they lie dying, and give a mighty pull to extract his sword back out.

Some of them cried for their mothers. Some simply died without any audible words, but only with the sounds of suffering, face down, in the mud.

Yet Fawkes was strangely not haunted by those memories. He was a soldier. And killing is what soldiers do. And this day, he considered himself a special kind of soldier—for now he would be a warrior for the Holy Roman Church, and for His Holiness himself.

He rose and gave one more inspection along the fuse line. Just in case a rat might decide to nibble. Or droplets of water from the cold arch-stoned ceiling might dribble down on it and dull its burning power.

Fawkes smiled as he finished the inspection. All was well. Holding the candle tray by the fingerhole, Fawkes turned and walked back to his sitting spot by the barrels that had been tucked back in the darkened cellar vault.

But Fawkes would not sit down. He would remain standing.

For just as he returned to his spot there was a sound. He could not tell its nature or direction. But there was a stirring. He strained as he stood in the opening of the vault, to try to hear.

What is that? he heard himself say inside his mind.

But now there was nothing. No sound.

And then suddenly, at the far end of the cellar, he could hear the sound of feet, but no voices.

Fawkes blew out his candle and jumped back into the shadows of the vault. He reached in his coat pocket. His flint was safely there. He had brought it just in case his candle would have to be snuffed out. When these intruders were gone, he calculated, he could then safely strike his flint and light either the candle or the oil lamp.

*Steady…steady…*he said to himself as he now heard a group of heavy feet moving into the cellar. He could see the flickering light being cast down the gray and black stonewalls from torches that were being carried.

At the end of cellar a half dozen men were entering. In the lead was Sir Thomas Knyvett, the Justice of the Peace for Westminster. Next to him was the sheriff and several of his men with swords. Two of them were carrying torches.

Robert Cecil had personally met with Knyvett to plan the search. They were to wear soft-bottomed shoes to lessen the noise of their approach. There would be no talking, but only the use of hand signs and signals.

And most importantly, Cecil instructed Knyvett to pay close heed to a particular part of the cellar—to a spot that had raised the interest of Cecil ever since he had learned about it from Lord Suffolk's first, hasty search.

The group of men walked slowly down the middle, glancing left and right, but not stopping.

They may simply be using the cellar as a corridor to get to the far end, and to the exit there, Fawkes thought quickly as he tried to calculate the impending risk of detection.

But no, that did not seem likely. Fawkes had to face the inevitable: given that there had already been a first search in that area by the king's men, the appearance of this group boded very badly.

They were there, in that place, at that late hour, to ferret out the possibility of foul play. That much now seemed undeniable.

Yet, none of the group had yet detected the length of fuse that Fawkes had laid. Fawkes had tucked it along the edge of the wall where it could be easily missed. His cleverness on that account seemed to be working.

Fawkes could now hear the shuffling of their feet growing closer. He speculated that there were four, possibly five of them, judging by the sound. Fawkes reached down and touched the handle of his short sword. One or two of them he could easily dispatch. But if they were trained in the art of combat, which they most likely would be, then Fawkes figured that killing four or five in close quarters would be difficult. Perhaps impossible.

As the group approached, Knyvett's eyes locked with the sheriff's. Knyvett pointed to a spot up ahead. The sheriff nodded and gave a signal to his men. They kept walking.

Then, as they approached the vault where Fawkes was hiding and where the pile of wood was stacked, two of the armed men, one with a torch, stayed back, and stood against the wall, waiting.

Knyvett, the sheriff, and one of his men walked straight past.

When they were even with the dark opening of the vault where Fawkes was standing in the shadows, Fawkes gripped his sword as he beheld the small group.

But to his surprise, they did not hesitate at the pile of wood on the outside of the vault but kept walking apace, not slowing or stopping.

Fawkes smiled.

It is not yet the end of my mission, he thought to himself as he listened to the wild beating of his own heart, which, along with the shuffling of the feet of the searchers, seemed to be the only sound in the stillness of the cellar.

The group walked past Fawkes's position. For a split second, his tensed body began to relax. Then he heard the end of the shuffling of their feet. His heart started beating faster.

Fawkes took a soundless breath. Then he waited for the sounds of the search party.

Nothing.

Then a torch was thrust into the vault. Two men rushed in, yanking Fawkes out by the coat.

He swung his sword slashing one of the men on the side of the head, drawing blood. Then he tried to dash to the opposite direction, pulling away from the grip of the other man.

But two armed deputies were waiting for him along the wall. They dropped their torch and tackled Fawkes and threw him to the ground. Then the third man took the handle of his sword and bashed it against Fawkes's hand until he let go of his weapon.

Fawkes was pinned to the ground. The man nursing the cut to his head tossed a rope to the others and they bound Fawkes fast as the sheriff pointed his long sword against the flesh of Fawkes's neck.

Sir Thomas Knyvett stooped next to Fawkes, who was tied up, and lying on his back on the cold stone of the cellar floor.

Knyvett's face was placid and emotionless. He was prepared to disbelieve the story he was about to hear.

"What is your name?"

"John Johnson," Fawkes said, staring him in the eye.

"And what is your work?"

"I am a servant to Sir Thomas Percy," Fawkes said.

Knyvett rose and looked down at Fawkes.

"We shall soon discover," he said with a cold assurance, "the truth of your tale, sir. And may God have mercy on you. For we shall soon also learn the truth of this matter. Mark that well."

Chapter 11

At Holbeach House, Stephen Littleton rose early, before the break of day. He was waiting for the word that he expected would come from London. If all went well, by midday a rider would bring the message that Parliament had been decimated, along with the king and all his heirs—save one—the little Princess Elizabeth. She was to be spirited away as the pawn of the new Catholic rule in England.

But as he walked the grounds nervously, he saw a rider approaching at full gallop. The rider was barreling down the tree-lined road that led to Holbeach House.

Littleton began walking at a fast clip toward the rider, who reached him and reined in his sweating horse.

"Master Littleton," he announced breathlessly from his horse. "I carry dreaded news. Someone has been captured. It may have been Mister Fawkes. Though we don't yet know for sure."

"The plot, sir," Littleton yelled, "the plot. Was it foiled? Are we undone?"

"I am afraid so," the rider said with panic in his voice. "Our plans are in ruin. All of our group are fleeing from London as fast as they can."

"What about Catesby and Wintour and the others?"

"Catesby is to his home…at Ashby St. Ledger. Wintour is close by, hereabouts."

"Lead me to him," Littleton shouted. "Take me over to my stables—quickly, man."

Littleton hopped on the back of the rider's horse and together the two rode quickly over to the stables.

As Littleton pulled open the wide stable doors, he was startled at what he saw.

Gideon Grove, his groom, was preparing a person to mount a spotted pony. But Littleton realized that it did not belong to his estate.

"What business is this?" Littleton said with consternation.

"Please forgive me, sir, for not telling you," Gideon said. "This is my dearest friend, Alice Mackenzie. She was given a room in the servant's area last night. But she is on her way, now. She shall not be a bother…"

"You cannot allow her to leave," the rider whispered to Littleton. "She could reveal everything."

"She poses no threat, sir," Gideon pleaded.

"That may be," Littleton said. "But we cannot take the risk. I command you to keep this person here. Until I give further orders. And I shall have two of my manservants posted in this stable to make sure of that."

Then Littleton strode off to his horse. He quickly pulled down his saddle, fitted the horse, and swung himself up onto it with dispatch.

"She shall not leave Holbeach House," Littleton shouted to Gideon with finality as he reigned his horse toward the mansion. Then he and the other rider rode off at a gallop to the main house to fetch the servants and order them to keep watch over the intruding Alice.

"What have I done?" Gideon moaned as he ran his fingers through his hair.

"This is for the best!" Alice said brightly. "Now we shan't be separated. Can't you see that, dear Gideon?"

"Don't you understand?" Gideon shouted out in a voice so withering that it made Alice jump. "I've risked your life. What a fool I was, to have ever had you come to Holbeach House!"

"What could be so dangerous—" Alice began to wonder out loud to Gideon. But he quickly interrupted her.

"Alice," he said with a frenzy in his voice that startled her. Then he grabbed her by her delicate shoulders. "The revolution I told you about last night…Master Littleton is with the Catholic rebels, and more men aligned with him will soon be arriving here…they are all part of it. And when the armies of King James find out that Holbeach House is their headquarters, they will march here with cannon, and fire, and sword! They will ask no questions. They will kill us all as traitors to the Crown!"

There was a stunned look on Alice's young, innocent face. Suddenly the horror of the situation was becoming clear to her. Her life was truly jeopardized, and Gideon's too.

And beyond that, her actions could spell disgrace and disaster for her own family. Alice's father was a close confident to King James' court. He would be destroyed by this turn of events.

And if somehow Alice and Gideon were spared in the armed skirmish that Gideon thought was inevitable, to what avail? Once captured, they would both have to explain away their presence in this nest of Catholic rebels. Alice was young and naïve, but she was not stupid. She had eavesdropped on some of her father's conversations with her mother in the library. She had heard the stories, about the goings on at court—and the long, well-established use, in England, of cruelty and torture for those suspected of treason against the king or queen.

"God help me," Alice whimpered as the full extent of her folly became clear.

"I will break trust with Master Littleton," Gideon exclaimed. "I will get you out of here. But you must leave now. Up on your pony!"

Gideon helped her up quickly and then handed Alice her travel bag with gold, black, and red stitching.

"Off with you, now," Gideon said urgently. "I will try to stall the master's men—"

"You're too late for that, Master Gideon!"

The voice had come from the open door of the barn.

Gideon wheeled around. When he did his heart sank.

There in the doorway was the big blacksmith who managed the livery for the house, and the stable master too, and two more manservants from the estate, most of them carrying clubs.

They grabbed Gideon and pulled him away from Alice's pony.

"Sorry to do this, Master Gideon, but we have orders to place you under lock and key. And your young damsel here too. Now, Miss, come down from that pony."

Alice slowly swung off the pony as one of the men helped her down. As Gideon was held fast on each arm by a man, he could see Alice's face.

Her eyes were filling with tears and her chin was trembling. As she took a step forward she nearly fainted. The man helped her back to her feet.

"Take heed to the lady!" Gideon cried out as he was escorted away. And then he called out once more to her.

"Alice—do not give up hope!"

Chapter 12

By the time the sun began to break over the rooftops and spires of London at dawn, Andrew Mackenzie had already mounted his small two-seater carriage and harnessed his two fastest horses to pull it. He was about to depart from his small stable behind the house and head off to Staffordshire in his hunt for his daughter. Andrew calculated he could reach Staffordshire by midmorning if he drove his horses hard.

But before he could snap his carriage whip, he saw a rider rein in his horse out at the hitching post in front of his house, and then quickly dismount.

Perhaps 'tis a message about Alice, Andrew thought, his spirits buoyed momentarily. *News of her whereabouts.*

Andrew quickly drove his rig around to the front of the house.

The messenger was at the door. The maid answered the bell, then turned back into the house. In an instant, Kate appeared and began to speak with the visitor.

As Andrew ran up to the front door of their mansion house, the messenger greeted him with solemnity.

"Master Mackenzie. I bring you an urgent message from Thomas Craig," he said. "There is to be a meeting, of the utmost emergency nature, at Westminster…at six o'clock tonight. Immediately after the opening of Parliament."

"What of the full ceremony of the opening?"

"Done away with, this year. It shall only be a brief and unceremonious affair."

"At whose command is this meeting that you speak of?" Andrew asked.

"The king," he said. Then, after pursing his lips, he added, "His Majesty has summoned his chief advisors. The Privy Council. All the lords. Master Thomas Craig begs you attend this conclave with him."

"And the reason? What has the king said of the reason for the meeting?" Andrew asked.

The messenger shook his head.

"I'm sorry, Master Mackenzie. I know only what I have just told you."

Then he tipped his cap to Kate and Andrew and hurried to his horse.

When the messenger was outside of earshot, Andrew took Kate tenderly by the shoulders.

"Do not fret, dear," he said. "I am off to Staffordshire first. There I hope to learn of the whereabouts of Alice. Then, I'll ride hard back to Westminster for the meeting. Meantime, my precious Kate, pray the Lord for me, that He shall lead me to her."

"Oh God," Kate said with a voice choked with emotion, grabbing Andrew's coat in her grip and looking skyward, "Ye had a Son, Yerself, poorly put-upon by evils of humanity. Ye know the grieving hearts we have now for our daughter's folly. Bring us to her, Lord. Deliver Alice to my husband."

"We pray this of You," Andrew added quietly, "by the tender grace of Yer only Son, the Savior, Jesus Christ."

Then Andrew gently removed Kate's grip, kissed both her hands, and then turned to run back to his carriage.

Kate stayed in the doorway, praying, as Andrew's carriage sped its way down the Blackfriars road and then turned to leave the city, and disappeared from view.

It was late morning on that cold November day when Andrew finally reached the villages of Staffordshire. As he entered each, he would methodically report first to the toll booth or constable's office and introduce himself.

"I am Andrew Mackenzie," he would say, "counselor to the Court of King James. I am looking for a girl…"

Then he would describe his daughter. That she might be accompanied by a man of roughly the same age. But no one had seen her.

He would then locate the village blacksmith or stable, thinking that Alice and her unnamed companion may have needed livery assistance for their travel.

But the faces of the smiths, blackened by soot, would simply look up and shake their heads.

Finally, at Kingswinford, Andrew encountered a tollbooth official who seemed to remember a young person riding on a pony, in the early evening. About sundown.

"I couldn't tell you, sir," he said, scratching his beard, "whether it be girl or boy. The person was heavily cloaked. But riding a spotted pony—that I am sure of."

"What direction, man?" Andrew asked with excitement.

"There," the official said pointing.

"What lies along that road?"

"One large estate."

"Of what family? What house?"

"Holbeach House," he said. "Mister Stephen Littleton. A most respectable man."

"And you are sure that the rider headed in that direction?" Andrew asked.

The tollbooth keeper paused for a moment and wrinkled up his face.

"No, sir," he said. "I am not entirely confident of that, as I think on it. I am sorry. We were on the lookout, that night, for a road bandit who had purloined a wagonload of cotton goods. That's what my mind was on that evening. But God's speed to you, sir, on your search."

Andrew snapped his whip and steered his carriage at a full gallop toward Holbeach House. He was now crestfallen. What at first had sounded like such optimistic news, had now been mired down by a tollbooth-man's confusion.

It was midafternoon when Andrew arrived at the guardhouse on the outskirts of Holbeach House. Two rather rough servant men exited the small house and greeted Andrew. He quickly explained his court credentials, gave an account of the news he had heard at the tollbooth, gave a description of Alice, and demanded to know if she had visited their master's estate.

"No one like that has arrived here," the larger of the two said to Andrew, staring him in the eye. "And we would be the ones to know. Being that we are stationed at the entrance gate and all..."

"Perhaps I can speak with Mister Littleton," Andrew said, looking beyond them to survey the long road leading up the Holbeach House.

"Master Littleton is not at home at present," the man said abruptly. "And we have strict orders not to permit strangers on the premises in his absence."

"I did explain to you," Andrew said with some ire in his voice, "that I am a counselor to the Court of King James—"

"That you did," the smaller of the two quickly interjected with a smile. "And most impressed we are. Please take no offense at our master's command on this matter, sir. But we have not seen the girl you have spoken of."

Andrew searched the faces of the two men. Something unspoken was stirring in the pit of his stomach as he studied them.

"Perhaps you can answer this," Andrew added. "Do you have any manservants about the age of my daughter employed here? Or a son of the family? A handsome lad?"

The smaller of the two men answered quickly.

"No, sir," he said, shaking his head with a grin. "Only the likes of us. Ugly and tired old fellows such as we, sir. Not the kind who could draw the eye of someone as fair as your daughter sounds to be, sir."

With that the two men laughed.

Andrew forced a polite half-smile.

"If you encounter my daughter or hear of her whereabouts," Andrew said sternly, "I will expect to hear of it. Immediately. Or know the reason why. I can be reached in Blackfriars."

Andrew handed his card to the short man who took it with an exaggerated flourish.

"Most certainly," the smaller man said spryly. "We will keep a sharp eye out, good sir. And until then, have a most pleasant travel back to London."

As Andrew turned his carriage around and urged his horses to carry him in haste to Westminster, he carried within him a strange and desperate feeling. A sinking sensation, as if he had accidentally stepped onto a hidden bog, and the mud was sucking him down—first to his knees, and then his waist.

And then finally to his neck.

Was it because he did not believe the account given him by the guardhouse men at Holbeach House?

Or perhaps it was something else altogether. Perhaps it was the fact that this had been the only clue he had been able to unearth about his daughter, Alice. And it had only led him to a dead end. And now he must return to Westminster, and the business of politics, and law, and the dreary, self-centered concerns of ambitious men, and the tedious affairs of state.

And then after that, he would return to his house. Where he would have to tell his heartbroken wife that, as of yet, he had been unable to locate their headstrong daughter.

That Alice was somewhere out in the world, where the naïve are preyed upon—and where lovely, sweet girls can too often become grist for the mills of evil machinations of others.

Lord, what shall I do? Andrew prayed, as he snapped his carriage whip, and then gripped the leather reins in his hands—hands that now seemed limp, and weak, and empty with failure.

Chapter 13

"Thus," Robert Cecil concluded, as he addressed the large gathering of counselors and advisors, "this John Johnson fellow is now being transported—as we speak—to the Tower. There he will be kept secure, to await the king's command."

"And this matter of torture," Lord Suffolk said, raising his arm, and pointing at Cecil with a leather gloved hand. "Sir Robert, you have not ventured your own opinion on that issue. Yet you ask us of ours. A pretty gesture, sir, of obvious obscurity. You solicit authority from us to exact confessions from this Johnson fellow by the means of the rack and manacles—yet you remain aloof yourself?"

Suffolk's stinging accusation was deflected easily by Cecil. He had expected as much from Suffolk, whose shoddy first search of Westminster had missed the obvious cache of gunpowder—not to mention also failing to detect the lurking John Johnson in the basement. Suffolk was clearly defending his wounded pride.

"The very capable counselor Lord Suffolk is far too clever," Cecil said with a smile, "to permit me the luxury of silence on this matter."

Cecil walked, in his slightly twisted gait, across the chamber room filled with the most powerful men in King James' cabinet.

He raised a pale, delicate hand in the air to make his point, as his other hand was placed behind his black robe.

"So I will address the matter directly," Cecil said. "My opinion is thus—that we face a national crisis of most horrible dimensions. Clearly a plot to destroy, by explosion and fire, the whole of our government—to decimate the Crown of England. Gentlemen, we must use any and all means to uncover the full scope of this dastardly and evil design. Before our enemies strike us with a blow that cannot be foiled, as this one was."

"I would hear from Thomas Craig, the most honorable and learned lawyer," Suffolk shouted out. "Let us hear from him."

Suffolk knew that Craig was a Scot, like James himself, and was a handpicked favorite of the king to advise him on legal matters.

Craig rose slowly to a mild round of applause.

"Gentlemen," he said. "I am humbled by your confidence in my judgment on this matter. But it is not merely a question of law. It is a question of grave polity. It goes to the very duty of the Crown to protect the existence of the Crown. As our Savior and Lord hath said—can a house divided against its own self stand and not collapse? The duty of this house of state is to remain strong and to stand. If we permit internal insurrection and intrigue to divide the government by force, can there be any hope for the continued reign of our most upright king?"

"Then you support me," Cecil quickly said, "in the use of torture against this Johnson conspirator? So that we may attain the names of the greater number of his black hearted compatriots?"

"Hold," Craig interjected. "I have not so concluded. I just state one side of the ledger. For the other side of the balance, I would ask for the opinions of my trusted legal assistant."

Then Craig turned to the crowded room and scanned the faces

until he located that of Andrew Mackenzie, who was standing in the back of the room.

"Andrew, step forward," Craig said. "And give us your arguments—if any you have—against the practice Sir Cecil proposes."

The men parted to each side as Andrew cautiously made his way to the front of the room. When he had reached a position near to Robert Cecil, he bowed to the king's highest advisor and then turned to address the assembly.

In any other circumstance Andrew might have been flattered by Craig's invitation to address the group. But Andrew knew enough about the politics of Court to harbor a caution.

He was aware that his mentor had placed him adroitly into Cecil's line of fire. Craig knew that his assistant would argue his same position—but without risking the loss of Craig's prestige if the king sided with Cecil rather than Craig. Andrew was being used as a human shield.

But there was also the matter of Alice too. Andrew had raced into the chambers of the palace, one of the last to arrive, still burdened by his daughter's disappearance. He had hoped to slip into the assembly unnoticed so he could hide his dark, brokenhearted melancholy over his family crisis.

Now, in front of this intimidating assembly of the most powerful men in England, Andrew was being called upon to spar with the king's most powerful confidant.

Andrew said a quick, silent prayer. He cleared his throat. And then he began.

He decided to make his position short and concise, but elegantly persuasive.

"Torture has been used by the Crown of England many times,"

he began. "But we cannot use that fact, alone, as binding precedent—"

"Oh, then you question the binding authority of the kings and queens of England?" Cecil jibed sarcastically. "You reject the rule of the late Queen Elizabeth, perhaps, the guiding light of England's past greatness?"

Several of the assembled men shouted something out, but Andrew, struggling to keep his focus, ignored them. He raised his voice in reply.

"Not at all," he shouted back. "But then I would not look to the use of torture by Queen Mary Tudor, Elizabeth's predecessor, as precedent either. As she tortured and set aflame countless numbers of Protestant followers of Jesus. They were caused to scream out from the rack rooms and torture chambers, not because they were enemies of the state, but because they were the friends of God. It appears, good Sir Cecil, that the use of torture depends not on the good intentions of rulers, but on the fixed principals of law—both those that would temporarily bless England for generations to come, and most importantly, those that emanate from God's holy and infallible Word."

Then, to make the point, Andrew added, "In the thirteenth chapter of the epistle of the apostle Paul to the Romans, we are admonished that the sword of rulers is to be used 'to take vengence on him that doeth evil.' It does not state that government is to take vengence on anyone it pleases…"

"Well," Cecil responded with a confident smile, "I see, Mr. Mackenzie, that—like your father—you, sir, are learned in both theology and jurisprudence. But does it not appear then, that this John Johnson fellow, if indeed that is his true name, was one who was 'doing evil'? Do you not agree that a plot to kill His Majesty is the essence of evil?"

"Torture has been condoned for acts of high treason," Andrew said. "But we must first conclude in this assembly that the evidence is such that a true plot was fomenting against our good king, and that this Johnson fellow was part of it. The process must be fair that makes this evaluation."

"And if we so find?" Cecil snapped. "Then may we, my timid friend, commence to extract the truth from this scoundrel we arrested?"

"I believe," Andrew said, his mind bleary with the day's travels, and his heart heavy with his own personal travails, "that if we so find, then the use of sharp coercion—rather than blunt torture—is the more equitable and the more effective. Hard and relentless pressure perhaps, but without irreparable injury or death, is the first means to be applied."

"Then let us all now agree," Cecil proposed with his arms outstretched, "that the man in our custody is a villain, and that he is part of a traitorous villainy most grievous to the Crown. Let us raise our hands to affirm that—to the last man—and proceed to the finer points of what torture is to be applied."

In the far end of the room, behind a massive purple velvet curtain, King James of England sat in an upholstered chair, listening to the debate at the crack of the curtain's edge.

The king's congenitally drooping eyes appeared sadder than usual as he listened to the arguments of the assembly. His thin, smooth hands were unconsciously clasped to the sides of his chair as he weighed the future of his government and the means best calculated to secure his own survival in a world mad with violence.

Chapter 14

King James held the quill in his hand. He paused for only an instant. Then he dipped it in the silver ink bowl, glanced down one more time at the letter of authorization for torture in the inquisition of one John Johnson, and then scratched his first name, "JAMES," followed by the customary "R," the Latin initial for his kingly status.

In the letter, drafted by Cecil after close conference with James after the debate of the full council, the king was permitting the use of the "gentler tortures" first, having been swayed by the arguments of Andrew Mackenzie. But the letter also authorized, if necessary, the application of progressively more stringent schemes of pain against the man being held in the Tower of London.

Cecil took the letter and bowed to the king. James was looking particularly pale and self-absorbed. They had, he realized, uncovered one particularly dastardly plot. But were there others? James, who had always been particularly consumed with trying to ferret out possible insurrections against him, was now in full defensive posture.

In addition to the letter of torture, James had ordered that the ports and harbors of England be temporarily closed. That all ships be searched. That the tollbooths and border gates along northern England, which could lead to an escape into Scotland, be placed on high alert. All suspicious persons were to be interrogated. And an extra guard was placed on the person of each of the members of the royal family.

Cecil took the letter from his king, bowed low, and then quickly carried it himself, by horseback, over to the Tower.

Down in the bowels of the cold stone tower, in a windowless room lit only by wall torches, the lord chief justice, Sir John Popham, an overweight man dressed in his ample red robes and frilled white collar, welcomed Cecil's arrival.

"Ever so good to see you, Robert," Popham said loudly, embracing Cecil. In the corner of the room a tall, wide-shouldered man in a sleeveless vest was standing with his arms folded.

"And you know Mister Thomas Norton, I believe," Popham remarked, pointing to the man in the corner.

"Indeed I do," Cecil replied. "Mister Norton is our highly skillful master of the rack in the Tower. We have met before."

And with that, Cecil gave a quick nod to Norton.

Then Cecil took a few steps with Popham over to the side of the cold, shadowy room, handed the letter of torture to Popham, and gestured toward it as he spoke.

"This is the authorization, Sir John," he said, lowering his voice. "With the King's own signature."

"Yes, excellent," Popham said, studying the document. "It is as I expected. In conformity, it would appear, with the custom and law of torture."

"I am full glad that the king has placed you in charge of the investigation," Cecil said.

"Your confidence is appreciated," Popham said. "I have already sent search parties out to the homes of the chief Catholic suspects throughout London. The results are already coming in. We have the beginning of a list of possible conspirators—Catholic dissenters whose sudden absence from their homes, after the foiling of the Westminster plot, appears to be unexplained."

"A shrewd beginning point."

"And now, with this document," Popham said, tapping the letter with his finger, "we shall get to the nub of this hellish turn of events."

"Keep me informed of your progress," Cecil said.

Then he gave a half-bow and quickly headed up the stone steps.

Popham gave the charge to Norton, and with that, the tall master of torture, along with two of his assistants, one with a missing eye, swung open the heavy wooden door of Fawkes's cell and dragged him out. Fawkes's hands were already tied together with rope, as were his feet.

He stumbled as they dragged him into the center of the room.

On the floor of the room, taking up most of its center, were two sets of wooden rails, a few feet longer than the length of a man. At each end were winches with ropes tied to them—at the top, ropes to pull the arms out of their sockets, and at the other end, ropes to dislocate the legs and knees.

"Behold the rack!" Popham declared loudly to Fawkes. "It shall not be used on you sir, *unless* you fail to speak—or fail to speak the truth in all its sundry details. Speak of everything you know, sir—hold nothing back—and you shall only be submitted to the gentler means of interrogation."

With that, the two assistants, under Norton's watchful eyes, snapped iron manacles on Fawkes's wrists, then connected the manacles to chains which had been laced through iron hoops in the stone walls some four feet above Fawkes's head.

As they pulled on the ends of the chains, they drew Fawkes to his feet, and then finally to a full standing position on his tiptoes, with his hands and arms straight above him.

"Now, sir," Popham began, "your name."

"I have said it before," Fawkes said, trying to maintain his calm in light of the strain on his shoulder joints. "John Johnson. Servant to Thomas Percy."

Fawkes had already decided that he would admit his complicity in a plan to blow up the government of James. There could hardly be any denying that. He was caught in the presence of twenty-six barrels of gunpowder, stored beneath Parliament, on the eve of the opening. Ready to light the fuses. Dressed for hard and fast riding. And his Catholic sympathies were never hidden.

On the other hand, if he could hold out for a period of time before mentioning names—or at least the names of his true compatriots—he could at least give them time to escape from England. Perhaps sail to France or Spain. And there to raise armies to try to wrest control of the English Crown out of the grip of the Protestants. To bring more fire and sword against James and his supporters. To kill for the sake of a new Catholic order in London.

"Were you plotting to kill the king and overthrow his rightful government, by means of gunpowder?" Popham asked, with no hint of emotion in his voice.

"Yes. Of course," Fawkes exclaimed through gritted teeth. "But I deny that James, the filthy, Scottish heretic Protestant, is the head of anything resembling a rightful government."

Popham's eyes widened ever so slightly. Then he nodded to Norton and his men. They drew the chain up higher, lifting Fawkes off the ground by a few inches and dangling him by his shoulder joints.

Fawkes gave out a muffled groan.

Popham stood, at first for several minutes, and then stretching on for close to half an hour, observing Fawkes dangle off the ground from his manacled position. He was now heavily perspiring. His body was beginning to shake with pain.

The Lord Chief Justice walked up to Fawkes and looked up at his face, which was twisted in a grimace.

Their eyes locked.

Then Popham casually turned and slowly began walking away, toward the steps, as if he were going to leave the room.

"Don't you want to ask me more questions?" Fawkes asked, his voice quivering.

"No," Popham replied blandly. He slowly mounted the stone steps.

Then he turned and said over his shoulder to Fawkes, "At least, not now."

In an instant, Popham was gone from sight. And Fawkes was left to hang by his own joints and sinews, feeling a nauseating rush of pain sweeping over his arms and wrists and shoulder joints as his feet dangled several inches off the ground. Left to wonder how long he would suffer alone in the dank, cold room.

An hour later, Popham returned, slowly descending the stone staircase.

As he stepped down he could hear the grunting and heavy breathing of Fawkes.

When Popham entered the room, he strolled over to Fawkes and looked up into his face. His eyes were bloodshot and teared, and his hair and beard were soaked in sweat.

"A question," Popham announced in a monotone voice. "Who?"

"What?" Fawkes asked in a low, hoarse voice.

"Who?" Popham announced again. "Who was with you in the planning of your most heinous plot to kill the king of England. Who? Names, please."

Fawkes's face was pale with pain. He glanced over at the rack on the floor. He had prepared himself to withstand the manacles. But he would undoubtedly be unable to stand up against the rigors of the rack. To his knowledge, no man had ever been able to manage that.

He had to give them something. A tidbit that would postpone—or maybe even eliminate—the use of the rack. A name. Someone he cared little about. A harmless name. Or perhaps even someone for whom he carried a bigoted disgust because of that person's lineage. Or his place of birth.

"Who?" Popham exclaimed louder.

Fawkes was trying to think now. But his mind was clouded with pain. He had to remember the man's name. He could remember well his friends and fellow collaborators. But those were the ones he wanted to protect.

Yet, there was another.

"A man," Fawkes shouted out. "There was a man…"

"Yes," Popham replied calmly. "Tell me about the man."

"Who helped…"

"Yes, yes. Tell me more."

"Who gave me counsel…"

"On what matter did this man give counsel?"

"For the gunpowder…"

"Yes. Good. For the purchase of the explosives, then, was it?"

"No. Not that."

"Then what?" Popham asked, his voice giving way to impatience and irritation.

Fawkes was thinking through his memory. Trying to walk the line. Not to give away anything that mattered to his fellow Catholic rebels.

"The man," Fawkes said through gritted teeth.

"The man *what?*" Popham shouted.

"Led me to the *fuses*…to ensure the proper burn…"

"Indeed," Popham said with a slight smile. "And what is this man's name?"

Now Fawkes was trying to sort through his memory for the name. But it wasn't coming.

"His *name!*" Popham exclaimed.

"I can't remember," Fawkes moaned. "Only…"

"Yes, yes. Only what?"

Fawkes raised his head and looked down from his dangling height at Popham's large face below. Then Fawkes spoke of the only thing he could remember about the man.

"The man was a Scot."

Chapter 15

The news of some vague national emergency had swept through London. On that day, in the survey and map shop, Peter Mackenzie was there along with his father, Philip, and the proprietor of the office, Kenneth Hadfield. Philip and Hadfield were talking about the news of the day. Peter was in the map room, rolling up a number of land maps and placing them in their appropriate shelved cubbyholes. But he could hear some of what they were saying.

Hadfield, his master, said that someone had been arrested. And the homes of greater London were being searched.

"It sounds like the Catholics, from what I heard," he remarked.

"In this city, the rumors always seem to start with them—and end with them as well," Philip said with a chuckle.

"Mind you, this is no laughing matter," Hadfield said. "This city is full of men with violence in their heads. If you want my opinion, our king has been more than lenient with those Papist traitors."

"We'll see heads rolling down the streets soon enough," Philip said. "That's why I try to steer clear of religious disputes."

"Surely you're no supporter of the Roman Church?"

"Kenneth, I am a true attender of the worship services of the

Church of England," Philip said nonchalantly, "if that's what you mean."

Then as he turned to walk away he muttered under his breath, *Though I cannot exactly remember when I last attended.*

That last comment was caught by Peter, who gave his father a slightly troubled look.

Peter was at the church worship services each and every Sunday. He could not exactly explain why, but the songs of exultation to God and the readings from the Book of Common Prayer had a strange and powerful hold on him. Unlike his father, he could not simply shrug off matters of God, and religion, and the weighty concerns of sin, hell, and condemnation.

His mother, Peter had been told, was a woman of great spiritual faith. Though he could remember none of that, as she had died when he was young.

All Peter knew was that it was as if some invisible force was moving him into the hard wooden pews each Sunday. He had even taken up the reading of the Bible. Someone had left a copy behind in the apartments he and his father had begun renting in London. Peter quickly snatched it and asked his father's permission to keep it.

Philip looked at his son after he had made that request, with the expression of a man who may have had much to say but decided to reveal very little of it.

"You can have it," Philip said. "I have little use for religious sophistry anymore."

There was much in the Bible that Peter found puzzling. But he loved the Gospel stories the best. Particularly the stories of the miracles. Like the little girl who had died, and whom Jesus then brought back to life to the amazement of family and friends.

"I'm off to the Black Swan," Philip announced to his son. "There's a meeting there. I'll be home by suppertime."

Philip had not told his son that he would be discussing some preliminary plans for the founding of a new exploration company in London, the purpose of which was to launch ships to the New World. He had kept it from him for a reason.

Though Philip Mackenzie may have lost his faith in much, over the years, he still prized his son and valued his welfare.

Philip remembered the last few words of his wife as she was hemorrhaging profusely on the birthing stool in the arms of the midwife.

*Mind our son—Peter—*she said, with the color draining from her face. *Mind him...your only son. Keep watch over his soul...*

That last command, Philip knew full well he had not kept. But at least, he thought, he could be mindful of his son's general welfare in the ways of the world. Philip's lust had always been to return to the New World and finish the exploration he had barely begun over a decade before, then as a young man. But now, with Peter solidly apprenticed in a honorable trade and fixed in the advantages and prosperity of London, Philip was feeling guilty about leaving his son behind in order to adventure across the ocean.

So Philip had been entertaining the thought of acting as a mere advisor to this new exploration group. Perhaps even trading his expert assistance for shares in the company. Lately, Philip had been considering more and more the possibility of not departing with the ships himself, though that would mean untold sacrifice for him. It would mean that he would be ramming a dagger into the heart of his most cherished ambitions.

So, as things stood, Philip felt that he could fulfill at least part of his wife's last wishes by remaining fixed in England and staying by the side of his son.

None of this was told to Peter though. Philip simply patted his son on the back as he left the shop for his meeting.

Within the hour after Philip's departure, there was a most unexpected and delightful set of visitors who arrived.

William Heatherton and his sister, Rose, stopped by the office to drop off several land grants and charters for the surveying project of their family estate in Scotland.

Rose was dressed in a long blue dress and bonnet. And as her brother discussed the documents with Kenneth Hadfield, she swept over to the desk where Peter was working.

"Ever so hard at work!" she said softly, and with a bright smile.

"It keeps me from mischief," Peter said with a grin of his own.

"Oh? Do you need keeping from mischief and frivolity?" she asked coyly.

"No, Miss. It's just that...well, last Sunday, the reverend spoke of how we—I mean all men that is—are commissioned to work. That work was something blessed of God in the garden of Eden. But after the fall, work became by the sweat of our brow, yet still blessed by God. That in the wisdom of the book of Proverbs, if we commit our works to God, then He will direct the thoughts of our hearts."

Suddenly Peter blushed, and felt that he had foolishly poured out a sermon when he should have given a simple answer to this beautiful girl's simple question.

"Well, Peter," she said with an ever-brighter smile that showed a subtle dimple in one cheek, "would you be a mapmaker, then...or a *minister*? You preach a wise and worthy sermon, sir. I should like to hear you every Sunday."

Then she laughed, and her laughter put him at ease.

"You remembered my name," he said, finding it difficult to hide his enthusiasm.

"Of course," she said. "You are Peter Mackenzie."

"That's right," Peter said. Then he paused, and added his own remembrance.

"And your name is Rose," he said. "Rose Heatherton. *Heatherton.* Like…well, the *heather* on the hills of Scotland. In the fall. When in full bloom. So lush and beautiful…I mean, it does appear that way…when I have visited Scotland with my family, I mean…that's what I was trying to say…"

Rose's face was flushed with embarrassment, but she could not keep from smiling so broadly that she had to cover her face with her two, lace-gloved hands.

"Rose, come along!" William, her brother, said smartly, when he had finished his business with the proprietor.

"Will you come back, again, Rose?" Peter whispered.

"I shall be so anxious to do so!" Rose whispered back.

And as she turned to join her brother, her gloved hand slightly brushed Peter's hand, which had been set flat on the desk.

Peter stared at his hand and then caught the very last glimpse of Rose as she floated out of the room.

And Peter wondered exactly what it was that was so fueling the burning, molten certainty within his heart, that in all the world, there could be no other woman quite as wonderful as Rose Heatherton.

Chapter 16

Most of London did not know what was unfolding in their very midst.

Down in the dimly lit interrogation chamber of the Tower of London, under the incisive questioning of Lord Chief Justice Popham and the cruel work of his unflagging rack masters, Fawkes had been broken. Within forty-eight hours of the increasing application of worsening and more intolerable torture, he had given up his true name and identity, and had named each member of the core group of his fellow conspirators. An arrest warrant was issued for Thomas Percy, the renter of the crucially positioned apartment that had access to the basement of Parliament.

By then, most of the plotters had left London and had gathered at Holbeach House. It was midmorning.

Alice had been kept in a third-level locked room that was bolted from the outside. Food was brought in twice a day. But none of the guards engaged in any conversation with her. She was, at least, glad for that. She had been pacing inside the room, intermittently weeping, and then praying, and then crying some more. But the thought did dawn on her that, perchance, none of the Catholic conspirators who were holding her knew of her father's powerful ties to the reign of James and his Protestant court.

If they have not engaged me in conversation, she reasoned to herself, *perhaps it is because they do not count me as important—thusly, they do not recognize who my father is. There is still hope...Oh, Gideon, my beloved, you were right about that...*

Alice had no way of knowing that her identity as Andrew Mackenzie's daughter, and her father's connection to the Crown, were already known to the conspirators: Andrew's unwitting conversation with the two guardhouse servants had divulged all of that.

Nor could she have been aware that, at that very moment, her future was being debated by the group of would-be revolutionaries in the banquet hall of the house. Wine and bread and two bowls of fruit were on the long, oaken table, and were being consumed by the weary group of rebels. In between bites, Tom Wintour raised a question.

"What do we do with her?" Wintour asked. "With Alice Mackenzie...daughter of that heretic pawn of the king, Andrew Mackenzie? I say we hang her from a tree."

"Keep her for a ransom," Thomas Percy, Wintour's brother-in-law chimed in. "If we get trapped here, she may well be our passage to freedom."

"There will be no 'passage to freedom,'" Robert Catesby said with a deep resignation in his voice.

There was an uncomfortable silence in the room.

Catesby had been the unyielding optimist among them. At first he insisted, on the news of Fawkes's capture, that the Parliament had, indeed been hit—and that perhaps even some of the royal family and Privy Council slain.

When the full failure of the plot became clear, he then insisted that when Spain learned of their efforts, an assault on England would begin.

And in any event, Catesby had always maintained that the closeted, silent Catholics who laced the countryside would rally behind him and his plotters.

But now, as the group that barely numbered a dozen in number gathered for strategy at Stephen Littleton's estate, the future of their planned overthrow of the government seemed desperately bleak.

Catesby's face bore a kind of stark realization—that winning an insurgent war against James and his supporters was now out of the question.

"No passage to freedom, gentlemen," Catesby continued, explaining, "except through death."

"I have no lust for the grave, Robin," Percy said, using Catesby's nickname.

"Nor do I," Catesby shot back. "But that end, for us, now seems sure. Fawkes is a hard man, and tough. But he will break. And our names will spill off his tongue. I am sure they are scouring the countryside as we speak. Tracking us down."

"But will they charge us with musket and cannon if they know we hold the daughter of a counselor to the king?" Jack Wright asked.

"They will not negotiate with us," Catesby replied quietly. "They will not. Be assured of that."

"I am sorry that your groom had to be secured, Stephen," Catesby said to Littleton. "Where is this Gideon fellow?"

"Tied to a barrel in a storage shed in back of the mansion house," the estate owner answered. Littleton was pondering his young servant's fate. He had never directly brought his stable groom into the details of their plot. He was now suffering the pangs of conscience that both Gideon and Alice would be part of the firing line in the impending conflict.

Catesby was quiet again and then made his recommendation.

"I say we keep them both secured. Until the battle breaks. And then, whatever happens, happens."

"What say we then, gentlemen?" Littleton asked.

Each of the men in the room raised a hand in agreement. Percy and Wintour were the last, and only with reluctance did they finally raise theirs.

It was further agreed that an extra watch would be placed on the outside gate. And that the men would be prepared to do battle from the courtyard, rather than from inside the mansion house. After all, the house was subject to being encircled and then could be burned down or blasted into rubble with them trapped inside. Though the chance of escape seemed remote, there was a slim chance that if only a small number of English regulars or an ad hoc group of locals arrived, some of the rebels could fend them off while the rest could escape by horseback from the unassaulted flank of the property.

However, if more than just a dozen or two arrived against them, they all knew that the chance of escape was almost nonexistent. A posse of fifty or sixty could probably successfully surround the grounds with musket fire so as to prevent escape.

As the conspirators dined and hastily made preparations, in the nearby town of Stourbridge the high sheriff was gathering a group of armed deputies. They were being assigned muskets, ball, and gunpowder for the assault on Holbeach House.

"We go to Holbeach House," he exclaimed to the assembly. "To capture and kill men who would assassinate our king. To fight for the Court of his most excellent majesty, James, God's rightful monarch. God's speed to us all. Long live the king!"

"Long live the king!" the men shouted out, raising their muskets in the air.

A cannon was being loaded on a wagon. When that was done, the sheriff and his next in command, Thomas Lawley, reined their horses around in the direction of Holbeach House.

Then they began to lead the march to the mansion house of Stephen Littleton.

And several hundred armed men, steeled for a fight, were following fast behind the sheriff.

Chapter 17

"I'll pray that ye shall see the likes of our fair daughter today," Kate said to Andrew, as he mounted the larger carriage. Kate was standing in the doorway, trying to be brave. But her face reflected a sense of abject fear.

Andrew had decided to take one of his servants as a driver on the journey, along with the servant's strapping son also.

"I shall not rest till that is done," Andrew called out to her.

But Andrew had an added heaviness in his spirit. He had been learned that the arrestee in the Tower had confessed—and had yielded up the names of the collaborators. Now the king's men were racing across the countryside looking for the members of the conspiracy.

Alice was out there, somewhere, in a land now aflame with threats of retribution and violence. England was now an even more dangerous place. And his daughter's safety was more precarious than ever before.

On the floor of the carriage Andrew had laid two muskets and a pistol. He had covered them up with a blanket so that Kate would not see.

Andrew decided to return first to Stourbridge. In his mind,

he repeatedly harkened back to his encounter with the gatehouse guards at the mansion house just outside the town. This time, he would talk personally to Mister Littleton, the owner. Andrew would not take the word of two shifty, rough-looking servants. Holbeach House is where he would start.

The carriage had a four-horse hitch. Andrew instructed his servant to drive the full team hard. He needed to reach Holbeach House by noon.

So the servant swung the whip and cracked it once, and the carriage lurched forward at a gallop.

As Andrew Mackenzie was leaving London, the high sheriff and his men were arriving within eyeshot of Holbeach House.

"Surround the estate," he ordered. "Let no one through. But fire no shot until my command. And keep yourselves well hidden, men. Until Mister Lawley, my second, shall raise the red ensign high along your ranks. At that sign, commence firing. Kill them—all of them."

"Shall we not take captives?" Lawley asked, mounted next to the sheriff on his horse. "Captives to interrogate—or perhaps those that are innocent, but who are unwittingly caught in the fight?"

"Killed," the sheriff said blandly. "Or captive. Either one. It makes little difference."

The hundreds of men were then scattered among the fields and trees surrounding Holbeach House.

At first, the posted guards within Littleton's compound did not see the encirclement. But as the assault group, mostly of local volunteers and nonprofessional soldiers, expanded itself around the grounds, scurrying figures, heads and torsos, and the long thin lines of muskets became clearly visible to the rebels at Holbeach House.

"They come!" one of the guards yelled to the others back in the courtyard. "They mean to surround us!"

The word was passed back to Catesby, who was crouching with his own musket at the front door of the mansion house.

"We shall die as devout followers of His Holiness the Pope, the Vicar of Christ," Catesby said. "And not as dogs."

The group had taken confession and their final sacrament of the Mass just an hour before. They considered themselves ready to die as martyrs to their cause.

Inside the stone-fenced estate, the men had gathered what intelligence they could about the movements of their attackers. But it was clear that they were pinned down from all directions.

At the perimeter, the sheriff gave the command to Lawley.

"Let fly!" he yelled.

Lawley raised the red flag on end of the lance and then galloped along the ranks of the men. They cheered when they saw the signal. Suddenly fire let loose from the ends of several hundred muskets. The air clouded with smoke.

The cannon was primed and loaded. The cannoneer lit the fuse and covered his ears.

The end of the cannon exploded with fire and smoke. A cannonball whizzed over the heads of the men and over the gatehouse.

It crashed into the second story of Holbeach House. Mortar and stone shattered and went flying. It had struck just above the main entrance next to the room where Alice had been kept hostage.

Alice was screaming hysterically. She hid herself under the bed and covered her ears. Eventually she could not catch her breath, and all she could do was to simply gasp and whimper in an almost soundless expression of horror.

On the first floor, inside the mansion, Littleton picked himself up off the floor. He knew what he had to do.

He crawled his way along the floor until he reached the rear exit, which led out to the back lands and to the storage shed beyond the gardens.

Two of the rebels were firing their muskets blindly at snipers who were positioned about one hundred feet from the shed.

"I am off to the shed yonder," Littleton yelled to the men. "Fire away. And distract the snipers..."

The men reloaded and then sent a volley off. Littleton ran across the backyard and scampered through the maze of the garden until he reached a small opening through which he crawled. The shed was only ten feet away.

Littleton bolted over to the door and swung it open.

Gideon Grove was struggling madly to try to gain escape from the ropes that held him fast to the barrel.

"I'm cutting you free," Littleton announced. Then he drew out a sharp knife and sawed into the ropes until they started fraying and then finally broke through.

Gideon jumped to his feet.

"Alice Mackenzie is being kept on the second floor of the house. No guards remain. The key is on a hook to the right of the door. Fetch her! Take the route through the hedgerow of the garden to get back to the house."

Before Gideon could thank his rescuer, Littleton ran from the shed, and headed away from the house, toward a ravine and a small creek that led along the bottom of the shallow ravine, away from the estates.

Gideon ran pell-mell through the gardens. He stopped momen-

tarily at the clearing, and then bolted to the backdoor of the mansion house. Several musket balls hit just a few feet from him.

Inside the house, he stepped over shattered glass and smashed
furniture. He ran up the spiral staircase and turned left and sprinted
down the long corridor. He halted at a door, looked to the right,
and grabbed the huge door key that hung on the hook.

He inserted it in the lock and turned the doorknob and pushed
the door open.

"Alice! It's Gideon! I've come for you…"

The girl scampered out from under the bed and ran into his
arms sobbing.

"We have to go. Now!" he cried, and as he pulled her along
behind him as he ran he explained his plan.

"We are going to try to make it to the stables. I didn't see much
shooting over there. We'll mount up and ride off from that direction."

When they reached the bottom of the stairs in the grand foyer,
musket shot came flying through the opening where stained glass
had been.

Alice screamed again and balked.

Gideon urged her on until they got to the backdoor.

"See where the stables are from here?" he cried out. "We must
run. As fast as you can. Are you ready, Alice?"

She gave a tearful, shaking nod.

"Run!" Gideon yelled.

Chapter 18

Andrew and his servants had passed through Stourbridge and were still a mile or two away from Holbeach House. But already they could hear the sounds of battle. Back at the tollbooth they had been warned that a huge posse of armed assailants had been gathered by the high sheriff and were set on a full-scale siege against the estate of Stephen Littleton.

"They rode through here, early morn," the toll guard said to Andrew, his eyes aflame with excitement. "Two hundred strong—maybe more. On the scent of the Papists, I gather. Those that had some design, it seems, to kill the king, God spare his soul."

Now, with the sound of musket fire popping in the distance, Andrew felt a frenzied sense of doom and panic rising in him.

"Use yer whip, man!" he commanded his driver. "Lay on! We have to get to Holbeach House before it is too late!"

His servant lashed at the horses, and the carriage was soon barreling down the dirt road. The trees on either side of the lane were whizzing by as Andrew prayed and uttered frantic pleas for divine help.

Soon they could see the puffs of smoke from musket fire rising up in the air and hanging in the tops of the trees that surrounded Holbeach House.

Andrew stood up in the carriage. He could see that the sheriff's men were posted around the house and were firing randomly toward the mansion house.

They sped the carriage up to the front gate where several dozen men were firing. Andrew spotted a man on a horse who appeared to be of some authority.

"You there!" Andrew called out, lighting from the carriage and running over to the man on horseback. "I am Andrew Mackenzie, advisor to the Court of King James. Tell me quickly, sir—what manner of siege is this?"

The man on the horse tipped a wide-brimmed hat with a feather in it and replied with a grim countenance.

"I am Thomas Lawley, good sir, deputy to the high sheriff. Our men are shooting at a group of rebels over yonder, thought to be plotters against the king...who aimed to blow up Parliament. And we shoot to kill, sir."

"I have a daughter. She was seen passing this way," Andrew shouted out, with travail in his voice. "I do not know if she is in that mansion house or not..."

"God help her if she is," Lawley replied, shaking his head. "The blood's running hot here. And there is very little mercy to be found in our orders."

Andrew ran back to the carriage and jumped aboard and shoved his driver over to the passenger seat and took the reins himself.

"Heahhh, heahhh!" Andrew screamed to the horses and snapped the reins and took the carriage at a catapulting speed around the circumference of the stone wall that enclosed the estate.

"Stay clear of the house, sir!" Lawley yelled out to him. But by then Andrew's carriage was already around the bend in the tall stone wall.

Andrew slowed the carriage as they approached a side gate to get a look at the battlefield through the view he had between the open iron bars. At the gate there were several men firing muskets toward the house. Two snipers were lying flat on their stomachs atop the stone wall, reloading their muskets.

Inside the mansion house grounds, a bloody chaos reigned.

Tom Wintour had been shot in the arm and was leaning against a wall of the house, bleeding profusely.

Jack Wright had been hit, was lying still in the yard, and looked to be dead. The bodies of several other Catholic conspirators were strewn around the front lawn.

The remaining rebels were scurrying around the grounds looking for some opening to escape the barrage of musket shot.

Thomas Percy and Robert Catesby were running around the front corner of Holbeach House, with Percy in front and Catesby in back.

On top of the stone wall by the gate, one of the snipers had finished reloading and saw the figures of Percy and Catesby. He lowered his barrel until he had them perfectly sighted, as they had stopped for just a second, Percy in front of Catesby.

Kaboom, the musket fired off.

The ball tore into Percy's shoulder, clean through him, and then ripped into the chest of Catesby, who was behind him.

Both men crumpled to the ground almost instantaneously.

A second later Catesby began clawing his way into Holbeach House. He would be dead in the foyer within minutes. Percy was dazed and struggled into the house also. There he collapsed on the floor.

Andrew had seen enough. He snapped the whip and continued to speed around the estate, determined to find some break in the line so he could get closer to the mansion. He had to find Alice whom, he had now concluded, must be there, somewhere. The two guard-house servants, who had denied ever seeing Alice or her paramour, were obviously part of the conspiracy. Andrew had been lied to.

Then Andrew saw something. Off in the distance. Two riders. A young man, it seemed, judging by the athletic posture, who was riding fast and away from Holbeach House, on a big bay. Slightly behind him was another rider. Smaller. On a pony.

Andrew ordered the two men on his carriage to get off, to lighten the load. Then he cracked the whip and rushed his four horses toward the two riders. He was leaning forward, almost standing, and was lashing the whip like a madman.

And then he noticed, as he drew closer, that the smaller mount was a spotted pony. The figure riding it was carrying a bag.

The two riders were in a field full of dead, harvested wheat stalks.

Get to them, catch up to them! Andrew was yelling to himself.

Then he saw four riflemen jump up from a small ravine close to the riders.

All four discharged their muskets at the riders. Andrew could see the puffs of white smoke from their musket barrels. An instant later he heard the *pop, pop, pop, pop* of their shots.

The lead figure on the horse leaned forward, slowed his mount, and then fell backward and down to the ground.

The figure on the pony—the smaller person—was falling forward onto the mane of the spotted pony, clinging on.

But then, a second later, that rider slid off, falling onto the cold dirt of the November field.

No, no, no! Andrew was screaming as he lashed the whip and raced his carriage toward the two.

Now he could see the smaller figure lying on its stomach by the spotted pony.

Andrew leaped off the carriage and began to run toward the prone figure, his breath pounding out little white puffs in the cold.

Then, as he neared the still figure on the ground, wrapped in a cape and cap, he saw something.

He was almost paralyzed. Barely able to move. Slowly, as if in a dream, he reached down to a bag lying on the ground about ten feet from the unmoving body. As he lifted it, he heard a moan rising from the bottom of his soul.

The bag was a travel bag, brocaded in gold, black, and red. Given to Alice by her parents two birthdays ago.

Numbed and dazed, Andrew stumbled to the lying figure and fell down to his knees in the hard, frigid earth.

He reached out with a trembling hand and slowly turned over the still body.

The blondish hair of his daughter cascaded from beneath the cap. And now Andrew was looking at the face of his precious Alice, so white and pale, lifeless. Her eyes were open but not fixed on anything on the earth. He fumbled with the cape and as it opened he saw the widening circle of blood engulfing the midsection of his daughter.

There would be no goodbyes between father and daughter.

Only a father's embrace as he held her and rocked her with speechless sobs that rose up from a dark and lonely place he had never ventured before.

Chapter 19

Two Months Later

The brutal, frigid month of January brought with it a kind of cold, hollow detachment in the mansion house of Andrew and Kate Mackenzie. With the death of their daughter, it was as if life between the husband and wife had come to a strange stalemate—in a place where time had stood still, and words between them were so insufficient that they were given up to silence and melancholy.

Kate alternately blamed herself and her husband for the events that led up to Alice's death. And on occasion, she even blamed the king's men, who were, as she put it, "so anxious for revenge against the guilty that they were blinded to the need for simple mercies for the innocent."

Andrew's plans to visit his aged father, Ransom, had been unexpectedly fulfilled when he, and Kate, and several of the household servants, made the long coach ride north to Scotland in mid-November, bearing the body of young Alice.

Alice Mackenzie was buried in the family plot in St. Andrews, Scotland, next to Margaret Mackenzie, her grandmother. Her grandfather, Ransom Mackenzie, had survived the death of his beloved wife, Margaret, but his own health seemed to be slowly declining.

At the graveside, a former theology student of Ransom, who was now a pastor in Perth, delivered the sermon. The text of his short message was from the epistle of James. As he read from the fourth chapter, the small group of mourners shivered in the cold of November, with a brisk wind whipping off the North Sea. The sea was churning off on the horizon like an undulating slab of icy, grey slate.

The pastor read,

> Go to now, ye that say, *"Today or tomorrow we will go into such a city, and continue there a year, and buy and sell, and get gain." (And yet ye cannot tell what shall be tomorrow. For what is your life? It is even a vapour that appeareth for a little time, and afterward vanisheth away.) For that ye ought to say, "If the Lord will, and if we live, we will do this or that."*

Then he closed his massive Bible and said, "Alice was a beautiful girl. Fair of face, and vibrant in spirit. I am told she knew and loved the Lord Jesus Christ. Therefore we can exult that she is now walking with Him in paradise. But to those left behind here on earth, it seems she was but a vapor, which vanished too quickly, and was taken too cruelly."

Then the pastor looked at Kate and Andrew, who were numb in their grief, standing by the open grave of their daughter.

"To Kate, her mother, and Andrew, her father, and Ransom, her grandfather," he concluded, "there is left only this: that while Alice lived, she did so under the canopy of God's sovereign will. And when she perished from among us, that too was as 'the Lord will.' Someday, when we see Him as He really is and know Him perfectly in His kingdom, all things shall be explained. All things revealed. Including the reason for dear Alice's death. Until then, as we remain here below, captive to our limited knowledge in these earthly dominions, we must trust in the love of God, for His love for His people is from everlasting."

Ransom, old and infirm, had been rolled to the graveside in a small cart. But he insisted on standing, leaning heavily on his walking stick, during the service.

During the service, Kate and Andrew's gaze was transfixed on the simple box that contained the mortal remains of their only child.

But Ransom's eyes were somewhere else—he was squinting his eyes, looking off onto the horizon, where the drab sea was rolling.

After the proceedings at the cemetery, the family and servants and friends made their way to the large apartments of Ransom, where his old friends and caretakers, Jean Macleod and her sister, had prepared food and drink for the mourning guests.

After a few hours of polite conversation, Andrew searched throughout the apartments looking for Ransom. His heart yearned for some tender, profound word from his father. Surely this learned man, who walked and talked with the likes of John Knox, who withstood, with his mentor, the charges of Mary Queen of Scots, and who helped energize the Reformation in Scotland, would have healing in his words to help bind his son's broken heart.

Andrew looked for his father and was finally told that he was sitting where he now spent most of his time, on the little stone bench that looked out over the sea. Andrew had come to realize that perhaps Ransom was not the man he once was. Age, and life, had overtaken him.

Andrew walked outside and followed the path that led to the stone bench.

He carried a heavy wool blanket and draped it over the frail shoulders of his father. Then he sat next to him quietly.

A long time passed with no word spoken between the two men.

At last, Ransom spoke up first.

"There'll be no sea there, ye know," the old man said.

Andrew gave his father a puzzled look. But after a moment, he nodded with recognition.

"There'll be no sea, the Bible says," Ransom continued, "when God creates His new heavens and new earth."

Then the aged man added, "Imagine that. No sea. No waves. No waters of the deep."

Then after a few more moments Ransom spoke up again. He was still looking out to the sea.

"Mind yer wife, son," he said. "Ye have yer own grief I know. And 'tis a hard thing ye must bear. But ye have to step out from it…and be like a tree that shades and protects yer wife in her grief. She is a mother. And a mother's heart is grand large. But it also breaks deep."

Andrew was struggling in his pain not to cry. But tears were rolling down his face, hot in the frigid air.

Ransom reached out and patted his son's hand.

There was more silence.

"Where is my son Philip?" Ransom asked. Then he looked over into Andrew's eyes. "Where is yer brother? He should be here to pay respects at yer loss."

Andrew knew the question was bound to come up. He didn't know how he would break it to his aged father. He did not want to mount grief upon grief on the old man's heart. But how could he avoid it?

"There's trouble with Philip," Andrew said quietly.

"Aye," Ransom said.

"Do you know of it?" Andrew asked.

"My spirit has been troubled over him in my prayers. But I did not know why."

"I cannot tell you all. But pray for him, Da," Andrew said. "For everyone's sake, I told Philip to hide himself for the time being. Nor to have Peter come here either. It was for the best. Once again, I fear, Philip has brought destruction on himself. Perhaps down on us all…"

Ransom looked down at the ground and considered all he had heard. He turned to face his son who was sitting next to him on the stone bench.

"Ye must promise me something," Ransom said, with a passion in his voice that Andrew had not heard for many years. "Ye must promise on a covenant before God," he continued, "that ye and Philip will heal the breach that separates ye both from one another."

Andrew was speechless before the old man's plea.

"Will ye do what I ask?" Ransom asked, pleading.

Finally Andrew answered him.

"Aye, Da," he said. "I will do as ye ask."

Then Ransom, helped by his son, slowly, stiffly stood up, leaning on his walking stick, and made his way back to the warmth of the gathering of mourners within.

In January, two months later, Andrew was thinking about that conversation as he was being driven, in his private carriage, to the

London survey and mapping shop where Philip's son, Peter, was working.

Philip, following the arrest of Guy Fawkes and the decimation of the Catholic rebels, had absented himself from London. Andrew had told Peter that his father had business that had taken him on a long trip. That, but nothing more. The proprietor, Mr. Hadfield, had been told the same thing. But Hadfield had received the information from Andrew with some measured suspicion, though he did not voice it aloud.

Now Andrew was heading to the other end of London to meet with young Peter and share with him some devastating information. Andrew did not know whether he could trust Peter with it or not. But he had concluded that the young man must be told.

Still burdened with his own grief over Alice's death, Andrew was feeling the weight of the earth slowly crushing him lower and lower as he saw the sign for the surveyor's shop coming into view along the crowded, noisy London street.

Chapter 20

"The land lies along the Berwickshire coast. My brother says I will be accompanying him soon and visiting our estate there."

In the shop, Rose Heatherton was excitedly explaining to Peter the lands that were to be surveyed and mapped by his employer. But Peter was finding himself gazing more at the young woman than listening to her account.

"Yes. Yes," Peter said, looking into her eyes with an odd smile. "Go on..."

"Have you been listening to me at all, Peter?" Rose asked with a laugh.

"Of course!" he replied, trying to suppress a laugh of his own.

"What coast did I just say?"

Peter thought a minute, then answered with a sudden burst of enthusiasm.

"Why, the...Berwickshire coast!"

Rose giggled.

"You are just guessing!" she said.

"No, I'm not!" Peter shot back, trying to look earnest.

"All right then," she said. "Well. As I was saying, along the coast in Scotland, just north of the borders, that is where the estate lands of my family in Scotland are located. And I get to visit there! I know it will be in the dead of winter, drab, and cold, and perhaps even some snow on the ground. But I don't care about that! I haven't been there for such a long time. Since I was a small little girl. It's such a wild and wonderful place!"

Peter nodded and then smiled as if he had a secret.

"What do you say to that?" Rose asked, fishing a bit to get his response.

"I say that such a trip will be most...concomitant..."

Peter had picked that last word carefully, to impart the full effect of his cloaked message, and to impress his listener with his vocabulary.

"'Concomitant?'" Rose said. "And how is that? I know you are very learned." She smiled and leaned down on the desk where they were sitting and put her chin on her hand coquettishly. "So, pray tell, explain yourself!"

"I just mean to say," Peter replied, "that your trip is most harmonious with my own plans."

Her eyes brightened.

"What plans are those?" Rose said, hiding her enthusiasm.

"My master here says, because my father is away on business, that a surveyor here in this shop is to travel soon to that very property to survey it."

Then Peter leaned back with a small measure of pride and continued.

"And I, Rose, am to be that man and travel to your family's estate as chief map draftsman!"

"Then we shall be there, perhaps, at the same time," Rose said, working intensively not to explode with joy in front of him. "That will be...most pleasant!"

Then Rose caught sight of her brother, through the window, dodging the horses and carts in the street, on his way to the shop.

"There is William," she said hastily, "I must go. Please visit me…I mean, feel free to visit my brother William and me while you are there on your mapping expedition. Your company is always appreciated."

"I will visit!" Peter said. "Yes—do count on that, Rose. I shall indeed!"

Just as Rose left the shop and met her brother outside, the door swung open and Peter's uncle, Andrew Mackenzie, strode in, removed his short-brimmed cap, and greeted him.

Peter could tell by the somber expression on his uncle's face that he was burdened by something.

"Good Uncle," Peter said. "So wonderful to see you again."

Andrew smiled thinly, then asked if the proprietor or anyone else was present in the shop.

"Why no," Peter answered. "What is it?"

"Sit down," Andrew instructed him. His uncle sat next to him at a drafting table, and leaned forward, and began to talk.

"I will be short and concise," he began. "You know that your father has been gone for some two months. On 'business' I had told you. In point of fact—he has been in hiding. And at my insistence."

Peter was surprised but not shocked. He knew his father's exploits too well to doubt the truth of what his uncle was telling him.

"You have heard of the plot of certain Catholic rebels who had designs to blow up Parliament, and the king, and his government with it?"

"Of course. All of London talks about it."

"The trials of several of those scurrilous plotters will be commencing soon. I am part of the legal consort advising the king. But mark you, Peter, I am caught in crushing pinchers of a great dilemma."

"What is it?"

"I have information that during his confession under torture, one of the defendants, one Guy Fawkes, made certain accusations. He claims to have received advice on the purchase of fuses for the detonation of the gunpowder bombs beneath Parliament—from an unnamed Scot."

Peter was riveted now on Andrew's every word.

"I knew that your father has, from time to time, used explosives while on expeditions and travels. He learned the trade on his first trip to the New World. I also knew that he circulated among men whose character is highly dubious—"

"My father would never consort with assassins," Peter urged.

"And I would like to believe that too," Andrew said. "But the fact remains that I have confronted Philip on this matter. After a very tumultuous argument between the two of us, he reluctantly admitted having a conversation with this Fawkes fellow, though he went by another name at the time. And in that discussion, he did advise Fawkes where he could purchase the most effective fuses to be found in London. Your father swears that this Fawkes fellow said he wanted the fuses for removing tree stumps on a large estate. But it doesn't matter. If your father is implicated in this plot to blow up the king, he will be drawn and quartered for it. Mark me well—he will! And then, when his head is placed upon a spear outside London Bridge, they will next come after you, and me, and my wife as well!"

"What should I do?" Peter asked, almost breathless.

"Nothing, my lad. Not yet. Just report to me any inquiries that come your way about your father's dealings. Or his comings and goings."

"I will," Peter said, his face bearing the ashen realization of the news that his uncle had just brought him.

"And one more thing you can do."

"What is that?" Peter asked.

"You can pray, boy," Andrew said, patting him on the shoulder. "Pray to the Lord with all your might. For His divine protection. For all of us. And especially your wayward father."

Chapter 21

In the weeks following Peter's meeting with Andrew Mackenzie, the young mapmaking apprentice thought back to his uncle's warnings. Yet in those days spent in the map and survey shop, he had no occasion to worry further about possible suspicions regarding his father's supposed involvement in plots against the Crown. The fact remained that no one, including his master, Kenneth Hadfield, had questioned the young man about Philip Mackenzie's whereabouts or his affairs. There appeared to be no reason to fear that Peter's father would be arrested, and then hailed before the master of the rack for interrogation.

Perhaps it was Peter's youthful optimism, then, that led him to so easily discount the potential risks against his father and against his extended family, all because of the intersection of Guy Fawkes's murderous plans with the shadowy activities of his father.

But there was also another fact. Perhaps more than anything, it explained Peter's blithe attitude about the treason trials that were being prepared in London and which seemed to occupy the conversation of everyone in that city.

Nearly all of Peter's thoughts had been preoccupied with his upcoming trip to the Berwickshire coast. After a few weeks of planning, Mr. Hadfield sent Peter off with Joshua Muggins, a younger surveying associate, to verify and then chart the boundary lines of the large Heatherton estates.

The last day before his journey north to the borderlands of Scotland, Peter was told the reason why the boundaries of the Scottish land holdings of the Heatherton family had to be mapped.

"There is to be a charter of sale for those lands, in fee simple," Hadfield said matter-of-factly to his young employee.

"Why is that?" Peter asked innocently.

"The father, Roger Heatherton, died with a burden of great debt," he replied. "His widow and children are facing destitution. The only thing that will keep them from sinking into complete poverty is their ability to liquidate the estate at a goodly price. His son, William, wisely I believe, has decided to sell off the Scottish lands at Seacrest House first, in piecemeal parcels if need be. I imagine he will next proceed to barter off their home here in London. The furniture. The horses. The good widow's jewelry. Everything."

The thought of Rose being plunged into poverty struck Peter like the smarting slap of a winter wind.

"Ah me, the poorhouse is, indeed, a dismal fate for any man's family," Hadfield said, shaking his head.

Peter was engrossed in reflecting back on his employer's somber comments about the Heatherton family while he and Joshua Muggins were traveling by horseback to the Scottish estate. By then, the two were a few miles beyond England's border with Scotland.

"Looky!" Joshua cried out as the two stopped their horses and gazed out over the rugged ocean-coast scenery.

From the gentle, rolling hills of the English midlands, the land had changed considerably. Now there were high, jagged cliffs comprised of sheer rock, but softened by a vast pelt of green and brown vegetation that covered them. The high rock faces, jutting out like the prows of ships from their considerable height, overlooked the crashing sea far below. There were swarms of circling sea birds cawing in the air above. As Peter and Joshua tracked the brids' flight as they rode by on their horses, they noticed that they were soaring back and forth from the nests they had made in the crevices of the rock cliffs, keeping their eggs safe from the wild updrafts, the winter cold, and the nasty beaks of other flying predators.

"Have you ever seen such beauty?" Joshua asked.

"I have," Peter said, smiling. "I have traveled through here with my father before."

Joshua studied his traveling friend, who seemed to be distracted and who was staring out to sea from their ocean cliff vantage point.

"But Peter," Joshua said with a laugh, "I don't think it's the grandeur of nature that you are mulling over now, boy-o."

Peter tried to hide his grin.

Then Joshua reined his horse over closer to Peter, to add another thought.

"I think it's not an ocean view you're thinking about," Joshua added, "but maybe a Rose…"

Now Peter was chuckling, and he led his horse back to the path toward the Heatherton estates.

"Do ye take me for a gardener?" Peter shot back with a chuckle.

"I do. But just make sure you don't get tangled in her thorns…"

She is the first Rose I've ever seen that seems to possess no such danger, Peter mused to himself silently.

The two riders made their way past the Priory near St. Abbs, where the late Mary Queen of Scots had frequented. They knew that they were getting closer. The cold was setting in, and they were tired, sore, and numb from riding since before the break of dawn.

Then, an hour's further ride beyond that, as the sun was setting they arrived, as they had been directed, at the long, single story, thatched roof house belonging to the groundskeeper of the estate. The keeper's name was Henry Paltree, an elderly man with a kind smile and more energy than would be expected for a man in his seventies. His wife, Esther, was a good-natured woman, slightly plump, with a round, ruddy face.

"Come in, dearies," Esther said as the two weary travelers dismounted. "We were told to expect you. I know you have important business for the Heathertons. And we shall be pleased to give you food and shelter for as long as your work here requires."

Esther laid out steaming bowls of stew, rich with beef, and a whole loaf of bread.

Peter and Joshua were famished, and they eagerly cleaned their bowls and were quickly furnished with seconds of the stew.

Henry stoked the fire, and the warmth of the blazing oak logs was a delicious end to the day as the two young travelers finished their bowls and then settled back in their chairs in front of the rough, stone fireplace.

"I noticed some strange equipment on your horses," Esther remarked, trying to sound nonchalant. "What manner of tools might those be?"

"Esther!" Henry called out briskly. "The business these young men be on, for the Heatherton family, is none of our business."

Then Henry turned to Peter and Joshua and apologized.

"Excuse my good wife," he said. "She has an unnatural curiosity. Though she means no offense."

"And we take none by it," Peter said quickly. "Actually, those are surveying and mapping tools. We are here to verify and measure the full extent of the Heatherton estate here at Seacrest."

Henry and Esther looked at each other cautiously after Peter's comments, but said nothing further.

Then there was a knock at the door.

Henry hurried over to the door, looking unusually spry, and swung it open. William Heatherton was standing in the doorway, and next to him, his sister, Rose.

"Come in, come in, Master William!" Henry said energetically. "My Esther here shall be glad to prepare a meal for ye. Come in an' set a spell before the fire. And I could play for you on my penny whistle too. It has been so long since we've seen ye, lad…"

William, whom Peter had taken to be somewhat of a cold, reserved fellow, broke into a warm smile and clasped Henry by the shoulders.

"Henry, you and your wife are such grand friends. You are right, it has been too long."

And with that, William and Rose stepped into the warmth of the humble Paltree house.

Esther served up more food. Henry piled another log on the fire, and then took to his penny whistle and commenced to play several lively tunes.

William kicked off his boots, and when Henry moved from musician to storyteller, William laughed out loud at several of his stories about the years of his youth on the Scottish estate.

Rose joined in with a story of how William, when he was fifteen years old, had tried to secretly escape the large manor house late at night by climbing down a tall, wooden, rose trellis; but it collapsed under his weight with a clatter, sending him to the ground. The servants heard the noise and were met by a dazed fifteen-year-old who was trying to explain what happened. In the confusion, when William tried to share with the servants that the 'spine of the rose trellis' had broken, the staff misinterpreted his account, taking it to mean that Rose herself had fallen and broken her back. The household staff was thrown into a panic until Rose finally appeared, rubbing her eyes from being awakened in the middle of the night, and fully unharmed.

All of them enjoyed a hearty chuckle at that. Eventually, William said they must retire to the estate house on horseback. Peter jumped up and offered to escort them down the winding road that led to the manor house.

William accepted his offer, describing it as a "kind gesture," which were the first positive words Rose's brother had yet directed to Peter. The three mounted their horses and rode down the forested lane that eventually wound from the groundskeeper's cottage for almost a mile to the main mansion. The moon was full and provided a fine light for their short journey.

Peter wanted to strike up a conversation with Rose, who was riding next to him, but he couldn't find the words.

The trio finally arrived at the wide circle path in front of the estate house that contained, at its center, a tall fountain with a statue. The four-story mansion house was built of yellow stone and climbing vines, and Peter was impressed with its grandeur. William dismounted. Peter assisted Rose as she climbed off her horse. Several servants hurried outside, and a groomsman led the horses of William and Rose off to the stable.

Peter quickly ran over to William and took him aside before he disappeared through the tall oak front doors of the Seacrest House.

"William, if I may," Peter asked. "Could I ask something quite important of you?"

"Concerning what?" William replied.

"Concerning your sister, Rose," Peter said, trying not to stammer.

"What manner of request do you have?"

"That after my work is done here on your properties, and before Joshua, my associate, and I return to London…"

"Yes?" William asked a little wearily, as he was anxious to head for his bedchambers.

"That perhaps, if it be possible, that you would see it clear to grant me permission—as the head of your family and in the stead of your late father—permission for me to walk with your sister. I saw a lovely place of cliffs and hills overlooking the sea on the way here. On the very edge of your lands, I would wager. I would very much like to stroll with her there. And you may accompany us, of course."

"As I will certainly do," William responded soberly. Then the beginning of a smile appeared, and he added, "It is a picturesque place. I've walked there myself on occasion."

Peter waited anxiously for his final answer on the matter. Then William concluded the issue.

"Your request shall be granted," he said, "assuming that you successfully conclude your surveying business first, of course."

William beckoned Rose, who was standing close enough to hear the interchange. She was beaming, and as a servant held the door open for her she entered the mansion house—but not until she first threw a bright smile toward Peter as she walked past him. Then the great oak doors of the estate mansion swung shut for the night with a loud thud.

Chapter 22

"Those birds are called razorbills."

"We saw them several days ago when we first rode toward your estate lands."

"Aren't they wonderful? So graceful. And they fly so fast—darting up and down the air currents. Sweeping along the cliffs. Looking for food. Protecting their young in the nests in the rocks."

After she said that, Rose wrapped her arms across her chest, snuggling into the thick cape that kept out most of the January winds. It was a mild day, and the sun was out and was actually warm on the face, as she and Peter walked along a slightly worn path that led up and down the cliffs overlooking the sea. But the winds were fierce in that place as they whipped off the ocean and then raced upward along the sheer rock walls, and their chill could still cut through even wool coats.

Sheep were grazing on the hills below the highest cliffs. William was slightly ahead of them with his walking stick. He seemed pensive that day, and had left Peter and Rose mostly to themselves. Joshua Muggins had decided to ride into the local village and nose around there a bit on his own. Though Peter suspected that his associate was not just enjoying the exuberance of traveling outside of England for the first time, but also was kindly giving Peter as much privacy with Rose as possible.

Rose stopped on the path, and closed her eyes, and bent her head back, smiling.

"What are you thinking," Peter asked, "this very moment?"

After giggling for a few seconds, Rose opened her eyes. Then her smile became wider, but she shared only a part of her mind.

"A prayer," she replied. "I said a prayer to God."

"Then why were you so amused?" Peter asked, suddenly becoming serious. "How can God be a source of amusement?"

There was a strange sense of curiosity in his question, but no hint of judgment, though his question could easily have been misinterpreted by someone with a less delicate and refined sense of discernment than Rose possessed.

"Does not our Lord Jesus speak of joy—repeatedly?" she asked.

After a moment's reflection Peter smiled and nodded.

"And on the matter of love, God is the Source, is He not?"

Again, Peter had to agree.

"Then why must we need to be unduly stern and dour when we speak to Him? Especially on matters so joyous—"

"Matter like what?" Peter asked, carefully eyeing Rose for her answer.

"There are some things," she said, "that a lady cannot speak of prematurely."

"What kind of things?"

"Oh, Peter!" she cried out with a laugh, "no more! Do not force me to answer. It would not be proper. Far too forward of me…"

"Then I shall not," Peter said resolutely, "pry any further. If there is anything I so admire in you, it is that you are a young woman of propriety…and grace…and so many other things."

Rose could feel herself blushing, and she quickly changed the subject around.

"And a moment ago...as we studied the birds, what were you thinking?" she asked.

Peter's face took on a intense expression, almost illuminated in the brightness of his eyes.

"I was thinking," he said, "of a verse of Scripture—from the psalms—about birds. It made me think of it, when we were looking over the cliffs."

"Please recite it to me," Rose said. "I would like to hear it."

Peter stopped walking and turned to face her. Then he spoke the psalm, one of dozens he had committed to memory:

> *Yea, the sparrow hath found her an house,*
> *And the swallow a nest for her, where she may lay*
>   *her young:*
> *Even by thine altars, O Lord of hosts, my King*
>   *and my God.*
> *Blessed are they that dwell in thine house:*
> *They will ever praise thee.*

Rose became very contemplative as they commenced walking. Then she finally spoke up.

"Birds find homes in the rocks," she said with a tinge of sadness. "But what of us, Peter—my family? Will we ever know another home, when all is said and done?"

Then, in that instant, Peter knew that Rose had been told by her brother everything about her family's dire financial problems.

"I'm sorry," she said with a trembling voice, "I didn't mean to burden you with our troubles."

"It is no burden," Peter responded gently, "to share the cares of those whom one cares for so very much."

After Peter said that, Rose gave him a comforted look that would have wanted to say much more, but was restrained by discretion.

"I am confident," Peter said with assurance, "if the Lord can find nests for birds, then He can find a home for you, and your brother, and your mother, after all of your father's debts are paid and settled."

After they walked on for a few more steps, Peter decided to go further in his comments. And so he spoke what was on his heart, but could not look at Rose while he did so, but looked out to the sea instead.

"My care for you is so powerful," he said firmly, and in a kind of ceremonial cadence, "that I shall now, in this place, pledge you this thing—that if it is in my power to do so, I shall protect you and your family from the haunts of poverty. And even more than that..."

And with that Peter paused and slowly turned around to take in her pretty and expectant face.

"I pledge to protect you, dear Rose. Like a rock cliff that hides the birds from the storm. As God is my shelter, I would, if you would allow me, wish to spread His shelter around you also."

There were no words between them at that moment, but there was no need for them. The tears in Rose's eyes were not from the biting wind.

She took her two gloved hands, grasped Peter's hand, and put it to her cheek. Then she closed her eyes, her lips moving slightly.

Peter guessed that she was praying.

And of course he was right.

Chapter 23

It had crossed Peter's mind to try and invent some artifice—some excuse—anything, so that he could stay longer at Seacrest and visit longer with Rose. But there was simply no way that he could do that. He knew that, having completed his surveying and mapping work with Joshua, his employer would now need them back at the shop in London. That was particularly true in light of his father's prolonged absence from the city.

On that score, Peter found himself not worrying much about his father's safety. He had been raised to enjoy a strong sense of self-dependence. Peter had occasionally been taken by him on his travels to Scotland, and Ireland, and even to the Continent once, where they passed through Spain and Portugal. He had seen his father fight his way out of difficult straits, sometimes by brawn or skillful sword play, but often by clever wit. It seemed incomprehensible to Peter that his father could not extricate himself from whatever suspicions lingered against him in London.

And as for Peter, his father did often take trips on his own and leave his son behind to fend for himself, leaving ample money, but little else, except a firm handshake for the lad and his confidence that he could manage till his father returned.

So as Peter and Joshua rode back to London, Peter had few worries, except regarding when, and how, he could next meet with Rose Heatherton. He was convinced that he was in love with the young woman. He had never felt such a wellspring of emotion for any other woman. Peter's good looks and kind manner had usually attracted women with ease. But he had never felt anything for the women he had met. Until now.

With his well-established job at master Kenneth Hadfield's shop, he had begun planning for his future—something that, more and more, he was convinced must include Rose as his wife. He had no idea how he would approach the issue with Rose's brother and mother, but he had already committed the matter to prayer.

Take away this great desire for Rose, he would pray, *if this desire is not of Thy will, O God.*

"Did you have a fair day with the lass?"

Peter's thoughts were interrupted by Joshua as the two headed inland by horseback, with the great cliffs of the eastern coast to their back.

"I had a fine time," Peter answered. "And you?"

"I knocked about in the village of Ayton," Joshua responded. "Had a chat with the local smith. Winked at one of his daughters."

"And did she wink back, laddie?" Peter asked with a laugh.

"Didn't have time to notice. The smith was a powerful-looking fellow, with a suspicious look. When he saw me eyeing his daughter he was quick to tell me if I didn't have a horse to shoe or a rig to fix or some iron piece to straighten, then I needed to be on my way!"

"He sounds like a fellow with a sharp judgment of people!" Peter shot back.

Joshua gave out a comically overblown reaction of feigned insult, pretending to be wounded and astonished.

Peter smiled at his antics. He had worked with Joshua at the shop, and the two had always been friendly. But during their trip to Seacrest House they had bonded in a close-knit way. Peter's life had always been a traveling one, due to his father's itinerant life. There was rarely time to develop lasting friendships. Peter was glad to have a peer he could now pal with.

As the two rode together on their way to London, the air was cold, but it was a bright day, with blue skies and just a few white, billowing clouds sailing overhead. Peter was feeling grand about life, and he was glad to have Joshua as his companion to banter with on the long ride back. He had no idea that outside of London, there was a meeting ensuing that could potentially impact all of his hopes and dreams.

In the grimy seaport of Blackwall a few miles east of London, Andrew Mackenzie was mounting a set of outside wooden stairs to the second story of a mercantile and shipping office. He paused for a moment, looking out over the docks, where sailors and deckhands were unloading large bundles of linen that had just arrived from Ireland.

Andrew knocked three times. Then paused and knocked twice. And then three times again.

"Name?" came on the voice on the other side of the weathered door.

"It's Andrew," he said.

The door swung open.

Philip Mackenzie was in the doorway, staring back at his brother.

"Well, if it isn't my esteemed brother, come a-slummin' to the docks," Philip said with a sneer.

Andrew stepped into the small hovel. There was a bare table with two chairs and a bed mat on the floor. The smell of fish, and grime, and foul water that permeated the docks was also present.

"Do pardon me," Philip remarked sarcastically, "that I don't have cakes and dainties prepared for you, seein' ye're a high consort to the Crown and all. And the room's a bit in need of a cleanin'—but then, it seems that the mansion staff is all off for the day."

"You can skip the jokes," Andrew shot back. "I can't stay long."

"No one invited you to stay long."

Andrew took a deep breath, wishing to avoid inflaming the interchange any further, but knowing that was probably impossible.

"I spoke to your son," Andrew began.

"And you told him what, exactly?"

"Enough so he could understand the risks we are all facing."

"You told him?" Philip said with a smoldering rage in is voice, taking several steps toward his brother until he was staring him in the eye, closer than an arm's length. "I told you I didn't want him to know. *I told you that!*"

"I had no choice," Andrew said trying to sound reasonable. "With you being in hiding right now, he has to know what we are up against."

"That was my decision not yours. See here, I am his father. I make the decisions what my son is to be told. Always playin' the big brother, aren't you Andrew? Well you can play that game with your own Alice if you want—but I will handle the parenting of my son!"

But before he could finish, Philip saw something in Andrew's expression at the mention of Alice's name. A look so pained that it defied measurement.

Andrew looked into Philip's face. Then he told him.

"My Alice..." he said, now feeling the ugly tide of emotion roaring up out of the pit again while struggling to keep his composure.

Then Andrew finished the painful message.

"My Alice is dead."

Philip was stunned. He stepped back.

"How?"

"The sheriff and his men were tracking the conspirators," Andrew said with a labored voice. "They caught a group of them. Cornered them at Stephen Littleton's estate in Staffordshire. Catesby and others. Alice happened to be there...in love with the groomsman it seems...they tried to flee together. But...they were caught in musket fire. Killed...both of them killed."

"I'm sorry. Someone should have told me..." Philip said in a wounded tone.

"I chose not to," Andrew replied bitterly. "I couldn't trust you. That in your impetuousness you might try to come to the funeral. We can't afford to be seen together—"

"You're right about that," Philip shot back. "I *would* have come back for the funeral of my niece. And no fear of the king's spies would have stopped me either. So what is troubling you the most, dear brother, the fear that your own hide may be tanned because of my dealings with Guy Fawkes?"

"How dare you insinuate that!" Andrew barked. "I am trying to keep all of us from the gallows. And all of this is because of *you*, brother, and your unsavory associations! Your actions have threatened us all with ruin!"

Philip felt the explosive impulse to shoot back, but a rare exercise of discretion came over him, and he stopped just short of a verbal retort. His face, however, showed the strain within as he labored to control his temper. Perhaps because he quietly recognized the pain of his brother's loss. Or also because he had felt for some time a lurking sense of unrest over the fact that he and Andrew had, for as long he could remember, been at violent odds with each other. But either way, Philip decided to hold his peace.

Finally, after an uncomfortable silence, Andrew strode to the door and prepared to walk through it. He turned around in the doorway to face his brother.

As Andrew stared at Philip, a torrent of feelings washed over him: his still fresh grief over the loss of Alice. The turbulence in his own marriage. His fears about the reaction of the Crown if Philip's dealings with Fawkes were uncovered. And how very distant God seemed lately in the midst of those sea of troubles.

But there was something else too. Long-held resentments he had allowed to remain untended. And unrepented of. His lingering feelings that during her lifetime, his mother had always favored Philip. Yet he could never point to anything specific to prove that. But when she fell ill, Philip was away on a voyage—on another of his far-flung adventures. Andrew, the faithful, the steadfast, was there, along with Kate, to help Ransom to care for his ailing wife as she slowly succumbed.

Philip the world traveler would not make it back in time for the funeral of his mother. That too struck a particular discord with Andrew. Yet, though he was a powerfully analytic person, he was unable to account, logically, for his feelings about that issue. Philip's absence at the funeral made no practical difference. It was, though, just one more example, in Andrew's mind, of his brother having abandoned both his family ties and his good sense as he chased the next horizon.

And at the same time, Andrew heard the voice of his father's plea to him, as Ransom Mackenzie sat on the cold stone bench that overlooked the sea and shared his heart's burden with his eldest son.

Ye must promise on a covenant before God that ye and Philip will heal the breach that separates ye both from one another.

Andrew decided to share none of that, though. His parting words to Philip were rigidly objective.

"Know this, my brother," he said through tight lips. "The trial of Fawkes and some of the conspirators begins soon. I have reviewed their written confessions. Yer name does not appear there. But they will, I have been advised, be given the right to address the jury in their own defense. There is a chance that Fawkes will have a sudden spark of memory—sufficient to give up yer name. Ye must be prepared to leave England—perhaps forever."

Philip cocked his head slightly to assess his brother's final warning. But he said nothing. Andrew turned away and shut the door behind him.

In his dingy little room, Philip Mackenzie mulled over what he would have said to Andrew had he possessed the mind to.

I have never run from a fight, he thought to himself. *I have no plans to start now.*

Chapter 24

As a lawyer for the Crown, Andrew Mackenzie was close enough to the prosecution team of King James to have gained advance intelligence about most of the upcoming legal proceedings.

The trial was to begin in Westminster Hall. A special platform had been constructed to house the eight conspirators who would be put on trial first. Guy Fawkes would be one of them, along with Thomas Wintour, who had survived the gun battle at Holbeach House despite being severely wounded.

Viewing rooms on the sides of the hall were created for ambassadors and visiting dignitaries. King James and his own family had their own secret, covered viewing area from which the entire trial would be visible.

The chief prosecutor for the crown was Attorney General Sir Edward Coke, the renowned English jurist and scholar. The judiciary overseeing the trial was comprised of eight lords commissioner. Robert Cecil, the king's chief advisor, was one of them. So was Sir John Popham, the lord chief justice who had supervised the interrogations of Fawkes.

On the day that the conspiracy trial opened, the hall was jammed with members of Parliament and officials of the Crown. Every seat

in the special viewing boxes was occupied. The eight lords commissioner, with Popham in the middle, were seated on the raised
judges' bench situated at the end of the hall. The commissioners
all wore red robes with white ermine fur collars.

King James sat silently up in his covered box, peering out at the
defendants as they were led to their platform by armed bailiffs.

Yet, while Andrew could anticipate much about the trial against
the Catholic plotters, there was still something missing; something
that was catastrophically critical, and of which he was completely
ignorant. For he had no idea what, if anything, the defendants
would say in their own defense. And he did not know whether, in
a final, desperate move to avoid execution, Fawkes or the others
might begin naming names.

Including the names of those that thus far had avoided being
included in the formal indictment.

Perhaps even the name of one man whose brother had close
ties to the king himself.

Down on the main floor, Andrew was seated at a long oak table
with several legal counselors for the Crown. He kept a calm demeanor, but inside he was controlling a flood of anxiety. Would his
brother Philip's dealings with Fawkes be mentioned in any of the
testimony? Would Andrew, thereafter, be questioned, and perhaps
even suspected of being a spy within the king's own company?

Andrew knew that there was only one procedure that carried
with it any certainty of avoiding that tragic possibility. There had
been speculation among the Crown's bench that, given the extensive confessions that had already been wrung from several of the
defendants—and notably from Fawkes—perhaps they would enter
guilty pleas and throw themselves on to the mercy of the court.
That would be the only way they could avoid execution, though it

would undoubtedly secure a lifetime in the dungeons. Yet, in time, and with a change of monarchs at some distant time in the future, even those sentences might be pardoned.

Much of the conventional wisdom suggested that if anyone was likely to use that strategy, it would be Fawkes. After all, he was caught red-handed in the cellar next to the gunpowder. And his confession was the most specific in plainly implicating himself. That is exactly what Andrew was hoping and praying for. If Fawkes pled guilty, his defense would never be heard. And Fawkes was the only conspirator who had been in direct contact with Philip Mackenzie. With a guilty plea, the involvement of Andrew's brother could slip into quiet oblivion. Future trials of the Catholic priests who had collaborated with the eight rebels were already being planned. The focus would soon be off of the likes of Fawkes and Wintour and onto the Jesuits.

There was still hope.

The trial was called into order by the lord chief justice. The clerk commenced to read out the names of each of the defendants. When he came to Guy Fawkes, he raised his voice, and then punctuated the various names used by Fawkes: John Johnson, Guido Fawkes, and lastly his legal one. As he did a loud murmur swept through the hall.

Then the clerk proceeded to recite the lengthy charges contained in the indictment.

The defendants were charged with a vile conspiracy "not only to kill the King of England, His Majesty James, and also his sons, but to alter and subvert the government of the kingdom of England, and to alter and subvert the worship of God established in this realm." Each of the defendants were alleged to be "false traitors, with evil intent to blow up and destroy the king, the princes, and the Lords and Commons by the use of gunpowder stored and readied for that malicious purpose."

Up on the platform, the defendants all seemed unperturbed. Several of them had been allowed to bring with them their pipes and bags of tobacco, and they were smoking leisurely as the clerk read the shocking contents of the indictment.

The king, who had openly written and spoken out against this new vice of tobacco, glared at the accused men. His Majesty could only interpret their public display as a personal insult against him and further evidence of their rebellious and subversive attitude.

After reading the indictment, the clerk stepped forward toward the platform containing the eight accused rebels. In his hand was the long document with the red ribbon seal dangling from it.

The clerk looked up at the defendants.

"How do you plead, sirs? Mister Wintour—what say you?"

Wintour stood up, his arm bandaged up after being blown almost entirely off in the battle at Holbeach House.

He looked out over the huge hall and then fixed his eyes on the lord chief justice.

"I plead *not guilty*."

An audible reaction rose up from the crowd.

Then, one after another, each of the next six defendants were asked the same question, and each answered the same way, until the clerk reached Sir Everard Digby, a close friend of Robert Catesby. Much to Andrew's delight, Digby entered a plea of guilty. Andrew hoped that might be a harbinger of things to come, as Fawkes's plea would come next.

Digby was given an immediate opportunity, having admitted his guilt, to plead for mercy.

"My part in this plot, good sirs, was regrettably only because of my close friendship with Robert Catesby, the chief architect of this harmful conspiracy. His enthusiasm and great skills of persuasion led me astray. Mister Catesby was a man of powerful leadership, and he entrapped me with his wiles."

Then Digby, with considerable tearful emotion in his voice, called upon the court to consider the impact of an execution upon his family.

"My guilt is mine own," he cried out. "But why should it also be borne—in my cruel death—by my wife and sons as well…left to wander this country in destitution and dishonor? Spare my life, not for me, good sirs, but for their sakes."

When Digby was finished, Sir Edward Coke leaped to his feet from counsel's table and strode directly into the center of the hall, poised halfway between the bench where the eight lords commissioners sat and the platform where Digby had now seated himself.

"Friendship with Catesby!" Coke thundered. "This deadly defendant does ply your ears with such phrases as *friendship*? Mister Digby does use such terms as *friendship* in a unique and curious way. For that which he calls *friendship*, the law of this realm does call *criminal conspiracy and treason!*"

Then Coke attacked Digby's plea on behalf of his family.

"And then this heretic and traitor does invoke mercy for his own wife and children as a ruse to save his own life. Yet, Your Honors, does he truly care about the wives and children of others? He was part of plot to murder not just the king, but his wife and two sons as well! Where was his familial care when the plot was hatched? Where was his love and concern for the kith and kin of the Crown when he sat in meetings where twenty-six barrels of gunpowder were agreed to be used to decimate countless innocent lives—wives and children included? I say to you, good members of this Court, that Mr. Digby's inconsistency in his argument is no mere lapse of logic. No. It rather is the reflection of an evil heart that is still unrepentant."

Judging by the faces of the judges on the bench, Andrew concluded that Digby's arguments had been demolished by Coke.

Now the clerk read off the last name on the indictment.

"Guy Fawkes, defendant in this indictment, you are called upon to enter your plea."

With that, Fawkes slowly rose to his feet on the platform. His strong, vigorous soldier's body was now broken and bowed.

Andrew Mackenzie did not realize it, but as he watched Fawkes rise painfully to a standing position, both of his hands were gripped so tightly on the lion-headed arms on his chair that his knuckles were white.

Chapter 25

The clerk called out to Fawkes again.

"How do you plead, sir? What say you?"

Fawkes looked down at the platform on which he stood. He was momentarily staring, as a condemned man might glance down at the scaffold that held his weight, and from which he would soon drop to his death.

Then he looked up and surveyed the entire crowded hall and spoke. He did so in a weakened but clearly audible voice.

"I do hereby plead," he stated without a flinch, *"not guilty."*

Gasps, and then a murmur of consternation and surprise swept through Westminster Hall. His plea, to many there, did not make sense.

By what audacity did Guy Fawkes now claim total innocence? Didn't he sign multiple confessions admitting his complicity in the planning and attempted execution of the plot?

"Are you sure that is your plea?" Lord Chief Justice Popham asked with a tinge of sarcasm in his voice.

"I am," Fawkes replied. "There are a few items mentioned in that aforesaid indictment...some meetings of the alleged conspirators...where I was not present."

"I see," Popham responded unimpressed. Then he leaned forward, and raising his voice, he demanded, "Anything else?"

Popham's voice rang through out the hall in an echoed reverberation.

Andrew Mackenzie at his place at Crown counsel's table was frozen in his chair.

"Yes, there is," Fawkes said. Then a twisted smile came over his weary face.

"But I shall speak my piece only when it is time to present my defense. And then...this matter shall be fully explained."

And then he added a further comment, in a voice that now seemed to possess a strange kind of renewed vitality. And it seemed to rock the floor under Andrew's feet.

"Including those who do not join us here on this platform of the accused...but *should well do so...*"

Andrew's mind was reeling. That which he had hoped and prayed against, now was threatening to unfold.

The panel of jurymen were led into the hall and placed on either side of the huge chamber. They were instructed by Popham of the nature of the charges and the identities of the defendants whose cases would now be heard.

Then Sir Edward Coke rose from his seat and strode up to a position directly in front of the bench of lords commissioner. He had narrow, piercing eyes, a long, immaculately trimmed moustache, and a pointed beard. His red robe was draped with a gold lattice necklace laden with honoraria. As the attorney general of the English Crown, Coke already had the esteem of all of the lords commissioner.

As chief prosecutor, he did not waste time before attacking Fawkes and the conspirators.

He charged, in a piercing voice that filled the vast hall, that some of the conspirators, and especially Guy Fawkes, had traveled to Spain specifically to garner support for a pro-Catholic revolt in England. It was, he said, a carefully constructed plot. And underlying all of it was a heretical and religious zealotry that sought power at the expense of blood.

"Behind all of this—behind the gunpowder, behind the dark plans of death and mayhem, and the plans to kidnap the little Princess Elizabeth and then raise her as a Catholic puppet queen—behind even the deadly anarchists themselves who smugly sit up there on their defendants' platform—behind all of this lies the Jesuits. The priests within this land who would depose all Protestant kings and would dispose of entire kingdoms. They sanctified and justified the evil plans of the gunpowder plotters, they administered the sacraments to the conspirators on the eve of their dastardly attack so their consciences could be scrubbed clean before wallowing in innocent blood."

Coke's explosive opening statement lasted several hours.

When he had finished, the sergeant-at-arms, Coke's chief prosecution assistant, then presented each of the various written confessions to the tribunal, displaying them with great flourish to the commissioners and then to the jurymen, then reading them aloud.

The last confession belonged to Fawkes. As the associate prosecutor read out Fawkes's earlier statement, he did not pause—he did not even accentuate—the one phrase that had been the obsession of Andrew Mackenzie.

The confession, as it was read to the court, was quite lengthy. It described in great detail Fawkes's role in the conspiracy and the meetings he participated in. After almost an hour of reading it aloud, the sergeant-at-arms arrived at the place in the confession most dreaded by Andrew:

"I do affirm that I conducted business, in pursuit of the conspiracy, with a certain Scotsman. He advised me on where to obtain the most excellent of fuses for explosive purposes—fuses that would not easily be snuffed out. Fuses that would ensure the proper burn. His name presently escapes me."

And then came the most feared line.

"However, it was thought by some among us, that the Scotsman may have members of his kin who are, or were, in close concert with King James."

As that was being read, Andrew was examining the faces of the lords commissioner. None showed a flicker of recognition, or interest. Except one.

Robert Cecil tilted his head slightly and then placed a finger to the side of his face, ever so gently. Andrew could not be sure, as the bench was a far distance from the counsel's bench, where Cecil's eyes were directed.

But for an instant at least, Andrew felt that Cecil was staring directly at him.

When the confessions had all been read aloud, further evidence was read into the record by the sergeant-at-arms. At the completion of the Crown's case, Andrew concluded that the guilt of the defendants had been proven by overwhelming evidence, most of it coming from their own mouths.

When the Crown rested its case, the defendants were given the chance to present a defense. After a short conference among the judges, it was agreed that Fawkes's defense would be heard first. Fawkes was helped down the stairway that had been erected for the temporary platform. He was escorted to the high witness stand where, with great effort, he climbed up, then hung on to the rails with both hands.

From his position in the dock, he first claimed that a few of the meetings alleged in the indictment were ones where he was not present. Andrew knew that given the bulk of Fawkes's involvement, according to his own confession, his first point was trifling at best.

Then he entered upon the meat of his strategy.

"I do not repent of my involvement in this matter," he boldly pronounced, "because the promises of this Crown to accommodate the rights of English Catholics has been repeatedly broken."

Sir Edward Coke bluntly interrupted him.

"What promises, Mr. Fawkes? Those that reside only in your twisted imagination?"

"No, Sir Edward," Fawkes shot back, "those made by James as King of Scotland on the eve of his leaving for London to assume the Crown of England."

"Show me the royal decree to that effect," Coke volleyed back. "Show forth the written instruments containing His Majesty's seal—any written document wherein the king agreed to give this 'accommodation' you brag about…"

Fawkes's face showed that he knew the truth of the matter: He knew he could not substantiate his claim by any written record. James had been purposely vague in making statements of compromise with his Catholic consorts in Scotland.

Fawkes was silent.

But then he spoke up again.

"Yet there are those—still free in this country—who participated in our plot. But because of their heredity and birth, they are not on this platform…"

Coke rose again and strode up to Fawkes.

"What heredity?" he asked.

"Is not the king of England Scottish by birth?"

"Do not be insolent with the patience of this tribunal!"

"Yet is King James not Scottish? And did not many Scots accompany him to Court when he ascended the throne?"

"What is your point?" Lord Chief Justice Popham demanded loudly.

"That my confession," Fawkes replied, "that was read out aloud here in this chamber, does make reference to a certain Scotsman who assisted me in my purchase of fuses for the planned explosion."

"Yes, it certainly does," Robert Cecil intoned with a slight smile. "You were unable to recall his name—does that name now come back to your memory, sir?"

Andrew was staring at his hands, which where folded perfectly on the oak counsel's table, feeling his heart race as he waited for Fawkes's answer.

"The name," Fawkes replied, "is lost to me, sir."

Andrew leaned back a bit in his chair. But not for long.

Coke came charging back.

"We are about to see," he said in his piercing voice, "whether that be truth or not."

Chapter 26

Sir Edward Coke was insistent on probing Fawkes's claimed memory loss.

"Some of your group had suspected this Scotsman as having kin who had close connections to the Crown. Is that correct?" Coke asked.

"That is correct. But I cannot recall the names that were suspected—"

"And why is that?" Coke thundered. "Is it because you wish to protect your collaborators?"

"Certainly not," he replied. "Why should I wish to protect a Scotsman?"

Andrew was listening intently. He had not missed that.

"My memory has lapsed," Fawkes continued, "due to the tortures that were used against me. Illegal it was. And despicable."

Coke was about to address that issue directly, but halted. He remembered that in one of his legal treatises he had argued that physical torture in extracting confessions was, in most circumstances, contrary at least to the spirit of the Magna Carta.

"Will no one respond on behalf of the Crown to this surprising contention by defendant Fawkes?" Popham bellowed. Robert Cecil, sitting next to him, was nodding vigorously in agreement.

Coke surveyed the panel of lawyers sitting at the Crown's table. He spotted Andrew Mackenzie, strode over to him, leaned forward into Andrew's face, and addressed him in a rushed whisper.

"I have heard, Mister Mackenzie, that you parried once in the king's chambers with Sir Robert Cecil on this very matter—on the issue of torture."

"Yes sir, but—" Andrew whispered back, ready to point out, however, that he had disagreed with Cecil's position. And in any event, his own theories on that subject would hardly advance the Crown's case against Fawkes. Further, if Andrew argued to validate Fawkes's confession, he would, at the same time, be arguing to corroborate Fawkes's allegation about the unnamed Scotsman—thereby substantiating the apparent complicity of his own brother, Phillip.

"Tush, tush," Coke said. "This is no time for modesty, man. Stand up and take a swing at this Fawkes's argument."

"I would, except—" Andrew began again.

"Will the Crown's case continue or not?" Popham was yelling from the bench.

"Now, man. To your feet!" Coke ordered Andrew.

Andrew rose, stepped slowly to the center of the hall, and bowed first to the bench. Then he turned slowly toward Fawkes, trying to figure his way out of this seemingly intractable dilemma. He whispered a short prayer. *God grant me wisdom.*

"What is that?" Popham said, straining to hear and cupping a hand to his ear.

"Wisdom," Andrew replied. "What we need is wisdom. For out of wisdom springs justice. And justice is what this proceeding demands."

The commissioners all nodded, but their expressions were still withholding approval.

"I have argued before," Andrew continued, "that in the course of interrogations, the harshest of physical tortures are in wont of substantiation under English law."

A ripple of confusion and dissent rippled through Westminster Hall. Popham's face was compressed into a kind of wrinkled restraint, but wanting to burst out in disapproval.

"Yet I have also argued," Andrew said, "that strong coercion, which is different than outright torture, is permissible, particularly in matter of national emergency."

Then Andrew stepped over to the table where the written documents of confession lay. He picked one up.

"Mister Fawkes, is it not true that you referred to this unnamed Scotsman in one of your earliest confessions?"

Fawkes paused for a moment.

"Do I need to show you the date and your signature?" Andrew barked out.

"No. Not necessary," the wearied Fawkes replied. "What you said is true…"

"And the order of the king, signed by the king himself, ordered that the 'gentler' tortures be used first in your interrogation."

"No torture is gentle," Fawkes said sarcastically.

"Then do you call the king a liar? For the king's own order uses that phrase."

Fawkes was silent at that.

"Thus," Andrew said, turning to the eight judges, "if the gentlest form of coercion was used first—and if that is when Mister Fawkes gave forth his confession in which he protested a lack of memory about this unnamed Scotsman, then it stands to reason that his lack of memory could not possibly have been from the extremities of torture…but from some other cause. For which we may never have the true answer. Though I wonder, if perhaps Mister Fawkes's intense hatred for Scots has burned the name of that Scotsman from his memory, much as a torch can burn the letters off a parchment."

For a long moment, there was silence in the vast hall. The eight judges were considering Andrew's ballet of legal advocacy. He had sidestepped the central issue of the identity of the unnamed Scot while adroitly focusing the court's attention on the lack of credibility in Fawkes's claim that he had already forgotten information at the early stages of interrogation due to "torture," when, in fact, the worst tortures had not yet been initiated against him.

Coke was also mulling it over. But then he lifted his head, smiled, and nodded.

Popham and all of the other judges, save one, where now nodding in affirmation. All agreeing, with one exception, that Andrew Mackenzie had shown Fawkes's arguments to have been meritless.

"Yes, well done," Popham said casually from the bench. He threw Andrew a smile, as did several of the other judges.

Andrew smiled and then prepared to return to the counsel's bench. But as he turned, his eyes fixed on Robert Cecil, sitting next to Lord Chief Justice Popham.

Cecil, the only judge who had refused to register approval at Andrew's argument, was staring at Andrew. And even from Andrew's great distance away, he could determine one clear fact.

Cecil was not smiling.

Chapter 27

In the end, all eight of the first set of gunpowder treason defendants were found guilty. No one familiar with the case was surprised at that. Immediately after the trial there were some speculations that floated around the Court as to the identity of the "unnamed Scot" mentioned by Fawkes, or whether he even existed at all. But in the weeks and months following the hanging of all eight of the Catholic rebels, that subject of the anonymous Scot seemed, for all practical purposes, to have been forgotten.

The bitter cold of January melted away, and in the spring and then summer of that year further trials were conducted against Jesuit priests who had collaborated with Catesby and Fawkes. However, Andrew Mackenzie was happy to have found a certain relief from those criminal proceedings. For whatever reason, he had been relieved from his position as a member of the prosecution team and asked to resume his efforts on the new Bible translation project ordered by James.

Andrew was made an assistant overseer of the First Westminster Committee, which was tasked with the translation of a new, "authorized" version of those books of the Bible from Genesis to II Kings. Two other committees, the First Cambridge Company and the First Oxford Company, were to translate the remaining books of the Old Testament.

Thomas Craig, Andrew's legal mentor and his supervisor on the painstaking union of the Crown's proposal, assured Andrew that being taken off the criminal cases was no slight at all.

"I've heard," Craig told him, "that the king himself was powerfully impressed by your arguments at the first gunpowder trial and your examination against Fawkes. You have to remember, Andrew lad, that as skilled as you are in the niceties of the law, you are also much valued for your theological training and your ability as an administrator as well. Why else would the Crown entrust you to ride rough-herd over the likes on that committee as Lancelot Andrewes, John Overdall, and those other ecclesiastical scholars?"

Andrew took some comfort in Thomas Craig's encouragement.

"Ye're a true Barnabas to me," Andrew told his mentor, "straight from the book of Acts. Though I be no apostle Paul, that is for certain."

"Lighten the weight ye carry," Craig replied. "Ye've lost a dear daughter. And ye've had the burdens of matters of state in a time of great turmoil. Now, enjoy gettin' back to the Word of God. Let it be yer delight. And though yer soul is wandering in dry, desert places, it'll be the oasis for ye."

Craig's advice was true enough. As Andrew devoted himself to overseeing the translation work of his committee, he started experiencing at least some measure of spiritual refreshment.

On the other hand, Andrew's wife, Kate, was consistently melancholy for months following Alice's death. In the spring of that year, Kate had decided to plant a flower garden in the acre of land that lay at the rear of their house.

On one particular day, in the warm days of the English summer, she was on her knees with an iron trowel in her leather-gloved hand. She had a long working dress on and a bonnet. She looked like a farmer's wife when Andrew spotted her.

Andrew kneeled next to her.

"Kate, dear, you could get help from the household servants."

"For what?" she asked.

"For your garden."

"I don't want their help with my garden," she responded, without looking at her husband, but she continued to dig feverishly in the dirt on her knees. "I want to do this myself."

Though he was about to dialogue further on the point, wisdom dictated that Andrew practice a quieter approach. Still kneeling next to her, he remained there and watched her work.

After a few minutes, Kate spoke up.

"It helps me," she said, "to see something grow. To know I am helping bring something to life."

Then after a few more minutes she stopped and sat up, tucking her legs underneath her dress.

"Does it cause you embarrassment," she continued, "being an advisor to the Crown, to see your wife on her knees in the dirt?"

"It causes me pleasure," he replied, "to know this brings you pleasure."

"Calm," she said. "It brings that to me. I need some calm. For when my daughter died, the world seemed to crack in half."

"Aye," Andrew said, nodding.

"So if the world cracked in half, why is it that the world continues on? As if nothing had happened? My precious daughter…my only child…is lying in a grave, in the cold earth. Yet the world goes on…"

Kate's voice wavered, and her chin was trembling. She swept the bonnet off her head, straightened a few errant hairs, and put them back in place.

"I would wager," Andrew said gently, "it was not the world that cracked, but rather yer own heart."

He sat down next to her in the dirt and put his hand on hers.

"But because ye have a heart that is as large as the world, it just seemed so…"

At first Kate covered her mouth with her glove and struggled against the emotions that were spilling over. But then she yielded, and the sobs came, so powerful that she dropped her bonnet and lay down on the ground and cried.

Andrew bent over her, but said nothing. He held her hands until her crying stopped.

Finally, she said, in a waivering voice, "I know the Scriptures say we are not to sorrow like the others, who know not God. For their mourning is without hope. And I know I will see my dear Alice again…but the pain keeps on, Andrew. And does not yield."

"The Lord Jesus is our ensample," Andrew said. "Though He knew He would resurrect Lazarus, our Savior still wept at his tomb. Though we know Alice will meet us in the resurrection, still we weep."

Kate pondered that, still lying on the ground, looking up at her husband.

"I'm sorry I could bear you no more children," she said, tearing up again.

Andrew took her hands to his lips and kissed them.

"My only regret," he said, "is that I may have ever caused ye pain or sorrow at any time in our lives."

Defying the conventions of the day, Kate pulled herself to a sitting position and gently kissed her husband on the lips in full view of the servants who were drying the laundry in the backyard.

"My great treasure and blessing," Andrew said, stroking his wife's face. "That is what ye are."

Chapter 28

As summer faded into fall, the oaks and maples that lined the Blackfriars lanes near Andrew Mackenzie's house burst into brilliant colors. In the backyard, Kate's roses and chrysanthemums, and the creeping ivy along the trellis, all grew lush and vibrant.

That autumn in particular, Andrew began feeling a powerful draw back to his homeland in Scotland. His agonizing visit several months before to bury his daughter had been the first time in over a year that he had returned. As he and Kate would sit together before the glow of the fireplace in the cool nights, his thoughts ran to the hills of Scotland. He thought back to how, in the fall, the heather would explode in an outrageous display of purple over both the highlands and the lowlands. And how the heather was lovingly cradled in the dark, damp, mossy ground, and in the spongy black bogs. And even among the cold, gray granite outcroppings.

So too, the mossy softening that comes with the passage of time had slowly begun to cover over the jagged edges left by Alice's death. Andrew and Kate were a comfort to each other. Andrew made sure that the demands of his time with the Westminster Committee did not unduly deprive him of time with her. They took daily walks together, and at night had taken to reading out loud to each other in front of the crackling, popping fires in the great stone fireplace.

The treason trials of the gunpowder conspirators had ended. All of the defendants were tried, found guilty, and executed. There was a certain confidant exuberance, a sense of safety that had settled upon London. The feeling that England had been spared, just in the nick of time, from the awful plot of political terrorists. That peace still reigned, and King James could continue as the divinely chosen monarch to care for his people.

Yet despite the communal optimism that had swept through the government, Andrew still dealt with his own personal, gnawing anxiety. Despite his pledge to his aged, infirm father, he had not made peace with his brother. And beyond that, he still harbored concerns about the entire gunpowder plot. Following the Fawkes trial, during meetings of the king's chief advisors, Robert Cecil treated Andrew with a cold, almost hostile detachment.

Andrew could not help but think that his brother, and all of the Mackenzies for that matter, were still not in the clear.

He had reported the results of the trial to Philip in his last, tense meeting with him. Philip seemed satisfied that the threat was over. So he returned to his work at the surveyor's shop in London.

But Philip was also much occupied with the work of the London Virginia Company. That enterprise, patterned after the success of the East India Company, sought to expand exploration in the New World and reap the riches and bounty that they presumed to exist in that land. The first expedition, which included Philip, had discovered natives that varied, from tribe to tribe, in ferocity and savagery.

A major mission of such further exploration was not just commercial expansion however. Philip sat in on numerous council meetings where English clergy urged, as part of the upcoming adventure, the conversion of the Indian tribes to a faith in the Christian gospel. Philip had distanced himself from the faith of his brother, Andrew, and of his father, Ransom, for that matter. But he did feel a slight twinge when the preachers spoke of bringing the savages of the New World to a knowledge of Christ.

The Virginia Company had been chartered those lands along the coast of the New World that lay to the south, while the Plymouth Company had jurisdiction over the coastal and inland regions to the north.

Following the Fawkes trial, Philip doubled his efforts in planning with the Virginia group for the sailing, which was set for December. He helped advise the Company on provisions needed for the expedition and the delegation of manpower. But his primary benefit was really to counsel the investors on the planning of surveying and mapping of the region. There was a particular interest in finding a major inland waterway that could take settlements deeper into the rich lands of the New World.

He had been asked repeatedly to join the exploration and to name which of the three ships he wished to sail on. But each time, Philip begged off. He had become convinced that Peter needed him, particularly now that he seemed so enamored with Rose Heatherton and talked often of making plans for his future.

"I do plan," Peter confided in him one day, "to find a time within the next year to ask for the hand of Rose in marriage. I shall need your advice, Father, on how to proceed. I should need, I believe, a raise of salary here at the shop. Do you think that Master Hadfield will deem me worthy of it?"

"Without a doubt," Philip replied with a wide grin. "Son, I've taught you all I know about land-mapping and charting. I fear that soon you will be the teacher, and me the student!"

He had not told his son about the overtures from the Virginia Company to join the expedition. Quietly, and in his own way, Philip had simply purposed in his heart to remain in England as long as he could be of some value to his son's budding future. At least that way, he concluded, he could fulfill his promise to his dying wife.

But one thing now seemed clear. His days as an adventurer would be over. To him, this next season of life would be filled with the mundane things. His daily life in London would, by all accounts, now be mired down in predictability, with little exposure to risk or danger.

One day, a word was brought to Robert Cecil. It happened late in November, as the windy cold of the coming winter had descended on England, covering towns and countryside with hoary frost.

In the anteroom of his personal chambers at Hampton Court, Cecil had his servants stoke the blackened fireplace, then bid them to leave. As he huddled under his cap at his study table, poring over several documents the king was to sign that day, he heard the shuffling of feet outside his door.

Then he heard a knocking on the other side of the thick black-walnut double doors.

He was not expecting an interruption.

The knocking came again.

"Who calls?" Cecil yelled with a great deal of irritation.

"The Ferret."

Looking up from the papers of state, Cecil decided this was an interruption that should be permitted.

"Enter," he called out.

Chapter 29

The massive double doors opened, revealing a thin, gangly man with a wide-brimmed hat, gaunt face, and untidy, untrimmed beard.

The man stepped in, but not until first grabbing the hat off his head and holding it in front of him as he bowed clumsily.

"Beggin' your pardon, sire."

Cecil looked at the man standing with his hat in his hands.

The man had a name, but it was never used in discourse with Robert Cecil. In the line of work that the man was engaged in, proper names, particularly those banded about in the halls of the palace, could often be dangerous liabilities for those, like Cecil, who employed them. The man's name was Hedley Meeks. But whenever he had dealings with Cecil, he simply went by the title "The Ferret." It was a name picked by Cecil himself.

During his lifetime, the Ferret had performed a host of odd jobs—from the wharves of Liverpool to the slaughter yards of the East End of London. But since James' coronation and Robert Cecil's elevation as the king's chief advisor, he had one main livelihood.

The Ferret was one of the more reliable informers Cecil employed in his web of spies that stretched from England to France,

Spain, Italy, and Portugal. In addition to his other duties, Cecil was the head of royal security and intelligence. He relied on his spies to provide continuous information. Those spies like the Ferret who had a track record of disgorging useful, credible tips and delivering them to Cecil were handsomely rewarded.

"I know ye're a man with a good many important duties," the Ferret said with a labored smile, in a voice tinged with a thick layer of manufactured courtesy.

"And knowing that," Cecil said sharply, "you will get to the point quickly."

"Aye, I will, I will indeed," the Ferret replied.

Then he placed his hat, spotted by dirt and wear, back on his head and moved a few feet closer.

"It concerns the gunpowder trial," he said.

"And what concern is that to you?"

"Just this," he responded, drawing another step closer. "That there was certain testimony given and received, good sir. At that trial I mean. And certain of it was concerning certain unnamed individuals. About a person, or persons, unknown, and not exactly charged in the treason, mind you…as you full know, of course, as you sat as one of the lords commissioner in that very proceeding. Well, I have information of a very timely nature, Mister Cecil…and bearing on that very matter."

"Be clear, man," Cecil snapped. "Concerning what?"

"Concerning a certain Scotsman, sir. Yes. A Scotsman who had certain dealings, you might say, with Fawkes…the traitor whose head remains on a spike on the London Bridge to this very day."

Cecil put down his papers and slowly rose to his feet.

"Continue," he said quietly.

"If I may…" the Ferret said, "may I call into your chambers, the very man, the very source of this information?"

Cecil nodded.

The Ferret scrambled out of the room and disappeared around the doorway. Then in an instant, he entered again. He removed his hat and swung it toward the door and bowed dramatically to prepare for the entrance of some person, as if they were actors at the Globe.

In the doorway, a large, hulking man appeared. He was bald, and his neck and the backs of his hands were hairy. He wore a stained, sleeveless tanner's shirt that was partially covered by a tattered black waistcoat, but his shirt was partly unbuttoned and revealed a hairy chest. His black leather apron stopped at his knees.

The man smiled, revealing several missing and blackened teeth.

"This," the Ferret announced, "is the man I have just spoken of."

"Do you have some knowledge," Cecil said, addressing the man, "of matters that arose during the treason trial of the traitor Guy Fawkes?"

The bald man smiled more broadly.

"Oh yes. I do."

Cecil gave a wave of his hand to dismiss the Ferret from the room.

But his spy hesitated, bowed, and then cleared his throat.

"Oh yes, of course," Cecil said with a sigh. He strolled over to his table, opened a compartment, retrieved two sovereigns, and tossed them over to the Ferret, who caught them with delight and hurried out of the room.

Approaching the big tanner, Cecil asked him for his name.

"Jaquart Mundy," the big man said. "To my friends, I go by Jacko Mundy."

"What do you know?" Cecil bulleted back.

"That a certain Scotsman was mentioned in the testimony of Fawkes. A man who had knowledge of fuses and the use of gunpowder. That this man helped Fawkes to buy the very fuses that were going to be used to blow the Parliament, and the king himself, clear into the next life, sir."

"Yes," Cecil said with his hands behind his back, smiling. "Very good. And as to this Scotsman…do you know him?"

"I do," the man said.

"And what is his name?"

The big tanner hesitated.

"If you excuse my manner of speakin'," he said, "I work every day in the filth of Southwark. For a peasant's wages."

"And you want to be paid? For your information?"

"If it wouldn't be too much trouble."

"It is too much trouble. Far too much. We have a government to run. Do you know I could take you to the Tower and get the information you carry by a far cheaper method?"

"Indeed you could," the tanner said. "But sometimes the rack goes a bit too far. And your witness doesn't survive. And then where would you be?"

Cecil paused and considered the man who stood before him.

"A name. I need a name," Cecil demanded. "Name first. Then we shall discuss terms."

"A name you want?"

"Yes."

"Then a name you shall have," the tanner said. Then he crossed his thick arms over his chest and gave up the name.

"Philip Mackenzie."

The eyes of the king's chief counselor widened.

"Did you say 'Mackenzie'?"

The dirty, muscular tanner leaned his head back with satisfaction and grinned, and then gave Robert Cecil an approving nod.

"Come," Cecil said to the tanner, motioning for him to take a seat in his private chambers. "Come sit down, Jacko. Let's discuss this matter. Shall we?"

Chapter 30

In Philip Mackenzie's rooms, Andrew and his brother were having a meeting. Like every conversation of late between the two, this one had been filled with acrimony, accusation, and bitterness.

But unlike the others, this dialogue had ended with a point of common agreement that seemed painfully clear to both men. There was a certain finality about it all.

"Why should I believe your sources are reliable?" Philip asked, not wanting to believe what he had just heard.

"They are beyond suspicion," Andrew said. "It is undeniable that Cecil and this tanner, this Jacko Mundy, have had two separate meetings. You have been named as an accomplice of Guy Fawkes. You aided him in locating high-grade fuses."

"Mundy," Philip muttered, and shook his head.

"So you know him?"

"Yes, I know him. I bested him in a tavern contest," Philip said with a little smile. "He never did like me. But that incident in the Black Boar Tavern sealed it…"

"So once again your unsavory dealings have cost you dearly."

"Why don't you just lie back for once?" Philip barked, stepping up to his brother in a threatening move.

"You have to leave England," Andrew replied, unflinching. "If you don't, Cecil will have you on the rack in a fortnight."

"Where? How?" Philip snapped back.

"The London Virginia Company is shipping out to the New World again, isn't that what you told me?"

"All they have to do is check the manifest from the ships," Philip said. "There will be supply ships bound for Virginia regularly next year. They will track me down."

"Not if you register under a different name," Andrew said.

Philip mulled it over. "Cecil and Coke, and Popham too, all of the great men of the gunpowder trials, they are stakeholders in the London Virginia Company."

"But none of them will be putting out to sea in the ships, will they?"

Philip grew quiet.

"Who are the captains?" Andrew asked.

When Philip didn't respond, Andrew persisted loudly. "Do they know you, man? Do they know you by face?"

"Christopher Newport. He's captaining the *Susan Constant*. Never met him. Then there's Bartholomew Gosnold on the *Godspeed*, and John Ratcliffe on the *Discovery*. Neither one knows me. At least by face."

"And what of the sailors, and carpenters and such. The others on each ship. Have any of them met you?"

"I have no idea," Philip said. "Haven't been privy to such information. I've met with some members of the council for the exploration. Never seen a list."

"What have you told them of your intentions?"

"That I would *not* be putting out with the ships. Even though they asked me to join."

"Good. Let's keep it that way," Andrew said. "I will procure a copy of the list for each ship. When are they shipping out?"

"Four days."

"Then we have to act quickly," Andrew said. "I'll get you the manifest list. You make sure you've not made the acquaintance of any of the passengers under the name Philip Mackenzie. I'll vouch for you under an assumed name. We'll call you 'John Kensington.' Use that. I'll say that John Kensington is an accomplished adventurer who has traveled with you previously. And that he is your most excellent second on the voyage."

Philip eyed his brother with suspicion. "You have this all figured out, don't you?"

"Still you don't trust me," Andrew said. "After all this time—"

"Why should I?" Philip sniped. "You have neatly arranged for me to leave England. Perhaps never to return. You know the odds and the risks, my brother. You're aware that over a hundred Englishmen and their families disappeared at Roanoke Island after being dropped off by the Granville and Raleigh expeditions. I know. I was there. I saw them waving goodbye to us from the shore. Standing in front of that meager little fort. And I saw the expressions on their faces as I stood on the deck of the ship, leaving them behind to a fate that is still a mystery. What makes you think this expedition will fare any better?"

"We have no choice, you and I," Andrew said quietly. Then he reached out his hand to take Philip by the shoulder, but his brother drew back.

"Philip," Andrew said, with a note of tenderness in his voice.

"I have been an assistant overseer of one of the Bible translation committees."

"Good for you," Philip replied sarcastically. "May you and your God prosper in the business of religion…"

"Hear me out, Philip. I've been spending much time in God's Word. In the book of Genesis, which our committee is laboring over. I've read the story of Cain and Abel. And Jacob and Esau. Brothers against brothers. This enmity between us…this is not what God wants. For my part, I repent, brother, of my harsh words against you. Can't we restore what we've lost between us?"

Andrew reached out his hand to Philip. But his brother drew his hands behind his back and turned away.

"I will go to Virginia. *Alone*. But I will not give you false words just to comfort you…"

"Not to comfort me," Andrew said. "But to comfort our ailing father. And to please our Almighty Father in heaven."

As he looked into the face of his brother, Philip wanted to see hypocrisy, so he could ridicule it. But he saw none of that. There was a transparency on Andrew's face that reflected the pain of a life possessed of mistakes and missed opportunities.

"And I am afraid," Andrew said delicately, "that you will *not* be journeying to Virginia *alone*."

"Oh, so God shall accompany me then?"

"Yes, quite so. But that is not my meaning."

"Then what?"

"I meant to say that you will be traveling with another."

Philip stared at his brother, groping for his intent.

"Who?"

"During the time of your alleged complicity with Fawkes, you shared these apartments…and worked side-by-side—"

"What are you saying?" Philip said, quickly grasping his brother's meaning. He was barely controlling his rage.

"They will take him to the Tower," Andrew said in a chillingly calm voice, "and will put him to the rack in place of you. We both know that. To crush his young body. To squeeze from his screaming lips what little he knows of your business. Your associates. The places you frequented. They will torture your son…"

"I will not do this thing. No. Peter has nothing to do with this. *Nothing.* He has a job. A life. He is in love with a young woman. I will not risk his life for this matter. I'll not ask him to give up all of that because of *my* dealings…*my* mistakes."

Philip's rage was suddenly pouring over into a pitiful sob that he could not contain.

Once again, Andrew tried to step closer to his brother, but Philip turned away and held out his hand.

"Leave me—now," he muttered with his back turned. "Just leave me alone."

Chapter 31

The ride up to the Scottish borders and then over to the Berwickshire coast was a frenzied one. As Peter rode hard through the night to Seacrest House, he was overwhelmed by a sense of dread and confusion. As the horse's hoofs stomped on the frozen ground at a gallop, Peter's mind was racing.

His father had told him that both of them must leave for Virginia on the ship *Susan Constant*. They would put out from the port at Blackwall in just a matter of days. Philip had been blunt with his son.

"There will be perils on the sea," he told Peter, "perils when we arrive. Starvation, sickness, attacks by savages. The only other chance for you is to leave England in the other direction and head, by yourself, over to the Continent. To disappear from sight. Hide from Cecil's spies there if you can. But you will be alone and on your own. I would have no hope in that location...I am known by too many there."

Then after a considering the matter, Philip realized that such an option was simply not feasible.

"Yet," he murmured, as his son stood before him dumbfounded, "I know of no ships heading off to the Continent in the next week.

Cecil already has my name, and if I don't leave in the next few days I will be undone. It would take him only a few days longer to trace my connection to you. But little more than that. And by the time you found a ship to the Continent, Cecil and his henchmen would catch up with you."

Philip looked up at his son's face. In it, he recognized the look—the expression on Peter's face now that he realized his dreams were being shattered.

"I'm sorry, son. But it's off to Virginia for both of us. We have no other choice."

Those words—"we have no other choice"—were ringing in Peter's mind as he rode on. His eyes were bleary for lack of sleep. The foam from the horse's mouth was a frozen froth around its bridle.

Then, in the gray cold of the breaking dawn, he recognized the road that wound through the high ground along the coast for several miles, and then up to a path that led to Seacrest House. He slowed his horse to a trot and tried to gather his thoughts.

At first he had hoped Rose Heatherton would be in London when he searched her out, frantic to tell her of his need to leave England immediately. Yet also to try to muster some way of expressing his love for her, and his intention, no matter what the cost, or what the sacrifice, to return and make her his wife.

But when he showed up at the Heatherton house in the city, he was told that she and her brother had made one last trip to Seacrest.

What would he say to her now? How would he explain his unannounced presence?

Peter knew he dared not explain the details of his father's intrigue, or the suspicions at Court against him—nor their destination. Or even that they would be traveling under assumed names.

As he rode the final mile down the tree-lined path to the house,

close enough to the sea that he could hear the crashing of the waves
and the cawing of the fulmars circling in the air, Peter pleaded with
God. Asking that somehow, by some divine miracle, he would be
spared from this voyage to the New World.

*Lord God, was it not Your choice to cause me to meet my fair Rose
and fall in love with her? How then can You send me off to a land
across the ocean, perhaps to be killed, never to return again?*

With Rose in England, and Peter on the other side of the world
in Virginia, how then could they ever be married? This would be
the end of everything between them.

Then a remembrance, a burning, incandescent memory of something Peter had read, floated back into his thoughts.

It was a dialogue. In the Gospels. Between Jesus and his disciples. In the tenth chapter of the Gospel of Mark, a rich man ran
up to Jesus, and falling on his knees before Him pleaded with
Him. The rich man wanted to know how to inherit eternal life. As
they talked together, Jesus ended by pointing out that the man still
lacked one thing.

Jesus told the man he should sell all his considerable wealth, then
give that money to the poor, "and come," He concluded, "follow
me and take up the cross."

But the man, because of the enormousness of his wealth and all
his possessions, could not summon the faith to follow Jesus, and
left in great sorrow.

As they watched the man trudge away, Jesus told His disciples
it was easier for a camel to pass through the eye of a needle than
for a rich man to enter the kingdom of God. That was it. That was
what Peter was remembering.

And after that, Jesus' disciples asked, "Who then can be saved?"

Jesus answered them with a truth that was both startlingly clear, yet astonishingly profound. "With men it is impossible," He explained, "but not with God; for with God all things are possible."

Peter was repeating that phrase to himself—"with God all things are possible"—as he dismounted his weary horse, tied it to the hitching post, and stumbled like a sleepwalker to the double doors of the house. Off in the distance he could hear the rush and crash of surf as it frothed and raged in the winds of winter, just beyond the ridge upon which Seacrest House had been built.

Peter stood before the front entrance of the great, yellow-stone mansion. Even in winter, its walls were still covered in an arching embrace of ivy.

He grabbed hold of the large iron door knocker in the shape of a lion's head. He banged it twice. He could hear someone approaching from within the house, footsteps echoing in the marble foyer. And in an instant, the doors swung open to him.

Chapter 32

In their attempts to stave off poverty and the crush of debt, the Heathertons had let go all but one of their staff at Seacrest House. William had negotiated with the creditors of his father in London to accept Seacrest and all their holdings in England as well in satisfaction of their family's overdue notes. William and Rose had traveled back there one more time to ready the estate for final transfer to the creditors.

And now the one lone servant, an aged butler, was standing in the open doorway, having just arisen early himself. He was eying Peter with confusion, but after a moment's reflection, remembered him as the young surveyor who had recently mapped out the boundaries of the estate to facilitate its sale.

"Do come in, Master Peter," the butler said with a tired smile. "You wish to see Mistress Rose?"

The butler's openness was, to Peter, a sign of something significant. That in those final days, at the end of Seacrest House, indeed, the ending of a way of life that the Heathertons had known in Scotland, some formalities were disappearing. No more stiff rituals, no more pretense about Peter's reason for being there.

"She was up early, I suspect. Earlier even than I," the butler said.

"Out there, in the gardens. Just sitting. You know the way, I presume. Down the hall. Through the glass doors, through the sitting room and the parlor, and then out the doors to the garden."

Peter remembered the route. When he swung open the French doors that led to the gardens in the back, he could see Rose seated on a stone bench on the far end of the manicured expanse of hedgerows, bushes, and winding brick walkways. She was wrapped in a woolen cape, with a bonnet secured under her chin. Her eyes were fixed beyond the trees ahead. She was gazing out to the gray, undulating sea on the horizon.

Peter was praying as he walked. Rose was not aware of his footsteps until he was almost up to her.

When she turned to see who was approaching, her face, on recognizing Peter, burst into an expression of joy that was, at the same time, both heartwarming and yet also cruelly crushing for Peter. He knew he was bearing unbearable news for her. How could he gently lead his beloved to the truth that they would be separated, and probably forever?

Rose stood up quickly, covering her mouth with gloved hands, then waving them before her face. She was laughing and crying all at once.

Peter strode up to her. Then he gathered her in his arms and held her tight. Surrounded in Peter's embrace, Rose said, "Peter you're here, you're here. I can't believe it! How wonderful!"

But Peter did not respond. He just held her close, and then finally pulled her slightly away, so he could kiss her boldly.

It was then that Rose's countenance fell as she studied Peter's face.

"Something's wrong. Is that right?" she asked quietly, fearing the answer.

"Yes," he said. "That is why I have come."

"What is it? You must tell me without delay."

"It's about me. And sadly, about you…both of us, I fear."

"What could possibly be so wrong?"

"I am away to sea," Peter said, not knowing how else to broach the painful subject, and finally blurting it out. "There is no use explaining it. I cannot. I am a hostage to forces greater than me. I cannot tell you why…or even where I go."

"When," she stammered, "when…will you return? Please tell me it shall be soon. Will it be soon?"

"I fear not."

"But when?" she said, her voice now rising, and so pitiful that Peter's soul groaned at the sound of it.

"I do not know…"

"But you must. Some idea. Some speculation. Something, Peter. You must—"

"I cannot."

"Will you ever be back? Ever return to me?"

Now Rose was pleading, and her voice was quivering in the frigid break of day. She was shaking from the cold, but more than that, she was trembling at the expression on Peter's face. At what was not being said, except in the language of the heart; in the silence of things almost too painful to speak of.

"*Ever?*" she cried out, her face contorted.

"It may be," Peter said, "that I will never—"

But then he stopped. He took a breath. And reached out to Rose. She was looking up into his eyes with grief.

"All I have is my pledge," Peter said. "That no matter what the sacrifice or risk, I will give up my life in an effort to return to you."

And then he added, "With God all things are possible, Rose.

That is the only rock we have to hold onto. The whole world is out of control. Kingdoms rage around us. Plotters. And deceivers. And they threaten us with their net. So we must hold onto the Lord God, Rose. We must pray for Him, and Him alone, to reunite us. There is no other hope."

But as Peter looked into Rose's dark eyes, he could not see hope. Only tears, coming hot and fast down her face.

Together, they sat on the stone bench and faced the sea. And listened, without a word, to the unceasing sound of the surf, as the relentless waves crashed onto the shore just beyond their view.

Chapter 33

Five months later
Along the coast of Virginia near the mouth of Chesapeake Bay

It had been, all of it, just as Peter's father had predicted. The harrowing voyage in rocking, pitching, reeling ships, through the winter tempests. Storms as they put out from Blackwall on December 20, 1606. And more violent storms as they rounded the island of Martinique in the West Indies. Philip, as a seasoned world voyager, bore up well. But not Peter, who experienced violent sea sickness. He spent days in a blurry world of nausea.

Finally, when they reached the Dominican Isles, the weather became fair. They dropped anchor off the islands there and were immediately approached by long boats filled with local savages.

The men were all painted in hues of red, which was apparently to ward off the vicious mosquitoes and other biting pests.

Captain Newport of the *Susan Constant* negotiated a trade with them, giving them hatchets and knives in return for an abundance of fresh fruit. But the crew of the ship had been sternly warned not to allow any of the savages on board. The Spanish had been dealing with the inhabitants of those islands for years, and every adventurer had heard the tales of how these savages would not only kill unwary travelers but also delight in eating their flesh.

Peter had been told about the fearsome traits of the savages, but he couldn't help but lean over the railing of the ship, holding on tight to an iron cleat, and stare at the wondrously painted natives in the canoes passing close by.

Leaving the West Indies, the ship then bore northward and passed the Tropic of Cancer on the final leg of the journey.

Though Peter had been taken to the Continent with his father on a few shorter trips, this was the longest sea voyage he had ever endured. He was thankful, and a little amazed, that the *Susan Constant* had not lost a single hand up to that point, and that the spirits of the crew were good.

During most of the trip, Philip busied himself with the captain, Christopher Newport, his first mate, and the leaders of the proposed settlement. Going by his assumed name of John Kensington, Philip spent hours planning the expedition, as they huddled together in the captain's quarters.

After a few weeks, Peter was allowed to join his father during some of the meetings, but only after being admonished that he must find a discreet corner of the quarters and not speak up—or out of turn.

According to the agreed plan, one of their first tasks, after the staking out and construction of an outpost, would be an expedition inland to investigate the accessible waterways. There was also talk of another attempt to locate the missing Roanoke settlers from England, whose fate had been a mystery for some two decades. Some of the group, particularly a fellow name George Kendall, openly argued that such an effort would be fruitless. There had been other attempts to locate and rescue the missing settlers over the years, Kendall said, but all had failed.

But Peter's father spoke up against him.

"If those settlers, or their kin, or their kin's kin, are still alive, we must—even at our own loss of blood—find them."

Peter was transfixed by his father's boldness. He knew that his father, as a young man of Peter's age back then, had actually seen the settlers establishing their first outpost during the Granville exploration. He had borne the burden of those abandoned souls ever since. But he dared not talk of that now. That would raise too many suspicions. These men aboard the *Susan Constant* knew all the stories of those early expeditions to the New World—including every last name of every last crew member of every ship. They would be able to detect the ruse if someone calling himself "John Kensington" claimed to have been part of the Granville expedition.

During the long, arduous days at sea, Peter's main task was to make an effort to keep his mind off his crushed spirit, which was still aching from his separation from Rose and fearful over whether he would ever see her again. Peter sat in the captain's quarters and read to himself as the men discoursed about the "Jamestown" settlement, as they were now calling it. He would mostly read his Bible, but one day he also noticed a pile of papers on the table next to him.

Peter quietly pulled the documents over to himself so he could take a glance at them.

Among the various maps and charts, one paper in particular arrested his attention, On the top of that one, in large letters it read, "CHARTER OF VIRGINIA."

It began with the words "James, by the grace of God, King of England, Scotland, France, and Ireland, Defender of the faith…"

Peter was able to determine that this was one of the copies of the charter from King James that set forth the governing principles for the expedition to the New World that now included a reluctant Peter Mackenzie and his father.

Within the body of the document, Peter came to the spiritual mission, which in part had energized the voyage. There was something courageous and profound in what he read:

> We, greatly commending and graciously accepting of their desires to the furtherance of so noble a work which may, by the providence of Almighty God, hereafter tend to the glory of His Divine Majesty in propagating the Christian religion to such people as yet live in darkness and miserable ignorance of the true knowledge and worship of God, and may in time bring the infidels and savages living in those parts to human civility and a settled and quiet government...

Of course the document also addressed more mundane matters—the precise degrees of latitude within which the settlement, and its inhabitants, would control the land; the need to establish a "plantation and habitation" there. And the establishment of "councils" in Virginia, which would operate with governing powers on behalf of England.

Somewhere in the midst of Peter's reading of the charter, and then his studying of the intense faces of his father, and of Captain Newport, and the others—the men bent over the captain's table in heated debate over the initial tasks that were to follow the ship's first landfall—there was a realization.

Peter was slowly coming to the understanding that the "providence of Almighty God" must, indeed, be at work in such a bold and fearful endeavor as this. How it would play out, and what small role he might play in it all, as a young man with little adventuring experience, he did not know. Nor did he have any idea what was to be done about his love for Rose Heatherton, or the fact that he had left her back on the other side of the world.

But one thing was becoming clearer. This Jamestown expedition might well prove more important than Peter Mackenzie, now renamed Peter Kensington, could have ever imagined.

It was on the twenty-fifth day of April when, after four months at sea, there came another raging storm. The ship was tossed to and fro by the massive, roiling ocean. Below deck, Peter, now accustomed to the great rolling movement of the *Susan Constant*, was swinging in his hammock. His father was asleep in the hammock next to him. Then, suddenly, his father bolted upright from his slumber. A fierce, excited look washed over his face.

At first, Peter could not understand his father's awakening. There were only the howling winds outside, and the incessant creaking and rolling of the ship.

But Philip Mackenzie broke his trance and whispered over to his astonished son just one word: *"Landfall..."*

Then he said it again, but louder now, as a boy might yell for joy at the sight of the traveling tinker whose wares and wagon also bore treats, and mysteries, and wonders from distant lands.

"Landfall!" he yelled.

Philip had somehow heard the voice of the boatswain's mate far above the hold of the ship, far above the sea-washed deck, from up in the very highest point of the ship—in the dangerous, wildly swinging crow's nest.

"LAND HO! LAND HO!"

Topsail, the mate was yelling himself hoarse with the call of the first sighting of the contours of the land, the outline barely visible against the breaking of the first light sometime after four o'clock in the morning.

As all hands were called to the deck and scrambled up the ladder, Peter found himself shaking—whether from the coldness of the dawn or the excitement of the moment, he did not know.

But the young man began muttering something over and over to himself as he was the last one bolting up the ladder, heading to the deck, and running to his first glimpse of Virginia.

He was saying, "Providence of God...Providence of God...be with us now..."

Chapter 34

The other two ships, *Discovery* and *Godspeed,* caught up with the *Susan Constant* shortly after the sighting of land. Captain Newport ordered his ship to begin prowling the coast in search of the Chesapeake Bay, which had been roughly mapped from prior expeditions. It did not take the three ships long to locate the mouth of the bay. To the delight of the captains, the bay was found to be wide and navigable. There had been fears of spending an inordinate amount of time in search of a safe harbor.

But not now. All three ships slowly steered into the bay, one after another, dropping soundings as they went, with sails unfurled. Finally, the ships dropped anchor on the southern edge of the bay. It was midmorning.

On the main deck, Captain Newport ordered a small survey crew to board the launch, which was lowered down to the sea level. He called out the names of the initial landing party. George Kendall was one, along with Peter's father, "John Kensington," two fellows named William Brewster and George Percy, Bartholomew Gosnold, the captain of the *Godspeed,* and about twenty others, including a lawyer by the name of Gabriel Archer. Archer had been acting as the recorder for Captain Gosnold, noting down the events of the expedition.

Peter's father carried a weapon, a short blunderbuss, and a sketch pad for initial mapping. The other men were also armed. Peter waved to his father as the launch was lowered over the side, but wished that he did not have to stay behind on the ship. A blacksmith who had only gone by the name of "Mister Reed," stood next to Peter at the railing. Reed was gruff, and had scarred and muscular arms, and a coarse way about him. But for some reason had taken a liking to Peter and had passed the time with him from time to time on the voyage over.

"Yer father with the landing party?" he asked.

Peter nodded, not taking his eyes off the little launch as it was rowed toward shore.

"Did he eat well this morning? A good breakfast?" the blacksmith asked.

Thinking that was a strange question, Peter simply nodded without comment.

"Too bad," Reed said, with a bit of manufactured sympathy in his voice.

"Why is that?" Peter asked.

"Well," Reed said, stroking his beard with his soot-stained hands, "just that, seein' he's all fattened up, the savages will rightly pick him to eat first!"

Then Reed broke into a riotous laugh at his own joke. Peter was not amused.

"Oh, come now, lad," Reed said when his laughter subsided, "don't take it too serious-like...I've had my eye on your father. Looks to be a man what can take care of himself in a pinch. Not like that lawyer fellow—Gabriel Archer. Pasty-faced and skinny-necked. Why'd they pick him?"

"Recorder," Peter said quietly. "To take notes. I heard my father say so."

"Well, I suppose there's got to be some kind of record now, that's true enough," Reed said, with a grudging acknowledgment. "Specially seein' as we are making history true enough, aren't we good lad? I reckon they'll rightly name cities after us, righty-o? Reedville...or maybe Petersburgh. What say you to that?"

Then the blacksmith started laughing again.

Turning back to the view off the side of the ship, Peter nodded silently again. He was not in any mood for Mister Reed's humor. He only wanted to feel some assurance that his father would return safely back to the ship at the end of the day.

When the launch arrived on the shoreline, the men disembarked. What they saw was an amazement. Trees several times taller than the huge oaks of England. Rich green forests with streams in abundance. As the men cautiously hiked inland, they discovered rolling meadows covered with wildflowers in brilliant yellows and blues.

As Philip surveyed the land, it was as if he uncovered the secret hiding place of Eden. It was a mild day, and everywhere he looked, there was an almost suffocating overgrowth of lush greenery.

The landing party spent the day walking inland, several miles in every direction. They found the same natural beauty everywhere. But there was one thing they were also looking for but didn't find any traces of.

There were no signs of the savages they knew inhabited the area. Sightings of the Indians had been documented for decades, from the prior English expeditions. But also from the expeditions of the Spaniards who had driven the French out of Florida and had slowly moved their way north toward the Virginia lands. Over the years, contacts with the various tribes of the Powatans, as well as their enemies, the Monacans, Mannahoacs, Susquehannocks, and Massawomecks, had yielded a rich lexicon of Indian terms the English hoped would help them in their communication with the savages and thereby forestall hostilities.

At sunset, Newport ordered the landing party back to the launch. The group slowly made their way across a large clearing with a meadow and toward the group of trees and thickets that surrounded the edge of the shoreline.

In the front, Philip and Captains Newport and Gosnold were discussing the need for another venture soon, this time up the main river, which was called at that time the King's River, to try to locate the source of its headwaters. The twenty other men were close behind. At the rear were Gabriel Archer and a sailor straggling behind.

Then something caught Philip's eye.

At first he thought he had been mistaken in seeing some movement. That in the dimming of light at dusk, perhaps his eyes were playing tricks.

But as they approached the treeline ahead of them, Gosnold saw it too.

"Movement. Over there," Gosnold whispered to the two other men.

"I saw it too," Philip murmured back.

Newport halted the group. Then he realized that they were at the edge of a clearing, and if they turned back they would be on open ground, even more susceptible to attack from their flank.

Giving the silent signal to his men to be watchful as they

proceeded to load their muskets, Newport took them cautiously into the thicket that separated them from the beachhead.

As they entered into the trees, a whisper of sound flew over their heads.

And then another. And another.

"Fire at will!" Newport shouted.

Then more arrows started raining down on them from the left and right.

The Indian raiding party had been crouching among the bushes and now they were filling the air with deadly arrows.

A scream was heard from the rear, as the right hand of Gabriel Archer was pierced through with an arrow and then his left arm, seconds later. The sailor running next to him was shot in the gut, and a second arrow hit his upper shoulder.

Two of the group scurried back in the hail of arrows to help the sailor get up on his feet. But he was too injured to walk. They snapped the ends of the arrows off, and then the bigger of the two rescuers slung him over his shoulders and began carrying him toward the beach.

Newport, Philip, and the others then charged the Indians, who were now on their feet, firing off more arrows in rapid fire succession. The English landing party fired their muskets. Several Indians dropped to the ground.

The rest of the raiding party screamed out with an unearthly shout, and then vanished off into the dusky forest, leaving their dead behind.

The smoke from the muskets cleared, but the English were unable to determine a precise direction for the exit of their attackers.

"To the launch!" Newport shouted. They carried the wounded sailor, who was bleeding profusely, into the boat. One of the men, trained in basic medical physic, was able, with a great deal of effort and much screaming from Gabriel Archer, to extract the arrows from his hand and arm.

As the boat was rowed through the quiet, black waters of the channel toward the *Susan Constant,* darkness was almost upon them. They headed toward the lights of the torches that were burning up on the deck of the ship.

Philip turned around and glimpsed back at the New World they had just left.

It no longer looked to be the idyllic paradise it had first seemed several hours before. The sailor would be dead by the next morning.

However, Archer would recover.

A half-dozen Indians lay dead in the bush.

To Philip, it was obvious that the settlement of Jamestown would be accomplished, if at all, only at a frightful price.

But he had no idea how dear a price it would prove to be.

Chapter 35

The next morning, starting at dawn, each of the three ships sent multiple launches to the shore and back in successive trips until all of the crew, passengers, and supplies had been unloaded. The ships' carpenters and builders immediately scrounged for suitable branches and felled logs to build as many lean-tos as they could manage for the first night.

They then built a temporary barrier around the grounds by cutting thickets and thornbushes and then piling them high to create a bramble fence. The goal of the oddly misshapen, makeshift wall was to slow down any nighttime attackers before they could reach the encampment.

The body of the sailor was brought onto shore last. He was buried a hundred yards from the initial grounds of the settlement. Reverend Robert Hunt gave a short message about the promise of the resurrection for all those who "seek solace and salvation in the name of Christ, their heavenly King and Savior, and the work of His blood on the cross..."

Then the entire assembly moved back to the settlement. A large cross was erected near the beach. Reverend Hunt offered up the thanks of the settlers to the beneficence of God that had brought all but one of them safely to that moment; and he reminded them all, in a solemn prayer, that "this great endeavor is for nothing less than the honor of Almighty God, and to bring the Christian religion to the hearing of these savage peoples, whose souls are darkened with superstition and idolatry, and whose minds are blinded by violence. For God does hold us accountable, those who know the truth, to share the light with those that are perishing."

Those words provoked a few disgusted mutterings from some of the sailors who had been friends of the deceased. They saw no good reason to pray for the salvation of the natives who had just afflicted the landing party.

During the prayer, Philip was watching, with his eyes open, how his son was reverently bowing with hands clasped in front of him. Reverend Hunt's words had taken an odd hold on Philip. In times past he would have given it little thought. He had emptied himself of the faith that had been the hallmark of his renowned father—not so much in one great effort, but in a slow, steady dissipation. Like a wooden bucket with a slow drip.

But to his surprise there were certain stirrings now within. Unexplainable. Yet undeniably real. A movement of the soul. An awakening. And Reverend Hunt's reference to the fact that "God does hold us accountable, those who know the truth" provoked something deep inside of Philip. As Philip gazed on his son, his young face engrossed in earnest prayer, he couldn't shake a growing feeling that his life of brawling and adventuring was wasted years, a period of time consumed by the locusts. And that it was his life of reckless associations that had now driven both him and his son to this dangerous new land.

After Reverend Hunt's words, the three captains—Newport, Gosnold, and Ratcliffe—conducted a ceremony where they jointly pronounced the settlement and those adjacent lands within the boundaries of the charter from King James be under the sovereign government of England. Then they planted the English flag deep in the sandy soil.

Those lands were to be held in accordance to the rights of lawful ownership as determined by the councils established under the charter given by the king. Private ownership and individual investment would now hold sway.

But unlike the English homeland, hereditary fiefdoms and titles of nobility would have no place there.

Later in the day, a case of food was cracked open, and on the fire the settlers stewed salt beef and enjoyed a hot meal.

Philip ate next to his son, sitting cross-legged on a soft, sandy spot. But Peter had been uncommonly quiet that day and said little during dinner.

"Never seen a dead man before, lad?" Philip finally asked.

"No."

"There's a first for everything."

"Were you scared? When they attacked?" Peter asked his father.

"Only of not seeing you again."

"I think I would have been fearful."

Then he added, "I prayed for you."

His father fell silent at that.

After the meal the fires were doused and a guard was set around the encampment. Philip and Peter laid out their mats and stretched out under their blankets. Peter ached from the work of the day. The night grew chill and damp. So he pulled the wool blanket up to his chin. There were sounds of night birds and owls in the forest. Suddenly overwhelmed by the feeling that he was on the very edge of the end of the world, Peter had the strangest sensation that if he moved too far this way or that, he would drop off.

Yet after saying his prayers, Peter was soon fast asleep.

His father, however, was still awake, and he remained so for a long time afterward as he studied his slumbering son.

Chapter 36

"We will head up the King's River tomorrow at daybreak," Newport explained to the small governing council that had met the next day. Standing with him was a contingent of his most able explorers.

Philip was there, along with George Kendall, George Percy, and John Smith. An experienced adventurer and mercenary with a full beard and a prominent waxed moustache, Smith had a reputation as a battler. In one military campaign, he was reputed to have slain three war-hardened Turks in hand-to-hand combat. However, on the voyage over, Smith had disputed the orders of Captain Newport and had spent the last few weeks of the journey in the hold of one of the ships in chains, charged with attempted mutiny. Newport had handled the entire matter so discreetly that most of the crew, as well as Peter, had been unaware of the incident until reaching land. Philip had known of the trouble with Smith, but chose not to divulge it to his son.

The charges against Smith were dropped after landfall, but Newport continued to harbor great distrust for the mercenary. It was only because of pressure from Gosnold and the entire council that Newport finally relented and included him in the exploration.

"What do you hope to accomplish in your mission?" one of the councilman asked.

"Two things," Newport replied. "To find the headwaters of the King's River. And also to discover any mountains that might harbor minerals or other valuable types of ore."

"Very much in accord with the scope of the charter from the Crown," the councilman added. "Then you have your two tasks for your inland journey—"

"There is also another," a voice rang out.

It was Philip.

The councilman turned to address him.

"You, sir," he said. "Mister Kensington. You have something to add?"

"I do," Philip said. "It has long been the judgment of the Crown—both King James and Queen Elizabeth before him—to make every effort to rescue any survivors of the English that disappeared at the settlement at Roanoke."

"You mean, rescue the dead!" came another voice.

Then the speaker, George Kendall, stood up and continued.

"Dead and gone, that's what I say. It's been twenty years. More than that. We all know those settlers must have been slaughtered by the Indians. There have been several rescue parties looking for them over the years. Yet not a single sign that they are alive. Now of course, it's all very regrettable what happened to them. But Kensington here would have us chasing after ghosts."

"Since when do we abandon those who are left behind before us?" Philip retorted.

"A rousing *aye* to that sentiment," John Smith said, joining in. Newport threw Smith a stern look.

"I don't know about anybody else, but I don't want to risk my life," Kendall shot back, "for Mister Kensington's wild fantasy."

"And I don't care for your cowardice," Philip barked.

The presiding councilman could see the division brewing. Tempers had already flared since the attack from the local tribe the day before. That, coupled with John Smith's dispute with Captain Newport on the voyage over, had made the establishment of Jamestown precarious from the start. The councilman needed to maintain order.

"There will be no more outbursts!" he announced firmly. Then he turned to the three sea captains in attendance.

"Captain Newport," he said. "What make you of this—of the fate of the Roanoke settlers? What chance is there of their survival?"

"Slim, regrettably," he said. "I share Mister Kensington's passion for rescue. But we lack any clear traces of them after all these years."

"Captains Ratcliffe and Gosnold," the councilman continued. "What say you?"

Ratcliffe thought for a moment, then answered.

"I don't dispute Captain Newport's assessment. Yet there is one other consideration."

"Oh? And what is that?"

"The Spanish," Ratcliffe said nonchalantly.

Philip was eyeing George Kendall. And when Ratcliffe spoke up, Kendall's face took on the kind of expression you might expect from one who had bitten into a sour apple.

"That's absurd!" Kendall said in disgust. "You worry about the Spaniards? In case you didn't notice, those were savages decked out in war paint who were firing arrows at us. They are the ones trying to kill us, not the Spanish armada!"

"Let us hear out the captain," the councilman said, motioning for Kendall to sit down.

"By 'Spain,'" Ratcliffe added, "I refer to any future claim Spain may make to these lands." Then he motioned for Gabriel Archer, the lawyer, to speak up. His hand and arm had been bandaged up, and his face was pale from pain—even paler than usual—but he had summoned the stamina to attend the meeting.

"The fact is," Archer said in a weak voice, "we control this part of the New World under the lawful charter from the English Crown, of course. But the ancient law of sovereignty vests lawful land ownership in that nation which can prove *first* discovery and settlement. The Spaniards have already wrested control of the lands along the southerly coastland from the French under the claim of first discovery and settlement in the land they call Florida."

"But what right of claim would Spain have to these lands within Virginia?" the councilman asked.

"Just this," Archer replied, "if we cannot claim an earlier settlement here, then Spain may later claim that these lands encroach on their lawful lands to the south."

"On the other hand," the councilman said, grasping the import of the lawyer's assessment, "if the Roanoke settlers are still alive… then England could claim continuous settlement of these regions in Virginia for the twenty years, thus foreclosing any reasonable claim by Spain, correct?"

"Exactly," Archer said, wanting to add a gesture, but wincing a little when he tried and thinking better of it.

"Yet," Newport chimed in, "mounting a search party is not within the express terms of our charter. Neither the Virginia Company nor the Crown authorized us to take on that task."

The residing councilman considered the matter. Then he ruled.

"It appears the good captain has put the point on the matter," he said. "We are bound by the charter. Yet I also say this—if there be any sign or clue that settlers or their descendants be near to where you are venturing—and if it does not waylay you or take you from your designated course or add any further risk, then you shall have the authority of this council to investigate."

Then he turned to the other members of the council.

"What say you all?" he asked.

All nodded in agreement.

As the group dispersed, Philip locked eyes with Kendall, who was harboring a smoldering fire behind his mask of composure. Philip had not won the day. But he had what he needed—a loophole to search for settlers if he could find any evidence of them as they ventured up the King's River.

But the debate had now sparked another question in Philip's mind.

Why did George Kendall express such passion in minimizing the threat from Spain?

Philip knew only two things about George Kendall. First, that he had been a mercenary on the Continent. That, in itself, could raise a question about his allegiance to England.

But there was also the second matter. On the voyage over to Virginia, Philip had eavesdropped on a discussion between Newport and the presiding councilman regarding those men who would be considered "most reliable" in the new venture. In that conversation, Newport swore on excellent authority that George Kendall once served as one of Robert Cecil's foreign spies. Philip was not as politically astute as his brother. On the other hand, even he (and most of London) knew that Cecil's loyalty to the English Crown was unquestioned. It seemed logical to Philip that Cecil would not have trusted Kendall unless his fidelity to James was beyond reproach. The idea, therefore, that Kendall might be a Spanish sympathizer, despite his odd comments, seemed far-fetched.

As Philip crossed the crude settlement clearing strewn with cut trees and spliced lumber, amidst the banging of mallets as the carpenters began the construction of the permanent houses, one thought persisted.

He couldn't escape the feeling that there was something about this Kendall fellow that lay below the murky surface—a mystery about him—but what that was, he could not decipher.

Chapter 37

It had been months since Andrew's brother and nephew had shipped out of Blackwall aboard the *Susan Constant*, bound for the New World. During that time, Andrew had been praying diligently for them. But he had no word about their fate.

At the same time, matters of state had also occupied Andrew's attention. He had been named as the assistant to Lancelot Andrewes, the Bishop of Chichester, to aid the bishop in his duties as director of the Westminster Committee, one of several now laboring intensely on the new Bible translation commissioned by King James.

Trained not only in law and politics but also theology, Andrew Mackenzie had been considered an administrative asset of unique value to the translation effort. After all, that process was not only intended to be a spiritual achievement—ironing out the small but significant variants in the versions of the Bible circulating through England—but it also had to garner favor with King James himself—a decidedly delicate political affair.

Ordinarily, Andrew would have considered his post to be one of unequaled prestige, not to mention one of extraordinary significance to the faith. Yet as he trudged, several days a week, into the large Jerusalem Chamber in Westminster Hall to take notes of the regular translation proceedings, he could feel only a sinister sense of foreboding. After all, this was the very building the Catholic radicals had planned to blow up. And while his brother's dangerous ties to Guy Fawkes, and his incidental connection to the botched plot, had never been publicly exposed, they were ever in the forefront of Andrew's mind.

But Andrew's sources within the palace had revealed that Robert Cecil had received a report linking Philip Mackenzie to the purchase of fuses intended for the Gunpowder Plot. Why hadn't Cecil seized on that information and hailed Andrew before the rackmasters for interrogation about his brother's whereabouts? At a minimum, Andrew expected to have been relieved of his position on the Westminster Committee, distanced from any of the "pet projects" of the Crown.

Yet, for whatever reason, that had not happened.

Cecil had proven himself cold and aloof in dealings with Andrew. However, considering the evidence Cecil had against his brother, Andrew was amazed he was still permitted to circulate within the powerful inner circles of James.

He was still musing on that unanswered question, when a voice from the committee pulled him back to the translation proceedings.

"Mister Mackenzie," the Bishop of Chichester said, "may we have an answer to that question?"

Looking around the mahogany table at the faces of the committeemen, Andrew flushed with embarrassment.

"Please do pardon me," he said. "The question…which question?"

"Why the question posed by Mister Saravia, of course," the bishop countered.

Andrew turned to Hadrian à Saravia, the Prebendary of Westminster, who served under the bishop there. Saravia was a swarthy, well-mannered fellow, half-Flemish and half-Spanish, who had served as professor of divinity at Leyden. Despite his genealogical ties to a nation known for staunch Catholicism, his Protestant credentials were impeccable.

"My dear Mister Mackenzie," Saravia said in a good-natured tone, "I might have expected to have been completely ignored *prior to* England's peace treaty with Spain two years ago...but surely not now!"

His clever joke sent the ten members of the committee into a sudden burst of laughter. Andrew blushed even more as he realized he was the butt of the joke.

Saravia often made light of his Spanish descent. He was smart enough to do that so as to disarm those within the Court of James who still harbored distrust against Spain. King James had negotiated an uneasy truce with Spain in 1604, the year before the Gunpowder Plot. It brought to an end the long sea war between the two countries. Robert Cecil was one of the chief negotiators for England.

But despite appearances, the two nations were still full-blown antagonists. Many Court observers were surprised, then, that Spain did not figure more prominently in the conspiracy trials of Fawkes and his fellow conspirators. Yet the prosecution team, perhaps on orders from Cecil or other counselors to the king, chose instead to paint the Jesuits, not Spain, as the real sinister force behind the plot to destroy the Protestant government.

But Andrew knew the lay of the land and made an adroit comeback.

"Indeed," he said with an unassuming smile, "it is not the Spanish peace treaty that is at issue. But rather our declaration of war against the words of the English language, which occasionally seem at odds with the Greek and Hebrew texts of Holy Scripture."

Several of the members chuckled at that.

"Well said," Saravia continued. "Then let me state my question again—where did we leave off in our last session regarding, for the want of a better term, the Exodus dispute?"

"Yes, of course," Andrew said. He combed through the journal he had been keeping. After a few moments, he spoke up.

"Here it is. The director, the good bishop, brought up the matter of Exodus chapter 1. The matter of the midwives."

"Yes, the midwives," the bishop intoned. "I recall my reference to the mistaken interpretation in the comment notes of the Geneva Bible—"

"That was it," Saravia interjected. "The delicacy of that matter, of course, cannot be overstated. In a sense, it involves the attitude of His Majesty regarding his own sovereignty. And the extent to which he would countenance...well, how should we say it...subversion within his own realm."

Several of the members nodded vigorously at that. Finally one of them, Richard Thomson, chimed in.

"His Majesty could hardly be expected to agree with that radical claptrap from the likes of Calvin and Knox and those other radicals—those who say the Bible is over the King."

"Well, yes," the bishop said, then added diplomatically, "this committee is certainly blessed, I believe, in not only acute scholarship, but also with a keen sense of...well...appropriateness. We are, after all, servants of the Crown. And in that, we serve at the good pleasure of the king."

"And yet," Andrew said, his voice lowered as he mused on the point he was about to make, "is not our chief allegiance, not to the visible kingdoms of man...but rather to the invisible kingdom of

God and His Son, Jesus Christ, who is King, and Savior, and Lord of all?"

A dead hush fell on the members. After several seconds of total silence, the bishop shuffled some of the papers in front of him and tried to gloss over Andrew's politically volatile comment.

"Yet," the bishop said, "Scripture says that God appoints the rulers, and inasmuch as we are subjects of the ruler of this realm, our splendid King James, our obedience to him is deemed thereby to be obedience to God—"

"Certainly," Andrew said, "obedience to lawful authority is the general rule of Scripture. But there are those few exceptions—as it is mentioned in the first chapter of Exodus. The Jewish midwives clearly disobeyed Pharaoh's edict to slay any sons born to Jewish mothers. And God honored that."

"But isn't that the very issue at hand?" Saravia said. "Whether the translations that contain that language are accurate. Is that not the very question? And the second question is similar—namely, whether the king would accept an interpretation that places his Crown beneath the cross of Christ, so to speak, rather than vice-versa."

Andrew turned to William Bedwell, a quiet man who was widely respected as not only an eminent Arabic scholar but also a noted mathematician.

"Mister Bedwell, do you have an opinion?"

The bishop, noting that his assistant was beginning to reach beyond the scope of his authority and was now running the meeting and directing the discussion, quickly tried to rein in the debate.

"Perhaps it is unfair to hedge Mister Bedwell into a corner so unexpectedly—"

"Not at all," Bedwell said with a smile. "I was just thinking...that

Laurence Chaderton, over at the Cambridge Committee, has indicated an interpretation that is in line with what our good assistant to the director, Mister Mackenzie, has said..."

"Chaderton?" Roger Tighe said with a sneer, "that Puritan radical? He is no friend of the Church of England—or of the king..."

"Mister King," Bedwell said, addressing himself to Geoffrey King, the Hebrew scholar, "you are the one with the best ancient linguistic skills. What say you?"

King, who had secret friendships with some of the Puritan scholars and privately shared their evangelical approach, paused and considered his words carefully. Then he finally spoke.

"On this matter in Exodus," he said, "I cannot say that the Geneva Bible is...inappropriate in that respect..."

The bishop, noting the lateness of the hour, and deciding to adjourn before a doctrinal crisis developed, closed the meeting.

As Andrew walked out, nearly the last one to leave, the bishop came up next to him and laid his hand on his shoulder.

"We must remember," he said to Andrew, "that this translation shall, in the end, be subject to the approval of His Majesty."

Andrew nodded. Then he looked his superior in the eye.

"Of course," he replied, "but I would rather—if forced to a choice—incur the wrath of King James than face the disappointment of the Lord Jesus that I failed to fight for the integrity of His Word."

"Then let us hope," the bishop said, "that you will not be forced into that choice."

"Perhaps," Andrew replied, "we can both pray to that end."

Chapter 38

It was late afternoon, and the sun was illuminating the glass-enclosed sunroom with a golden light. Rose Heatherton reached forward to the plate before her. She delicately picked at a corner of a raspberry-filled pastry, lifted it with two fingers to her mouth, and then daintily wiped her mouth with the linen napkin.

She could easily have devoured the whole thing in two bites. For weeks, she and her brother William, and their now-ailing mother, had been managing on meager food rations. The estate in Scotland was being transferred to creditors. Their large mansion in London was already gone, along with all their furnishings, paintings, and silverware. All the staff was now let go. The three of them were living in cramped quarters in the East End. William was working two jobs. Rose was employed as a tutor and caretaker for several children on a large estate on the outskirts of the city. She was given food and board and a small wage. She visited her brother and mother on the weekends.

Life had become dreary for them, at least compared to the opulence of their previous state.

But Rose did not feel sorry for herself. Nor did she try to take advantage of the hospitality of her hostess that day by dropping hints of her family's poverty. She maintained an appropriate air of good humor and warmth. Though Rose did wonder why her hostess stared at her so and seemed to have such a faraway look to her eyes.

"These pastries are delightful," Rose said. "You are so thoughtful to let me visit today. I find myself a little at a loss for words…why I am here…and why you should treat me with such kindness."

"I have more of the pastries if you would like," Kate Mackenzie said with a smile.

"Oh no, I couldn't," Rose protested.

"Nonsense," Kate replied. Then she spotted her maid and waved her into the room.

"Betsy," she said, "wrap all of the pastries—yes, and throw in the scones too—and there are some wonderful fruits in the pantry. Andrew and I will never finish them. Pears and grapes. Add those. Have it ready, please, when Miss Heatherton is ready to leave."

Rose leaned forward as if she was ready to depart.

"No, I absolutely refuse to have you leave yet," Kate said firmly. "Now sit back and let's enjoy this time…getting to know one another."

Rose relaxed into the high-back upholstered armchair. She smiled and almost giggled a bit, feeling just a little giddy that she was being treated so affectionately.

"So," Kate continued, "tell me more about you."

"Well, I've told you about my tutoring. It's a challenge. But I think I have some skills in teaching. I love children. It has been hard working away from my home…I don't want to sound ungrateful though. The job and the money—I mean, the job is a blessing and a wonderful opportunity."

"Yes, I am sure it is," Kate said with a knowing smile. "But now tell me about *you.*"

"Oh my," Rose said, stammering a bit. "That is a subject that is not very interesting..."

"Well, I must disagree," Kate said. "That is exactly the subject I would like to learn, right now, more than any other."

"Really?"

Kate nodded.

"I don't know where to start..."

"Start with our meeting today—why you decided to visit me today. We've never met before, you and I. Though I am regretful for that. You seem to be such a very nice young lady. So...why did you come?"

"I...I am not entirely sure...well...it is such a difficult thing to explain..."

"Then let's see if I can help you," Kate said. "You came because you know that my husband is the uncle of Peter Mackenzie. And from what my husband had told me, you and Peter were very fond of each other."

Rose was wide-eyed and very surprised at Kate's keen understanding.

"And," Kate continued, "you do not know much about where Peter is right now, but more than anything you would like to know he is safe. And that he is doing well, wherever he is."

Snatching a lace handkerchief from her sleeve, Rose tried to dab away the torrent of emotion that was welling up in her eyes and then quickly trickling down her cheeks.

"I am such a ninny. Please forgive me."

Kate rose, walked over, and then knelt next to her guest, taking one of her hands in hers.

"My dear Rose," she said, "don't apologize for your heart's cry. It longs for the light of day. So...right here, in this sunny room, is the perfect place."

Rose laughed a little at that, and soon felt a little bit better. How strange, she thought, that she should feel so suddenly at home in a place she had never been before.

"And now for your reason for coming," Kate said. "My husband has not heard yet of the fate of Peter or his father. But we have every reason to believe they arrived safely...to wherever they were going. And as soon as we hear anything, we will let you know."

"Thank you so much for that!" Rose said in a burst of enthusiasm.

"But you should also know we cannot tell you everything. And even to the extent that you know *anything* about Peter or Philip Mackenzie...well, these are dangerous times. And your inquiries about them may place you in danger."

Squinting her eyes and wrinkling her brow a little, Rose was listening intensely and seemed to appreciate the risks.

"I think I understand," she said. "But I would like to hear anything you can tell me. Even if there is a danger in that. I must know about Peter—"

"And as we get information, we will share it," Kate said.

Then Kate stood up, patted Rose's hand, and then walked over to the large glass window that overlooked the formal gardens in back. She swept a loose strand of hair into place and turned back to face Rose.

"Yet...we shouldn't make too much of this danger business... after all, who could possibly suspect two ladies chatting together of anything dangerous?"

Rose giggled and nodded. Then she reached for another bit of her pastry.

Kate watched her and studied her young, graceful movements, and her enthusiasm. And, at least for that fleeting moment, was so grateful that the two of them had met.

Chapter 39

In his luxurious office a few blocks from Westminster, decorated with artifacts and statues from the Continent, Hadrian à Saravia settled down to write a short report.

He had just arrived back from the meeting with the Westminster Committee. He sent the message to have his cooks prepare a meal of roast beef, fresh boiled vegetables, and strong wine. Saravia had a special love of English beef.

Now he was settling down to pen a few terse paragraphs.

Though he had been spending much of his time in the translation proceedings and the chaplainry duties of Westminster, none of that would find its way into this writing, at least not directly.

He slipped his hand into an interior pocket of his cape, pulled the lining inside out, and then unlatched a tiny button that opened into another compartment. He fished deep into the second pocket until he found a few small pieces of paper. He unfolded them and then reviewed his notes, written in his own abbreviated form of notation. He read them over several times, until he had their contents memorized.

He took the candle that was burning in its holder on his desk and, with the notes in his other hand, he walked over to the large fireplace. Then he lit the edge of the notes on fire and tossed them into the fireplace. A careful man, he stood, candle in hand, as he watched the paper burn into ash. He stepped on the ash with his boot, crushing it into the stone of the fireplace.

Then he walked back over to his desk and pulled some fresh parchment from a box. Saravia looked around for his quill pen. Having found it, he went to an ornately carved black-walnut cupboard and opened the door. In the back was a small ceramic cup with a top. He carefully withdrew the cup and, after removing the top, carried it over to the desk.

Now he settled into the task before him. He reflected for several minutes on the assignment. Then he began writing. As he wrote, he dipped his quill into the cup.

It would be a short memorandum, just one page. He ended it with an obscure reference:

> Expecting further news from traveler. When received, your Excellency shall be apprised.
>
> Your humble servant

The note was not signed.

When he had finished, he held the paper up to the light. There was no writing visible to the eye, even on close inspection.

Satisfied that his task was done, he took the cup over to the fireplace and emptied out its contents—a lemon juice mixture—onto the dead ashes. Then he wiped the inside of the cup with a rag until no lemon scent remained. And he put the cup back into its place in the cupboard. Saravia folded the note, then took the candle and dripped wax on the edges of the paper to seal it, but he did not impress his signet ring on the soft wax as he did with official documents of state.

He heard a knock on his chamber door.

"Enter."

His personal servant, a tall, handsome Moor, entered with a large silver tray and laid it on the table. Saravia lifted the polished covers to examine the beef, beets, and carrots.

"Just in time," he said with a smile. "I am famished."

"Is there anything else I can do for you, sir?" the Moor asked.

"There is," Saravia replied. Then he snatched up the sealed note and handed it to his servant.

"Take this to the ambassador. Take the usual route. Tell no one on the way. Advise no one of its origins."

The Moor bowed and turned to leave.

"And one more thing," Saravia added.

"Yes, sir?" the servant said.

"Make sure this is delivered *personally* to the ambassador. No one else. Do you understand?"

"Yes, sir," the Moor answered. Then he bowed again and slipped out of the room.

Hadrian à Saravia then seated himself before his meal. After several bites he moaned in delight. The meat had been prepared in a thick wine sauce and was ringed with Spanish olives.

He took a bite of the English beef and then popped a Spanish olive into his mouth for good measure, chewing both at the same time.

Realizing the irony in that, he began to chuckle, then laugh out loud—so hard he choked a little and had to take several gulps from his goblet of wine to clear his throat.

Then he wiped his mouth on his cape and began to devour the beef again.

Chapter 40

The weather in Virginia was uncommonly hot that day. The members of the expedition were already sweating profusely as they prepared to launch their long, narrow outriggers, which would carry them up river.

Peter tried to be of good courage and not show any sorrow at his father's departure again. But he was only partly successful.

Before boarding his boat, Philip gave Peter an unexpected bear hug and a rough laugh. Peter had seen it before. That was his father's way of trying to soothe his fears and make light of the risks.

"You are needed here at the settlement," Philip said. "Make yourself useful."

"I will," Peter answered.

"Don't worry about me. After all, you say you've been praying—isn't that so?"

"It is, Father."

"Then God heard you. With a heart as good as yours, how could He not?"

"I am a sinner. Like everyone else."

"Yes, of course," Philip said. Then he lifted his head a bit and cocked it to the side as he studied his son. Then he said something else.

"I know all about that subject—sin. I could teach the preachers on that one."

"But you believed on Jesus once, didn't you? You told me you did. Your soul was washed by His blood on the cross."

"Aye. 'Tis true enough. Stood up in the church where your grandfather Ransom was preaching. I was ten."

After a pause, Peter innocently asked a question Philip was not prepared to face.

"What happened to you?" Peter asked, gazing at his father's face.

Philip looked away to hide his reaction, but he noticed the launch about to leave the beach. The men at the shore were waiting for him.

"Life," Philip said. "That's what happened."

But he knew, down deep, that he was not being honest.

It was not life that had happened to him. Rather, it was what he had chosen to do with his life that had made the difference. And no one could take the responsibility for that except himself.

Philip took a step over to Peter, grabbed his head and rubbed his hair, then quickly walked down the boat.

Peter watched his father climb into one of the boats. Then all of them pushed off and started along the shoreline, heading to the wide mouth of the King's River. Peter stayed by the beach studying the line of boats until they had rounded the bend and were out of sight.

Philip tried to shake off his son's parting words. But they lingered on. He was sitting in the middle of one of the launches while the oarsmen, in a standing position, were using long poles to navigate the boat in its place in the entourage.

He took out the maps of the river that had been sketched by

previous mapmakers. Then he took his sketch pad and unwrapped it from the worn leather case. He would mark off a rough sketch of his own at each geographical point along the river's bends, and then later he would work on a finished draft, comparing it to the older maps, and then correcting any inaccuracies on those.

The river was wide and impressively navigable. On each side the forest was dense. Many of the trees were cypresses, and their branches draped over the shoreline in a tangle of vines and branches. Wildflowers cascaded down to the water between the undergrowth. There was a sweet smell from some of the vegetation. A man on one of the boats ahead called out, "Berries—an abundance of them, men! Mulberries, I believe. Raspberries too. Growing wild…look at them all!"

Occasionally, as the boats oared downriver, a large fish would jump and then plop back into the depths of the muddy water. On the shoreline they would occasionally see herds of deer grazing, their tails flicking the flies off as they peered, big-eyed, at the line of boats as it passed them by.

The first two days were spent uneventfully. Sometimes Captain Newport would order the line of boats over to shore. He would send his miners into the open lands looking for signs of useful ore, or—as the legends had it—for places where gold might be excavated. But there were no discoveries of precious metals on those days.

By the third day, the boats were slowly making their way on the river when one of the men in the front launch stood up and gave a hand signal for the boat in back of his. The silent sign was then sent back to each of the succeeding boats. The message was for the men to stay on the alert, that *hostiles* had been spotted, and they should keep their hands on their weapons.

Philip put down his maps, grabbed his pistol, and laid it on his lap.

Up ahead, the lead boat had been given orders by Newport to go ashore.

From his vantage point several boats back, Philip couldn't see what had caused the first boat, and all the other boats, to head over to the shore on the right. But after a few minutes of tense oaring, Philip could see what had captured Newport's attention.

There was a good-sized Indian village in a clearing perhaps a hundred feet or so back from the waterline.

Several Indians, bows in hand, were rushing down to the shore. There was a great deal of yelling and wild leaping and jumping. But Newport gave the order not to shoot unless attacked. Slowly each of the boats landed on the shore, but the men stayed on board, waiting for the word to disembark.

By then, the numbers of the Indian warriors had increased dramatically. By Philip's count, the English were outnumbered three or four to one. Some had spears, and others, large clubs. The Indians were only a few yards away from the boats, and their chanting and yelling had now increased to a fever pitch as they jabbed the tips of their spears and arrows menacingly toward in the direction of the white explorers.

At close range, Philip was astounded at their appearance. The men were smooth skinned and muscular, with no hair on their bodies, and none sporting beards. They were barefooted, and wore only leather apronlike loin coverings with fringe. Some of them had their hair covered with tight-fitting leather caps. Others had their hair shaved on the sides but with a cock's tail running from front to back, many of them with hair that had appeared to have been colored red.

But their faces were what captured his attention. The look in their eyes was uncommonly fierce.

For a moment, Philip wondered whether Newport had made the right decision.

He was about to find out.

In Newport's boat, the man most fluent in the Indian dialects stood up, though with a little hesitation. He slowly raised his right hand, and then showed his palm to the entire assembly of warriors.

The warriors stopped yelling, but the look on their faces did not change.

Then the Indian translator, standing up in the beached boat, spoke only one word. And when he did, he spoke it loud enough for all to hear.

Werowance! he called out.

Then he yelled it out again.

Werowance!

One of the largest of the Indians, armed with a long spear, stepped out of the crowd of warriors.

He strode up to the translator, close enough so that he was closer than the length of his spear.

And when he halted, he hunched his head down slightly, still staring at the translator and never letting him out of his gaze.

And the look in the warrior's eyes was like that of a wolf eyeing his prey.

Chapter 41

The Indian warrior, a member of the tribe called the Rapahanna, stood his ground, staring at the translator with a fierce countenance.

The translator's face bore the look of carefully controlled panic, as several minutes elapsed with no dialogue, no gestures, only the face-to-face standoff.

Then the Indian broke the silence. He spoke loudly, with vehemence, moving his muscular arms wildly in the air. The translator apparently understood little, as he shook his head slowly back and forth. But one part of the warrior's speech was understood.

The word *werowance* surfaced in his Indian dialect, and at that word the translator nodded and spoke a few words in the same tongue. And then, repeated the word *werowance* and pointed to Captain Newport, who stepped off his boat and began walking down the beach toward the warrior. This sent the assembly of Indian braves into an uproar. They waved their bows and spears over their heads, shouting and stomping the ground.

But the translator quickly began shouting *noh maguk*, which Philip would later learn meant "one who sells or gives."

The warrior yelled back, using the words *mandoag* and *nottoway* and pointing to Newport as he did.

The translator quickly tried to dispel those adjectives—which were usually applied by the tribe to their mortal enemies—and tried strenuously to convince this Indian official that they were coming in peace, and that the English had not come to declare war on the Rapahanna.

But it was then that something happened behind the huge mob of Indians that immediately quieted them. The assembly parted like a field of tall grass in a strong wind. Someone was coming.

Out of the mob there appeared the *werowance*, or ruler, of the Rapahanna, taking slow, proud steps as two of his serfs were clearing the others out of the way.

The chief wore a headdress of deer skin and deer hair, painted red, and bunched up in a kind of a bun atop his head. Copper plates were sewn into the cap. Two feathers stuck straight up like antlers on his head, and his ears carried bird claws. His face was painted blue and his body red, and his torso was draped with beads, shells, and small bits of silver.

He motioned to one of his servants, and a mat was quickly spread on the ground. The chief sat down cross-legged, gave out a large sigh, and motioned for his pipe. A long wooden pipe, packed with tobacco, was handed to him already lit. He commenced to smoke from it, emitting large puffs of smoke and, with an aura of complete command, then lectured his tribe on matters, most of which were also beyond the ability of the translator.

But when he had finished speaking, the translator turned to Captain Newport.

"He would have us visit his village, which is just on the other side of that clearing," the translator said.

Newport smiled, nodded vigorously, and then called for all of the settlers to follow the Indian chief as he rose up, handed his pipe to his servant, and then began to stride toward the Indian settlement.

It was a short walk, about a hundred yards. Newport ordered his men to carry their weapons discreetly, and not to threaten the tribe that had invited them into their community.

As the white visitors entered the village, they were all visibly impressed. The Indian town was large and well laid out. At the entrance there was a tribal dance circle of carved poles. Leading from it was a wide, cleared lane—the equivalent of a main street. On one side were sturdy huts built of wooden superstructures covered with animal skins stretched tight up to the curved roofs. On the other side were carefully tended corn fields and plantings of several different vegetables.

The *werowance* led them all to the end of the main lane, then stopped in front of the largest hut which lay at the edge of the village. He called for his mat, clapped his hands, and then sat down on it, still giving instructions as he did. He invited Newport and his translator to sit next to him, joined by the rest of the English who were invited to sit down in a large circle. Behind the white settlers, in a larger outer ring, were the Indian tribe members.

Within the hour, the smell of a fire pervaded the village, and a large circle of smoke rose up in the sky as food was being prepared. Several Indian squaws, who appeared to be the chief's wives, scurried forward with baskets of food—first to the chief, and then to Newport, and finally to the other white settlers and the rest of the Indian village. There was smoked sturgeon, corn baked in its husks, and freshly killed venison. Several kinds of cooked gourds were presented and—what was new to the men—potatoes, some of them delightfully sweet to the taste.

Philip and his companions feasted until they were about to burst. For his part, Philip kept an eye on the fierce warrior who had engaged them at the beach. His stare was returned by the Indian brave, who, even when scooping food into his mouth by the handful, stared back.

When the sun started lowering along the treetops, Newport gave his men the command to depart. But before he did, he presented several handsomely fashioned knives to the *werowance,* who received them with a great relish.

Once they were back in their boats, the Newport expedition pushed off farther upriver to find a suitable clearing before nightfall that would also be a respectable distance from the Rapahanna village.

As they slowly made way upriver, one of the sailors in Philip's boat spoke up about something he had heard from the translator.

"He says he heard the chief brag about how he became chief."

"How did that happen?" Philip asked.

"The chief had one main competitor—but he killed him in a fight, and became the ruler of the tribe."

"What else did he say?" one of the oarsmen asked.

"That the guy he killed to become chief...he was his brother."

"Savages," the oarsman muttered. "What civilized man would hate his own brother?"

Philip was glad the sun was setting, the last glimmer of light piercing through the trees of the forest. That way his fallen, tortured countenance could not be clearly seen.

The entourage of boats headed over to the shoreline at last to make camp for the night.

Philip was still mulling over what he had heard in the boat about the chief. And he thought about his brother, Andrew. He wondered if they would ever see each other again.

And he also had to admit that there was a sinking guilt that lay down in the deepest part of his soul. It had to do with the way he had parted with his brother in England. And the anger he had allowed to simmer for reasons that now seemed indefinable and remote.

Whatever the cause, his resentment toward Andrew had been wrong.

As Philip lugged some of their equipment from the boat to the clearing he spoke just two words—quietly, unheard by any other human save himself.

Forgive me, he muttered, as he looked up toward the sky where the light along the horizon was dimming and dying in colors of red and orange against the shadows of the coming night.

Chapter 42

"She is a delightful young lady. A little more mature than her years. The trials of life have done that. I knew right off what was weighing on her heart."

"And what was that?" Andrew asked, finishing his breakfast.

"Well, of course there was the matter of her deep affection for your nephew, Peter," Kate replied, sipping her coffee and then thanking the serving girl who had just brought in a fresh brew in a polished silver urn.

"Yes, Peter confided some of that to me," Andrew said, a little absorbed in his thoughts. "In one of the meetings I had at the surveyor's shop. Don't you remember?"

"Yes, but I'm referring to Rose Heatherton's affections for him— not the reverse. Young men become infatuated with young ladies. Of course. But that doesn't mean that the young lady necessarily returns the courtesy."

Then Andrew was struck with a thought.

"You didn't...you did not tell her that *we knew* where Peter and his father were, did you?"

"Oh, no—not at all."

"Nor let on that they both had shipped over to the New World?"

"No. I made a point of not letting on in the least."

"Good," Andrew replied. "There are, I believe, still strong suspicions against me at Court."

"I know, dear, that you are afraid of retribution against you because of Philip—"

"Not fear," Andrew said a little sharply, "but fact. I know Robert Cecil was informed of Philip's connection to Fawkes."

"Perhaps he decided it was not a matter of consequence," Kate replied, trying to soothe the situation.

"Impossible," Andrew muttered with assurance. "There is something else afoot. Ordinarily, Cecil would have used this against me. He has never liked me…"

"Now, dear," Kate said trying to reassure him.

"You are trying to be bright-eyed about this, and I appreciate that. But we must face the cold truth."

"And what is that?"

"That I have made myself a menace at Court. Both because of my brother's reckless associations and my comments at the Westminster Committee."

"Perhaps the Lord God is protecting you. So that you can do His will and His work."

"Yes," Andrew said, still mulling his own thoughts.

After a pause, Kate continued.

"About Rose Heatherton," she said. "There was something else on her heart, as I was saying."

"What was that?"

"They are being forced out of their apartments in London. Soon they will be forced to live over across the river in Southwark. Oh, my," she sighed, "and you know the slums there. The plague is rampant. And criminal types. And filth of all unimaginable kinds. The poor dear…"

Andrew finished eating and leaned back. He knew his wife well enough to gauge what lay behind her words of compassion. She was a tender soul, much tenderer than he. Andrew may have been gifted in the theological realities of God's nature and the mysteries of His Word, but his wife knew the even greater nature of God's heart.

"What is it you are saying, wife?"

"Just that," she said, choosing her words cautiously, "I thought there might be some way we could help."

"The Heathertons, you mean?"

"Yes, exactly."

Andrew thought for a moment.

"What do we really know about these people?"

Kate narrowed her eyes and pursed her lips. Then she spoke.

"Andrew, we know many things. We know that Rose and Peter are in love. That they have been separated by a very cruel turn of events. Those two young people are certainly not to blame for that. The family has been bankrupted. And that poor Mrs. Heatherton has lost her husband, and she has now taken ill herself. If they move to Southwark, Mrs. Heatherton surely will not survive."

Kate was making more sense than Andrew wanted to acknowledge. But then she added the final blow.

"When you look at these poor people and their plight, and the fact that their path has intersected with ours…well…isn't that the very point of Jesus' parable of the Good Samaritan? You yourself have preached on that very portion of Scripture from time to time. Very ably I might add. Once, I recall, in your father's church."

That was an argument Andrew could not dodge. It wasn't that

Andrew was coldhearted or unloving. But particularly with his further embroiling in matters of the court of James and his newest, well-founded concerns, he felt overwhelmed with his own problems.

"We will talk further on this," he said rising from the table.

"Will we please?" she asked hopefully.

"Yes, dear wife. As always, you give reasons of the heart that the head needs to heed."

She could see the strain on his face. "What meeting did you say you had today?"

"The bishop. He wants to meet with me privately."

"About what?" she asked.

"He didn't say. But I have a feeling he will be delivering a message to me from the Crown."

Then Andrew turned to fetch a leather bag of papers waiting for him on the hallway bookcase. Before turning to the front door, he spoke again.

"And I believe the message will not be a happy one."

He managed a smile, and then opened the large oak front door and left.

Chapter 43

The meeting with Lancelot Andrewes, prominent bishop and director of the Westminster Committee, was held at Hampton Court. That sent a dire signal to Andrew. He had calculated that if it were held at the Jerusalem Room, the usual meeting room for the committee in its work on the new Bible translation, that would mean the issue was merely the bishop's disagreement over Andrew's statements about the "Exodus dispute" that had erupted at their last meeting.

But given that the meeting was to be held at one of the palaces of the Court of King James, that sent a very different signal.

The message was clearly that what the bishop had to discuss with Andrew would transcend a dispute over one text of Scripture. Andrew was also anticipating that when he entered into the palace room where the bishop would be waiting for him, he would not be alone.

Once again, Andrew was correct.

But he was unprepared for who he was about to meet.

The bishop was standing in the rear of the chaplaincy room, whose high walls were draped with long tapestries embroidered with brown and gold leaf. There were two chairs at the end of the room, and one hard-backed chair facing the other two.

A man was standing next to the bishop, with his back turned. The man turned, but before he had finished moving, Andrew could tell who it was—the short, twisted frame, stooped with a crooked spine, the carefully tailored beard and piercing eyes.

"Mister Mackenzie," Robert Cecil said with a thin smile. "Please be seated."

He pointed to the empty chair facing the other two.

Andrew strode up to the chair, gave a short bow, and sat down. His face was calm, but inwardly he was preparing for the inquisition that was to follow.

The other two men were seated. The bishop was the first to speak.

"Andrew, we do not want you to be ill at ease about our dialogue here."

"Should I be?"

"That would, of course," Cecil countered, "depend on your answers."

"My answers will be the truth. So—will the truth protect me then?"

"Truth?" Cecil said cynically. "And how shall we define that?"

"I suggest we start with God's definition rather than man's." Andrew replied.

"And would you be the sole arbiter of that, sir? You? *You?*" Cecil's tone of voice was intended to denigrate by insinuation. "You?" he continued. "A mere assistant to the bishop, here, whose prominence among the ecclesiastical divines is without parallel? You would ask the Crown to defer to *you?*"

"With God, there is no favoritism," Andrew said. "'Have not

the faith of our glorious Lord Jesus in respect of persons.' James chapter two, verse one."

"Hmm," the bishop began. "Yes. That sounds suspiciously like the Geneva version...not His Majesty's favorite. But let us not be unduly divisive. It is a simple matter. The king, Mister Mackenzie, the *king*, does prefer a rendering of the Exodus passage that does not unduly elevate the commoners—the midwives in those verses—over their sovereign ruler. In that instance, the pharoah of Egypt."

"And why is that?" Andrew asked.

Cecil was taken aback. "The insolence!" he cried out.

"A simple question," Andrew said. "Which should provoke a simple answer."

"The king," the bishop continued, "the *king of England* believes that the other translations incorrectly show the midwives to be possessed of a disobedient spirit, to have been actually rewarded for disobeying their king—"

"They refused to slaughter innocent babies," Andrew said, his voice rising, "a refusal that God honors even though it is in conflict with an edict of a sovereign ruler. Which is a fact that the text in the original language most certainly supports—"

"Treason!" Cecil cried out.

But the bishop held up a finger of compromise to quiet the king's most ardent counselor.

"Andrew, be reasonable," he continued. "We have committees filled with the most noted Bible scholars of our time. Your position as the assistant to the Westminster Committee is a...well...administrative position. Not a scholarly one. Please keep your opinions to yourself when they conflict with the good judgment of the Crown."

Andrew gave a strained smile but did not respond. He thought the matter was over, at least for the time being. But Cecil had one more issue to raise.

"There is one more thing," he said, his gloved hands clasped in front of him.

"Yes?" Andrew replied.

"There have been concerns."

"Oh?"

"Yes. Concerns at Court."

"And?"

"Concerns that some of the most intimate workings of the government and His Majesty's decisions and plans...have been leaked out."

"'Leaked out?'" Andrew asked. "In what way?'

"That is what we thought *you* might be able to answer for us," Cecil said coldly.

"I don't know what you are talking about."

"You know, Mister Mackenzie," Cecil continued, "that loyalty to the king is of utmost necessity for those who would be his closest servants. You do realize that?"

"Of course," Andrew said, wondering whether Cecil was going to connect him to his brother's conduct.

"In fact, it is a biblical mandate—it is the essence of a servant that he be found *faithful*," the bishop added.

After a moment of silence, Cecil unclasped his hands and pointed an index finger of each hand to the sky and shrieked.

"There are spies among us!" he said. "*Spies!* And they mean to deal grievous harm to the king. And we will hunt them down. And when we find them, we will destroy them in a very public, and a very painful, and a very horrifying way."

Then, as his voice grew softer, he added simply, "Spies, Mackenzie.

So be warned. The Crown is ever vigilant. And we are prepared to execute wrath upon our enemies."

After a few moments of reflection Andrew answered, but so calmly that he further insulted Cecil simply by the control in his voice.

"I wish you God's speed in your search for spies," Andrew said. "And for the execution of official wrath…something you seem especially well equipped to carry out."

Cecil hopped up, but clumsily. He did not give a farewell but strode out of the room with his characteristic limp.

The bishop smiled politely, rose, nodded, and then followed the king's counselor out of sight.

Chapter 44

Back at the settlement that had now been officially named James-town, Peter was busy in the construction of additional huts. At first, the mood among the settlers had been jubilant at their safe arrival, having survived the rigors of several months at sea. But since the first Indian attack and the realization of the countless dangers they would be facing, a more somber attitude began to set in.

Then the news came that the provisions they had brought with them in the ship would soon be running out. Though there were ample fish and deer in the area, it would still be necessary to de-velop friendly relations with some of the local tribes and learn their horticultural techniques. Vegetables would have to be planted soon, before summer waned.

Though summer had not even started, Peter was already having to adjust to the damp, suffocating heat and the vicious insects that swarmed around him and bit, leaving large welts on his face and arms. He had always believed that, like his father, he would be able to weather the rough living he knew would accompany an adventure into undeveloped lands. But now that the reality was sinking in, Peter was fighting discouragement. Life in the settlement meant a constant state of always being dirty, wet, tired, and underfed.

In the settlement, his bed consisted of two pieces of canvas sewn together with grass and leaves stuffed inside. His hut had leaks and gaps, and when the rains came, the water would trickle down on him until he was soaked.

It had been more than a week since his father had left on the expedition upriver. He prayed for his father's safety, and wondered where he was and whether he would return unharmed. But his mind consistently drifted back to the soft, green, civilized hills of the countryside in England, and the noisy streets of London, where life had become routine for him, and he had respectable work, and where he had a clean bed to sleep in at night.

But more than anything, he thought of Rose Heatherton and the day they had spent together on the high hills in Scotland, overlooking the sea. As he thought of her his insides ached. He remembered every detail about her—and how the wild winds picked up a few hairs from underneath her bonnet and delicately made them play about her face. And the pink in her pretty face that grew even more vibrant from the cold. But beyond that, Peter also recalled her love of God and gracious spirit.

Their last meeting together in the garden at Seacrest House had been excessively melancholy. Peter had made a solemn pledge to find some way back to her again, though he had no idea how that could come about.

While he was using a large mallet to hammer wooden pegs in place on an outbuilding, the chief ship's carpenter called out to him.

"You there, Peter. Take a few lads with you and pull that pile of plank over to where Reverend Hunt is working. Drop it off there."

Peter dutifully rounded up a few of the younger men, and

together they loaded a pile of plank that had, the day before, been rough hewn from a felled tree. There was a rich, sappy smell to the planks.

They were stacked on a wagon, and the men leaned their backs into the task of slowly rolling it through the sandy soil to the other side of the settlement. That was where Reverend Hunt, almost single-handedly, was building a small chapel.

After they offloaded the planks, Peter had the rest of them roll the empty cart back. Reverend Hunt strode over to him. Hunt was a middle-aged man with a thin beard and kind eyes. He was working in his cleric's coat, and the white linen frontpiece was now grey with sweat and grimy. Hunt wiped off his hands and reached out to shake Peter's.

"Thank you, Master Peter," he said. "I found myself running out of lumber for our chapel."

Peter stood back to admire the framing job Hunt and two other men had done. The structural supports for the modest steeple were in place, and the walls were ready to be lined with board.

"How are you doing, young man?" he asked. "This must be a grand adventure for you."

"'Tis," Peter said a little dejectedly.

"You don't sound excited about it," he said with a smile. "I know, the work is enormous, isn't it? And taxing on all of us. But I can't escape the feeling that this is the noblest of all experiments. The Christian religion is being introduced to a whole new continent."

Peter smiled and nodded.

"Your father will be returning soon from the river expedition. He'll have wonderful stories to share, I'm sure. And don't worry—he'll be fine. He is quite a capable man, even in these hostile surroundings."

"It's not that."

"Oh," Hunt said with a knowing nod of his head. "It is the lass you left behind…what was her name?"

"Rose Heatherton."

"Yes. Forgive me. You mentioned it the first time you and I met. On the ship."

"It's about my pledge," Peter said. "I mean to keep it."

"Of course you do. You mean to leave here, and return to her—"

"I haven't mentioned it to my father."

"I think he knows."

Peter was startled at that.

"He does?"

Reverend Hunt swept his broad black hat off his head and wiped the sweat off his brow with a work rag that was serving as a handkerchief.

"Your father has spoken to me several times."

"About what?"

"It is customary for clergy to maintain the confidences of those who solicit their spiritual advice."

"Spiritual advice?" Peter said with astonishment.

"You find that amazing?"

"I should imagine…yes."

"Your father is working his way back to where he started. He is a man of action. Of the physical world. But there is a strong soul at work there also."

Then Reverend Hunt gave his sore back a stretch. And he added something else.

"I think your love of the Savior, Peter, has been of immeasurable encouragement to your father. I really do."

Reverend Hunt prepared to return to his work. But Peter said something that stopped him in his tracks.

"Must we offer everything to the Lord Jesus…holding nothing back?"

Hunt turned to glimpse the young man who stood before him.

"Yes. We must," he answered softly. "Remember the Scriptures. Jesus said if we wish to follow Him we must deny ourselves, take up our cross daily, and follow Him."

"Then must I give up Rose?" Peter said, with brokenness in his young voice.

Hunt thought about it for a moment. Then he answered.

"You asked whether you must offer everything up to Jesus. That indeed was the right question. That is your proper spiritual duty and service. But only Almighty God can decide whether He will *require* it to be given. Search for the footprints of His inscrutable will. And then walk in that way, never deviating."

Hunt smiled, then slowly turned to head back to the carpentry work that lay before him.

Peter returned to the other side of the settlement, walking slowly. He wished for easy answers. But he hadn't received any.

Amidst the incessant heat and the back-breaking work of the New World, he would continue to pray for a miracle so he could return to England and be reunited with Rose Heatherton.

And his eyes would continue searching the shoreline that lead to the mouth of the wide river as he hoped expectantly for the return of his father.

Chapter 45

As Philip, Captain Newport, and the rest of the expedition wound their way upriver, Newport doubled up the men on the larger boats, had them heavily armed, and placed them at the front of the entourage. He anticipated that the word had spread to several of the more hostile tribes by then of the approach of the English boats.

Philip and George Kendall were told to follow up the rear of the line of boats in a small canoe, which both of them were paddling. The canoe had been given as a present by the *werowance* of the Rappahana tribe. Both of the men were experienced adventurers and handled the balancing eccentricities of the small craft well as they went on.

For his part, Philip was dismayed he was forced to share the small canoe with a man for whom he had such a distaste. There was little question that Kendall shared the sentiment. The two men had been at loggerheads from the first.

The only saving grace was that Newport had imposed a gag order on the expedition for the day, ordering silence on the water out of fear of attack. That meant that neither of the men needed to communicate with the other as they paddled up the wide, clay-colored river.

Though he didn't care for George Kendall personally, Philip couldn't help but find him intriguing, particularly as he learned more about his background from members of the expedition. He heard that Kendall had fought as a mercenary in the Netherlands. One night, while the men had gathered around the fire for supper and some conversation before sleep, he overheard Kendall sharing some of his military exploits. But whenever he was questioned by the other men regarding which army he was fighting for at that time, he grew conspicuously vague.

Philip had a theory about that, which he kept to himself.

He knew that in the Netherlands, one of the factions hiring mercenaries for battle were the Irish partisans—Catholics all. If Philip was correct, that meant Kendall had questionable loyalty to the Protestant Crown of James.

Philip did not know how much Kendall knew about him—or his true identity—but if he did know that "Kensington" was an assumed name, he had done nothing to let on. But something told him not to trust Kendall, and Philip was glad that Kendall's back was to him at the front of the canoe—and not vice-versa.

It was about midday. The heat was rising, and the river was like a brown, muddy mirror. In the woods on the nearby banks, there was a musical drone of insects and tree frogs. Occasionally they would see a white crane standing on one spindly leg in a marsh or hear the plop of a large fish. But there were no deer along that stretch.

Philip had noticed that.

It was then that something caught Philip's eye.

He had been scanning the shoreline, which was not more than

fifty feet away. The line of boats had just passed by a spot marked on the map as "Weanock" and then, in a bend in the river, another location known as "Turkey Isle," where the river widened around a small island. And after soundings, it was determined that the water was deep. The river continued around yet another S-shaped bend.

That had placed them near a section known, by the map, as "Port Cottage," though there certainly was no semblance of a port or a cottage there, and Philip did not know how it had gained that name.

But it was there—along that stretch at Port Cottage—when Philip saw it.

He thought at first it was an animal in the brush. Something moving. The branches shook suddenly. Philip peered into the gloomy underbrush as he paddled.

Then a figure. Smaller than a man. A face. Two eyes.

Philip stared back.

He studied the features of the face—but he could hardly believe what he was seeing.

It was the face and torso of a boy, perhaps ten years old. But there was nothing Indian about him. He had blond hair, bright blue eyes, and light skin with English features. His chest was bare, and he was wearing a loincloth.

The boy straightened up and gave a long, quizzical look in the direction of their canoe. By then, Kendall had seen it too. And his head was turned to look directly at the boy.

"Look at that," Philip whispered in utter amazement. Then the thought struck him like a thunderbolt.

"One of the lost settlers from Roanoke!" he exlaimed in a frenzy.

He dipped his paddle in the water to steer over to the shore. But Kendall blocked the effort, paddling furiously in the opposite direction.

"What are you doing?" Philip said, now in full voice.

Up ahead the men in the boats where starting to turn to see what the commotion was.

"That was a white boy—you saw it with your own eyes!" Philip cried out.

"I saw nothing of the kind," Kendall snapped back.

"You're lying!"

"I saw an Indian boy—that's all, plain and simple," Kendall barked back. "And be careful who you call a liar. I've killed men for less than that!"

"Turn about," Philip said. "I'll not leave those settlers behind."

That is when Kendall laid his paddle down in the canoe, sat down in the bow, and pulled something from under his pack.

In an instant, Philip was staring at the barrel end of Kendall's pistol.

"You paddle this canoe straight on, sir," he said to Philip through gritted teeth, "or I'll put a shot in your forehead and call it an accident. And don't think I won't."

Philip stared Kendall in the eye, then turned to cast a glance toward the shore.

He was able to catch a last glimpse of the blond-haired, white-skinned boy racing into the underbrush and then disappearing.

Chapter 46

"It was mutiny sir, plain and simple. I had no other choice. I had to train my pistol on Mister Kensington, there, to keep him from steering our small craft toward the shore."

George Kendall was sitting on a rough-hewn log that was serving as a bench in the main yard of the settlement. As he was talking, he was motioning over toward Philip—"Mister Kensington."

Philip was seated on another log. Two members of the settlement, both carrying weapons, were on either side of Philip, serving as bailiffs.

The seven-person Jamestown Council was hearing its first significant case. And the charges of mutiny lodged against Philip were ominous.

The three ship captains were part of the governing council. They had decided that John Martin, an experienced adventurer who had once accompanied Sir Francis Drake, would be the acting chairman of the investigation. Martin also had a political pedigree—his father, a goldsmith in London, had once been the lord mayor. This was a ticklish case and required more of the diplomacy of a politician than the blunt directives of a soldier.

But there was something else about Martin that would be a

critical component. And it would not be known until the decision was made—and the die was cast.

Nearly the entire settlement was gathered around in a semicircle in the clearing, straining to hear the proceedings. But Peter, who had the most at stake in the case—next to his own father—was not there. He was on the mat in his hut, feverish and desperately ill. Peter and several of the settlers had come down with the bloody flux, a form of dysentery. Clean water had been running out for the community, and they had been drawing water from streams and ponds. But the dirty water had made them seriously sick.

"And you considered his conduct to be mutiny," Martin questioned Kendall, "because Mister Kensington was deviating from the orders given by Captain Newport?"

"Indeed yes. He was directly disobeying the captain's orders. We had been ordered to continue straight upriver, to follow the lead of the gunboats in the front, as we were in great fear of hostile savages in that area."

Martin paused and looked to the other six members of the council to allow them to question Kendall further. But none did.

Then Martin turned to Newport, seated next to him on a tree stump that served as a chair.

"Captain Newport," he asked, "has Mister Kendall truly stated the orders you gave the men?"

"He has."

"Was Mister Kensington's canoe under your permission to deviate—to head toward shore?"

Newport took his time answering that. He liked Philip. He had found him a brave and competent member of the group. But his calling of duty was to answer in a straightforward fashion.

"Mister Kensington did not have my *express* permission to deviate—no, sir."

"Did the commotion in the canoe in the rear," Martin asked the captain, "imperil the safety of the other members of the expedition?"

"Hard to say," Newport answered. "In truth, it did not expose us to any dangers…that I know of…We didn't see any hostiles at that point along the river."

"Well now," Kendall interjected, "we did see one little Indian brave—and where the young ones are, the bigger savages are not far behind."

"That was no Indian boy," Philip cried out. "That was an English boy as sure as I have eyes in my head. Clearly he was being raised by a tribe…but he had the features and hair and skin of a boy who could have been the kin of a Yorkshire gentlemen if I've ever seen one!"

"Lies!" Kendall shouted out. "Who are you going to believe—this man? This Kensington fellow? Ever notice how none of us really knows much about his background—except that someone apparently used influence among some of the Virginia Company and got him aboard the *Susan Constant*."

"I'll vouch for Kensington," a voice rang out from the crowd. It was John Smith pushing his way to the front. "I was in the boat in front of their canoe. If I had known an English boy was loose in the bushes, I would have swum to shore myself—"

"Quiet!" Newport shouted at Smith, still harboring a distaste for the flamboyant explorer. "You are not a witness in this."

"Maybe I should be!"

But John Martin raised his hand and stopped Smith cold, admonishing him to cease his interruptions. Then he turned to Philip.

"Mister Kensington—we've already heard your description of that boy. And your justification—if it is one—for wanting to pursue him. Do you have anything else to add?"

Suddenly Philip, who had harbored resentment for his brother for so many years, now wished with all his heart that Andrew would have been there to defend him. Surely the expert in law and theology would have cut the case down to its vital center—and made a rapier-like thrust into Kendall's story.

But Andrew wasn't there. And Philip, who could handle himself in a knife fight, or a tavern brawl, or an Indian attack, was now floundering as he tried to defend himself against the clever lies of the mysterious George Kendall.

How would Andrew handle this? he asked himself.

"Mister Kensington, do you have anything further? This is a grave matter—mutiny, if found, could result in execution by firing squad. You know that, do you not?"

Philip nodded quietly. Then something came to mind. He let it roll round his brain for a few seconds—trying to sort it all out.

"Anything further you want to say?"

"Just one thing," Philip replied. "A question, actually."

"A question?" Newport asked.

"What kind of question?" Martin inquired.

"Here it is—as plain as I can say it," Philip began. "This Kendall fellow, from the very first, before we even dipped our boats in the water, was against any search for the Roanoke settlers or their descendants who might have been kidnapped by the tribes and made part of the Indians. Now why would that be? What kind of Englishman—or supporter of King James' enterprise here in the New World—would be so disinclined to rescue his fellow Englishmen?"

There was a silence among the seven councilmen. Newport was staring at Kendall.

"Then this blond-haired boy pops up—now why would I lie about that? What would I have to gain?" Philip continued. "Nothing. I would gain nothing. But what would Mister Kendall have to gain, I wonder, by blocking our ability to prove there were still survivors of the Roanoke settlement?"

There was another silence. Newport and several of the others already knew the answer.

"Mister Kendall would have nothing to gain—unless," he continued, "he would prefer to see England lose its ability to lay claim to the earliest settlement here—a claim contested by other nations. Nations like Spain, for instance."

"This is a slander on my name!" Kendall shouted. "This man should be executed for causing dissension in this settlement."

Several of the onlookers began shouting out—some in favor of Kendall's position—some against.

Finally John Martin had to stand up and, waving his arms, quiet the crowd.

When peace was restored, Martin sequestered the councilmen in the chapel at the end of the settlement to deliberate.

Philip was ordered to stay on his bench, guarded by the armed bailiffs. As the crowd milled about, Reverend Hunt was permitted a few moments alone with him.

"Would you pray for me?" Philip asked of Hunt.

The settlement's pastor nodded and bowed his head, and together the two men prayed for justice to be done. "But not our will, but Thine be done," Hunt said at the end.

An hour later the councilmen returned and sat on the tree

stumps in the clearing. There was a sudden hush. The only sound was the tide rolling in along the shore and crashing on the sand.

"It is the considered decision of this tribunal..." Martin announced. Then he took a breath and continued.

"It our unanimous decision that the actions of Mister Kensington...were in violation of the orders of Captain Newport."

Philip hung his head down at those words.

There was a gasp among some of the audience.

"And yet," he continued, "that is not the end of the inquiry. The question is whether *mutiny* occurred. As that term is customarily used on the high seas regarding the lawful command of a sea captain.

"We have determined," Martin concluded, "that mutiny *did not occur*. Mister Kensington's account of the blond-haired boy is credible, at a minimum. The mission of that expedition did include the investigation of missing settlers *to the extent it did not jeopardize the safety of the participants and did not deviate from the primary direction*. In point of fact, Mister Kensington wanted to deviate—but was prevented from doing so. Which leads us to wonder regarding Mister Kendall's very different account, also, of the light-skinned boy. Of course," Martin said with a polite smile directed at George Kendall, "Mister Kendall may simply have been mistaken. In any event, these proceedings are dismissed."

The councilmen quickly disappeared into their cabins. Reverend Hunt congratulated Philip and escorted him back to his hut, where the two men would keep watch over Peter, and the crowd dispersed.

All except two men.

George Kendall had a bitter expression on his face, and he was taking the long way back to this cabin, along the shoreline.

And Mister Reed, the muscular blacksmith who had befriended Peter, was hanging back. He was studying Kendall suspiciously as he watched the man stride down the beach. And Reed was considering the words of John Martin when he noted that the evidence in the case "leads us to wonder regarding Mister Kendall's very different account, also, of the light-skinned boy..."

Chapter 47

After the meeting with the bishop, it didn't take Robert Cecil long to have Andrew Mackenzie removed from the Westminster Committee. It resulted, of course, in a reduction of Andrew's stipend from the Crown. But it also bode poorly for his future at the Court of King James. And Cecil's warnings at the conclusion of their meeting meant that Andrew might expect the worst. Not just termination of his government career—but the imperiling of him and the safety of his wife as well.

Andrew had seen—in the gunpowder treason trials—the full fury of the Crown levied against anyone perceived to be an enemy of the state.

He confided everything in Kate. She was a loyal helpmate to him, and he knew that for all their disagreements from time to time on small matters, he could rely on her sound judgment on the big things that really mattered.

Andrew could see in her eyes that she understood the dangers they were facing. He was still employed—for the time being—in Thomas Craig's legal committee that was painstakingly considering the union of the crowns between Scotland and England. Andrew wondered how long he would have that position.

He believed it would only be a matter of time before that was taken from him soon, and then he and Kate would be in serious financial jeopardy.

That, he calculated, would be when the treason allegations would start to surface against him.

From there it would only be a short distance over to the dank, filthy confines of the rack room in the basement of the Tower.

Kate knew all that. But she also had the uncommon ability to also look out for the welfare of others, even as the storm clouds were starting to build over their house in Blackfriars.

She took Rose Heatherton under her wing, visiting her mother in their dilapidated apartment. She persuaded Andrew to pay the rent for the Heathertons, at least for that month. Kate also paid the apothecary, out of her own household account, to deliver some herbs and ointments for the mother's consumption.

But she never let on to Rose, or her brother or mother for that matter, that the Mackenzies of London were facing distressing times of their own.

Andrew and Kate often talked about Philip and Peter and wondered how they were managing in the frontier environment of the New World. One day Andrew inquired at the Virginia Company of any news from the settlement. The bursar was seated on a stool at a high desk in the offices.

"No news yet, Mister Mackenzie," he replied. "But if things are on schedule," he said, letting his voice wander as he leafed through a journal of the proceedings of the agency, "there should be a ship returning soon for a replenishment of supplies for those folks in the settlement. We allotted a subsistence amount for flour, some salted pork, fresh water, and such to be taken back. And additional gunpowder and small arms."

"Who is to return here to England?"

"I believe Captain Newport," he said. "But we will have to wait and see if that occurs, now won't we? I mean, given the uncertainties of travel across the oceans, and the hazards and all..."

The bursar closed his journal and then looked at Andrew. "Why do you ask?"

"I have an interest in...the investment capital of the settlement."

"Oh?" he said in reply. "I wasn't aware you owned any shares."

"Not shares," Andrew said, bowing and turning to leave. "But other forms of investment. Intangible forms, you might say."

The bursar gave him a strange look as Andrew hurried out of the door and onto the muddy street, which was alive with the clopping of horses drawing wagons and carts.

Three thousand miles away, Philip was sitting next to his son's sickbed in the little hut in the Virginia settlement. It was late at night. Peter had been ill for over a week, and his father was spending every extra moment at his bedside.

But there was one visitor he was not expecting that night. He heard a rustling at the front door and the creak of the wooden doorway.

It was Mister Reed, the blacksmith.

"How's the lad?" he asked.

"Still feverish," Philip said. "But he took a little food today. I think that is a good sign."

"Aye, 'tis a good sign."

For a moment Philip studied the big blacksmith, who clearly had not finished whatever business had brought him.

"Is something on your mind?'

"Aye, there is," he said. "It concerns that swamp rat, George Kendall."

"How so?"

"I've been doing some snooping. I got to thinking about your testimony at the trial—and about what Mister Martin said—that Kendall's account of the boy didn't add up. And so I have been watching him—Kendall, I mean. Got my eye on him."

"Good," Philip said. "That's good."

"Which is why I seen what I seen—"

"What do you mean?"

"Letters."

"What kind of letters?"

"Letters Kendall writes in the middle of the night. Looking over his shoulder, he does. Like he doesn't want anyone to see."

"Well," Philip said, "let me know if you learn anything else."

"You do think he might be a bad penny, don't you, sir?"

"Yes, I do." But then Philip looked at the rough, well-intentioned but clumsy blacksmith, and added one more admonition.

"If you find anything else suspicious," he said, "better let me take it from there. You don't want Kendall finding out you are snooping on him."

"Will sure do that," Reed said. Then he bent over Philip's shoulder and looked down at Peter.

"Give the boy my best when he's on the rise, will ya?"

Andrew smiled and nodded.

Reed swung open the door. As he strolled out, though there was a full moon in the sky, he did not detect that he was being watched.

Hidden in the underbrush, George Kendall was peering out at Reed, watching him leave Philip's cabin.

Chapter 48

Bending over Peter, Philip stroked the head of his son. His fever was high, and Peter was mumbling in his troubled sleep.

Philip sat down on the dirt floor of the cabin, next to Peter's mat, and leaned against the wall. Soon he was asleep next to his son. It was after three o'clock in the morning when something caused Philip to awake. He glanced over at his son, who was breathing heavily. Philip stood up in the moonlight that was flooding through the single window that had been cut into the cabin. He took a step over toward where Peter was lying.

Now Philip put his hand down to Peter's forehead. His son's hair was drenched in sweat, but his forehead was cooler. Philip reached down under Peter's shirt to feel his chest. It was wet with perspiration and cooler also.

His fever has broken. Thank You, Lord, Philip whispered and smiled as he watched his son slumbering. *I think he's going to be all right now.*

Standing over his son, Philip felt a rush of relief. He had felt no real resentment that he had to leave England on such short notice. That much he understood. And under different circumstances he would have relished the opportunity to return, after all those years, to the Virginia coast and explore the New World as he had often dreamed.

But he had never reconciled himself to the impact their quick departure had on his son. He knew of Peter's love for Rose Heatherton. And the fact that Philip's associations with Guy Fawkes had been the catalyst for the journey to Virginia, and the cause of Peter's separation from the women he loved, was something that was difficult for him to bear. His reckless life had visited misery upon his son.

Yet Philip also knew that something good had come out of all of that.

Since Philip's arrival in Virginia, and in the midst of the trying times he had endured, Reverend Hunt had struck up a friendship with him. The two had many conversations together. Some of them casual. But others more probing and serious.

Without giving out any details, Philip revealed that his presence on the expedition to the New World was an involuntary one.

"I am here," he told Reverend Hunt, "because of circumstances that have come against me; my life has caught up with me, and has now forced not only me—but my son as well—to seek asylum outside of England."

Philip explained how his son's romantic intentions toward Rose Heatherton had been cruelly cut short by the father's actions and the need to flee the country. And then he confided in the reverend how his own spiritual walk had dissipated over the years.

He also shared with Hunt his guilt over his fractured relationship with his own brother. All of those matters, over which Philip was now deeply repentant, seemed to have arisen from the major spiritual detour he had taken.

"I've walked away from Jesus," he said, "and don't know whether

242 Craig & Janet Parshall

there is any going back. I've let go of all that...I think I've fallen too far."

But Hunt, after much listening, patted Philip on the back.

"Have you been saved by the blood of the Lamb of God, son?"

Philip nodded yes, then added, "When I was much younger. During one of my father's sermons at church. I believed on Jesus Christ...I received forgiveness."

"Well then," Reverend Hunt said with a look that went into Philip's soul, "you need to admit you have been mistaken."

"Mistaken about what?"

"In believing that it is your grip on the Lord Jesus that keeps you safe and saved and forgiven. Because it's not."

Philip was staring at Reverend Hunt.

Then Hunt finished his statement.

"It's not how hard you are holding onto Jesus that counts...it's recognizing how hard He is holding onto you."

When Hunt said that, Philip started to weep. Try as he might, he could not hold it back. He hadn't cried since his wife died. And now it poured out.

He cried not only for the realization that God was still following him and caring for him, but also at the understanding that the locusts had eaten away so many of his years. They were gone and done. He could have done so many other things with his life for his son—and for God—but he had not.

But Hunt assured him that "God can restore what the locusts have eaten. In fact, perhaps He already has. Just look at your son, Philip. A fine young man with a passion for God. Just look at what a fine man he is turning out to be."

So Philip was looking at his son, slumbering in his sickness, unperceiving what was happening around him. But the father knew now that his son was going to recover. And that gave him a peace that lifted his heart.

It also put a smile on his face.

And the father closed his eyes, in a vulnerability unusual for him, his back to the open doorway of the cabin. He began to recite out loud:

> *The Lord is my shepherd,*
> *I shall not want.*
> *He maketh me to rest in green pasture,*
> *And leadeth me by the still waters.*
> *He restoreth my soul,*
> *And leadeth me in the paths of righteousness*
> *For His Name's sake.*

Uncharacteristically detached from his surroundings—and uncaring now for anything except his son and the blessings of his recovery—Philip did not hear the soft footsteps of someone stealthily entering the cabin.

For a half-second he sensed something behind him.

But before Philip could turn, the intruder, with a fierce sweeping motion drove a long dagger into Philip's back, simultaneously covering his victim's mouth with a rag to muffle his cries.

As Philip collapsed to the ground, his attacker, with an effort, pulled his knife out of his back. Then he took the knife and slashed it viciously across Philip's throat. Philip struggled, but it was in vain. The rag was held over his mouth until the loss of blood had become too much.

At last, Philip, his eyes still wide open and beholding his murderer

244   Craig & Janet Parshall

to the end, succumbed. He exhaled his final breath. Then he was gone.

George Kendall took his long knife and wiped the blood off it on Philip's shirt. Then he searched his body. But he did not find what he was looking for.

Peter was still slumbering fitfully on his mat, and uttered something undecipherable in his sickness.

Kendall froze. Then, when Peter was quiet again, Kendall looked around the hut for the subject of his frantic search. But it was not there.

He then turned to the body of Philip, and started to cut away a portion of his scalp. But he thought he heard a noise and stopped.

Then, with his tasks not completed but fearing detection, he slipped out of the cabin and into the night.

Kendall had failed to locate the letter he had penned and that had turned up missing from his hut. But the night the letter had disappeared he had noticed Reed, the blacksmith, lurking nearby. He had been sure that Reed had stolen it and then, in his visit with Philip, had transferred the letter to him.

As Kendall slipped into the night, Reed, on his return to Philip's cabin, thought he caught a glimpse of Kendal as he scurried into the bushes.

Reed was returning because he was having second thoughts. He had failed to tell Philip the whole truth—that he had searched Kendall's hut and found the suspicious letter and had given it to someone for safekeeping.

I'd best tell him the whole story, Reed was thinking to himself. *He deserves to know.*

But seconds after Reed entered the hut, he rushed back outside. His cries could be heard through out the settlement.

"Murder! Murder!" He was screaming.

Chapter 49

Captain Newport was summoned. He, Reed, and a sailor quietly picked up Philip's body and carefully carried it outside, not waking Peter.

There, removed a far distance from Peter's cabin, in the light of torches that were lit, they carefully examined it.

Soon the entire settlement arose and swarmed to the scene on the beach.

Newport, holding a flaming torch in one hand, with the other pointed to the scalp and hair that had been cut away.

"Indians," an onlooker said.

"'Twas no Indian, be sure about that," Reed muttered to Newport.

John Smith arrived as Reed said that and stared at Philip Mackenzie's body. Smith's face was grim and his eyes had a fierce look about them. Then he turned and ran from the gathering crowd and disappeared.

Reed whispered something to Newport, and the two talked quietly for a moment. By then John Martin had arrived. Newport took him aside and shared what Reed had just told him. The two discussed it beyond the hearing of the crowd.

Then, when the two men had finished, John Martin directed the chattering crowd to be silent.

When the talking stopped, Martin explained that a murder had just occurred. He commanded that the body be covered, but not removed from its resting spot on the sand, pending a formal inquiry the following morning, at daybreak. A guard would be posted.

Then Martin called out to the crowd. "I am ordering first, that no one be permitted to leave the settlement under the further order of the council."

Then he gave his second command.

"And I am further ordering that every able-bodied member of this settlement commence a search for Mister George Kendall. And when apprehended, that he immediately be placed under arrest for suspicion of murder."

The group started to break apart. But before they all dispersed, a sound of conflict and shouting was heard from the other end of the settlement.

Two men were engaged in a struggle. One man had hold of the other and was forcing him toward the group.

It was John Smith. He had George Kendall from behind, twisting his arm behind him and holding a forearm across his neck.

Kendall was fighting back, struggling to get loose, but to no avail. Smith had him in an unbreakable grip.

Several men from the group rushed over and grabbed Kendall by his arms and dragged him up to Martin and Newport.

"I will not be treated like this!" Kendall was shouting out. "What is the meaning of this outrage?"

With a man on each of his arms, Kendall was being held in front of John Martin. Martin looked Kendall in the eye.

"You are being held on the suspicion of murder of Mister

Kensington here," and with that, Martin pointed to Philip's draped body.

"Are you daft?" Kendall screamed. "I know nothing of this! Nothing! This is a conspiracy against me most foul—I demand to know what evidence you have to make such absurd accusations!"

"You shall hear it soon enough," Martin said in a steely voice. "At daybreak, we shall conduct our inquiry. And if we find that the evidence is as it seems...then may God have mercy on your soul."

Kendall was ordered to be put into iron manacles and was then chained to a nearby tree. A guard of three men was posted to keep watch on him until the trial. The crowd was dismissed back to their cabins.

Meanwhile, one guard stood at the motionless body of Philip Mackenzie as it lay on the damp sand of the New World.

But the guard was not alone. Reverend John Hunt was also there, sitting next to Philip's body the rest of the night.

And as he did, his face was in his hands.

Chapter 50

When dawn broke over the bay, the sunlight sent a crimson tint over the water.

Soon the sun, fiery on the horizon, evaporated the gray borders and the shadows of the night. The sky would be blue and cloudless that day.

The council was convened for the second time in just a matter of days. George Kendall, still in chains, was dragged over to the clearing where the council met once again. And, as before, John Martin would preside over the trial.

He announced in the presence of George Kendall the nature of the charges against him. If found guilty, he explained, his sentence would be death by firing squad. No appeals. No delay.

Sitting on the ground a few feet away from Martin, Gabriel Archer was rapidly jotting down a record of the proceedings.

Mister Reed was called as the first witness.

He explained how he had observed Kendall one night, hovering over a table in his hut, writing something, and looking around in all directions as if highly concerned that he might be found out.

"How exactly did you see this if he was in his hut and you were outside?" Captain Bartholomew Gosnold asked him.

"Well," Reed said chuckling, "he had the door shut. So I saw him by peering through a large space between the logs in his wall. That's how."

"Spying on me!" Kendall shouted out. "You heard him!"

"Quiet!" Martin snapped out at Kendall. "Another outburst like that and I will shoot you myself."

"What else do you have to accuse this man?" Martin asked.

"We all know, don't we," Reed continued, "that there has been a bad bit of blood between these two men from the start. Mister Kensington, God rest his soul, wanted to pursue the rescue of settlers that might have survived from the Roanoke settlement. Kendall wanted no part of that."

"Yes, but the other part—what you told me last night," Captain Newport said.

"Oh, of course, that. Well, I had visited Mister Kensington earlier last night. A discussion is what we had. Concerning Mister Kendall, actually. Then I left. I decided to come back to his hut later and share something I hadn't told him. That's when I found his body, poor fellow—"

"But what did you see on the way back to his hut?" Newport asked him, trying to get to the point.

"See?" Reed asked.

Newport shook his head.

Martin pressed in. "We were under the impression you saw someone in the vicinity of the hut where Mister Kensington's murdered body was found."

"That's exactly what I saw," Reed said.

"Who was it?" one of the other councilmen asked, growing impatient.

Reed paused for a second. He scratched his neck and then answered. "A man lookin' like George Kendall there."

Several of the onlookers started talking among themselves, and Martin had to shout them into silence.

"*Looked like* George Kendall—or *was* George Kendall—which is it, man?" Martin asked.

Reed did not answer at first.

"The penalty for murder will be immediate execution," Martin admonished him. "You must be very certain in your testimony."

Reed took several seconds to consider his answer.

"His back was turned to me as he slipped into the bushes," Reed said. "I didn't see his face. But the figure of the man was the height and weight of George Kendall. And because of the moonlight out last night, I can say that with full assurance, gentlemen…be sure of that."

"You said you had to return to Kensington's hut to further discuss something about Mister Kendall," another of the councilmen asked. "What was it you intended to converse about?"

Reed straightened up on the tree stump when he answered.

"The letter that this traitor Kendall was writing."

"Where is the letter?" Martin asked.

"I don't have it."

"Who does?"

Then a voice came booming out of the audience.

"I have it."

It was John Smith.

"I have that letter—and its contents show this Kendall fellow to be a spy and a traitor—or worse."

Martin demanded to see the letter. Smith pulled it out of his shirt and handed it to Martin.

As Martin read it over, he realized the awful dilemma his Jamestown settlement was now facing.

"Where did you find this?"

"Reed told me he found it in Kendall's hut."

"True enough. True enough, sirs," Reed shouted out. "That is exactly where I found it."

"Captains," Martin said addressing the three ship's captains. "Do you have any sample of Mister Kendall's handwriting—on the ship's manifest…or otherwise?"

"I do," Gosnold said. "I have his signature, place of birth, and other information signed by his own hand."

Martin asked him to fetch it. Within fifteen minutes, Gosnold returned with his logbook, opened it to the page with Kendall's handwriting, and gave it to Martin.

Martin, with the other six members of the council looking on, laid it next to the letter.

After several minutes of comparing the two, Martin whispered back and forth with the other members of the council and then addressed the assembly.

"It is clear to all of us—none excepting—that this letter is in the true hand of George Kendall."

But then, surveying the faces of the other councilmen, Martin made a surprising announcement.

"Because of the highly sensitive nature of this letter, however, this council must now retire into closed session to further discuss the case against George Kendall."

There was a confused explosion of chatter among the settlers as Martin led his fellow councilmen into his cabin. When they were all inside, the door was closed, and Martin proceeded to address the difficulty in a strained whisper.

"Has everyone read this letter?" he asked.

All nodded.

"Then you understand the predicament we are in," he continued. "George Kendall has been—to my understanding, and you must correct me if I am ill-informed—he has been known to be a confidant of Robert Cecil, Earl of Salisbury, the king's close confidant."

None of the men in the cramped cabin could disagree with that.

"And," Martin said, eyeing Newport, "more than that...Kendall was once listed as one of Cecil's spies. Am I correct?"

Newport nodded, with a grim look on his face.

"Then we have a dilemma," Martin said. "If we declare him a traitor," and with that he held up the letter Reed had found in Kendall's hut, "then we shall be—in effect—declaring Robert Cecil to be implicit in having a traitor in his employ."

"Cecil is a major benefactor of the Virginia Company," one of the councilmen said. "How can we do that?"

"I care not for niceties," Newport said gruffly. "But I will not countenance a traitor in our midst. Further, it seems likely he also murdered poor Kensington. He certainly had a motive to kill him. And Reed thought he was near the scene just after the murder."

"Are we agreed that this fellow is worthy of death?" Martin asked.

There was a short burst of debate on some of the points of testimony. But after less than an hour it was clear what the verdict should be. The only issue was how to describe the official charge.

"Let me suggest," Martin said, "that we simply record that Kendall was executed for causing malevolent dissension within the settlement, such that the survival and good order of Jamestown was thereby jeopardized."

"I don't care what we call it," Newport said, "as long as this man does not live to see the end of this day."

All agreed on Martin's proposal. But one of the councilmen had one remaining question.

"What of the letter?" he said.

There was a silence. Finally Martin gave the only response that could be given.

"I fear that it must be shown to the Crown," he said. "But discreetly men...*discreetly.*"

Chapter 51

Reverend Hunt interceded on behalf of Peter. He urged the council not to tell him the fate of his father until his health had improved.

"We dare not endanger his recovery with the shock of this kind of tragic news," he told them. It was agreed he was to be sheltered until he had made a more complete return to strength.

Meanwhile, on the same day of the trial, at sundown, a firing squad of five men was assembled. George Kendall was blindfolded and tied to a post. Then the squad took aim, and at the command, fired. Kendall was killed instantly.

Philip Mackenzie was buried in the center of the settlement under a crude wooden cross with the name "John Kensington." His grave was next to the sailor who had been killed in the Indian attack.

Kendall's body was buried outside of the village.

Three days later, Peter was able to sit up on his own. His appetite had returned.

It was then that he began to inquire about his father.

It was the natural choice for Reverend Hunt to be the one to tell him. Hunt entered the little cabin and sat on the floor next to his bed. Peter was sitting up. Though he was still pale-looking and had lost considerable weight, there was an alertness about him now. And his strength was improving.

"I want to talk to my father," he said. "Is he away? On another expedition?"

"No, Peter, he is not," Hunt replied calmly.

As Peter pressed, there was a hesitation, a sense of foreboding in his voice.

"Then where is he?"

"There was an incident...here in the settlement. An attack."

"What happened to my father?" he asked more urgently now.

"Your father was killed. They caught the man who did it. He has been executed."

For a short span of seconds, interminable, bewildering, and numbing, Peter was unable to speak.

His young face bore the look of shock that comes only in those few, most brutal moments of life. The only consolation is that they are few; were it otherwise, the heart would threaten to stop and fail to recover altogether.

Reverend Hunt said it again.

"Do you understand, Peter? Your father is gone, son. I am so sorry..."

Peter knew he had been delirious during his illness. Now he struggled to gain clarity of mind in the face of news that was so terribly unreal.

"Gone...my father is gone? Dead?"

Peter heard himself speaking, but the words sounded distant and far away, and it was as if someone else were speaking for him.

"Yes, son. He is dead. I am sorry for you. I will stay with you as long as you like."

Peter tried to get up. Reverend Hunt helped support him to his feet.

"Where is he? I want to see him."

"Your father was laid to rest three days ago. It was my decision not to tell you until you were better. "

"Show me where he is buried. I want to go there."

With Hunt holding Peter up, the two slowly walked out into the blinding sunlight. Peter had to squint against the brightness until his eyes adjusted to the light.

Hunt led him to the center of the village clearing where there were two crosses. Settlers who were busy tanning animal skins, shaving wood planks with a plane, and carrying firewood on carts, all slowed their work and stared as Peter took uncertain steps toward the two graves.

He stared at the freshly dug earth, the pink and sandy soil, and he looked at the rough wooden cross that had been erected for his father. Then he looked again at the name etched on it.

John Kensington.

"Kensington?" Peter asked. "Kensington?" he said again with bewilderment in his voice.

At first, Reverend Hunt did not understand. But then as he mentally pieced it together it began to make sense. He thought back to Philip's final conversations with him and his repentance over a life that had been embroiled in trouble before coming to Virginia. Philip, it now was clear, had been a prisoner to his old, troubled life in England; so much so that he had to cover himself with a forged identity.

Peter stared at the cross and the freshly dug, mounded grave, and as the full force of it weighed in on him, he began to sob. He broke down in Hunt's arms and wept for a long time, until there were no more tears left.

When Peter began to regain his composure, and as he wiped his face with his arm, Hunt spoke to him.

"Your father made his peace with God, I believe, before he died. And he resolved a good many things in his soul."

Then he added, "Your father was very proud of you, Peter. Now you must be strong and carry on. For him. For yourself as well. Your father is treading the paths of heaven today, lad, with the Lord Jesus. He is part of His great expedition. Your father may have ventured on ahead of you. But you will see him again some day."

After a bit Peter grew weary and sat down next to his father's grave. Reverend Hunt stayed with him.

Peter's eyes were on the wooden cross for a while, but then his gaze lifted, and he looked out over bay where the rippling water was quiet. And farther out, to beyond the sandbars and out to the pounding surf, where the ocean was rolling and undulating in a timeless rhythm.

Chapter 52

"It was all wrong."

"What, lad?"

"John Kensington. The name. It was all wrong. It had to be changed."

Kneeling at Philip Mackenzie's grave, Peter was trying to explain it to John Martin and Captain Newport.

"His name was Philip Mackenzie. That was my father's true name. Don't you see?"

Newport and Martin were trying to make sense of Peter's actions. Now they understood. They had watched for a few minutes while Peter finished securing the new cross. Peter had dug up the other and replaced it with one he had fashioned with his own hands. It was slightly larger than the first. On the horizontal bar he had etched the words "Philip Mackenzie" followed by the date of his death.

On the vertical plank he had written,

Father—Child of God

"He had to use a new identity when he came here," Peter explained. "I used the same name. But he was Philip Mackenzie. And I am his son."

Peter, still weak, struggled to get up. Newport bent down to help him. But Peter refused aid and, leaning on the shovel, he managed to slowly rise on his own.

When he was on his feet, Peter added a thought.

"If history tells the tale of this place," he said, letting his gaze sweep over the rough-hewn huts and buildings in the settlement, "then I want my father to be remembered for who he really was."

Martin nodded. Captain Newport shot a quick smile at the young man and then strode off quickly. He had much work to do.

Newport had several busy days ahead of him to prepare to set sail. It had been decided that, due to the impoverished state of Jamestown, if the settlement was to survive at all, then it was time for a ship to be sent back to England for additional supplies. The settlers were lacking clean water, ammunition, vegetables, fruits, salted meat for the lean winter when the deer would not be plentiful, additional tools, medical tonics, and other necessities. Before the end of summer, the ship would have to make landfall in England. And then return with ample time to restock the Virginia community before the beginning of the harsh winter.

There would be only a lean crew of able-bodied sailors accompanying Newport on the return voyage.

In the next few days, Peter forced himself to venture out in the daylight, trying to mend himself and making a point of engaging in a little conversation with some of the settlers. Mister Reed, far from a sensitive soul usually, was uncommonly kind to Peter as he mourned the death of his father.

On the day before Newport was to set sail, Peter had gone down to the beach overlooking the bay, and had taken his Bible with him. His grief over the loss of his father and the cruel way in which he was taken, he felt to be a crushing, nearly impossible burden for him to bear.

He had turned to Romans eight, verse thirty-five. It was a verse that had been mentioned by Reverend Hunt in some of their conversations together after Peter had learned of his father's murder.

> *Who shall separate us from the love of Christ? Shall tribulation or anguish, or persecution, or famine, or nakedness, or peril, or sword?*

Peter's father had been viciously slain by a knife-wielding murderer. Though he grieved deeply, Peter tried to understand the truth of that Scripture—that even a murderer's knife could not separate him, or his father, from the love of the Savior.

Still pondering that point, Peter did not notice a commotion developing at the center of the settlement.

A chief of the Powatan tribe, a fellow named Wahunsonacock, along with several of his Indian braves and members of his family, had boldly come to meet Newport and the other settlement leaders. His hope was to begin bartering for the powerful weapons he had heard were used by the English.

The chief was painted from head to foot in red and black, with a headdress that sported several long feathers. Around his neck were layers of necklaces. Newport and the other ship captains and the members of the council were engaging in labored attempts at communication.

At some point Peter became aware of the meeting and looked over to the camp. This was only his second view of Indians close up—the other being the side trip to the islands on the voyage over to Virginia. But what otherwise may have been a dazzling sight to him now had lost its luster. His heart was burdened, and he simply had no curiosity for such things now. His father was dead, he was separated by an ocean from the woman he loved, and he was now left alone to fend for himself in an uncivilized settlement in the middle of a wilderness.

Peter turned back to the verse in Romans, trying to absorb it and make it stick to the ache in his heart. He was not aware of how long he had been looking at his Bible, but at some point he was aware that someone was standing over him on the beach.

He looked up and saw the brown-skinned face of an Indian girl gazing down at him. Her striking almond eyes showed a look of amused interest in what he was doing. Startled, he leaned back quickly away from her, and she took a step backward at the same time.

Ashamed at his initial reaction, Peter smiled at her and nodded. She took a step closer.

Then the Indian girl, who looked to be around nine or ten years old, spoke up.

"*Ka ka torawincs yowo?*"

Then she pointed to the Bible on Peter's lap.

"This?"

"*Ka ka torawincs yowo?*" she repeated and again pointed to the Bible.

"Bible," he replied.

She stared blankly at him.

Peter struggled to remember a few of the Powatan phrases the settlers had been taught.

His face brightening up, he motioned back and forth between himself and the Bible by pointing first to his chest and then to the Bible's cover, and then back to his chest.

"*Mawchick chammay,*" he said, which meant "the best of friends."

The girl's face took on a curious look as she tried to understand what this strange white man was saying.

Then Peter pointed to the sky and back to himself and then up to the sky again, repeating the words *mawchick chammay*.

The Indian girl tilted her head to the side and wrinkled her brow, and then she looked up in the sky herself for a long time. She took another step closer and reached down with caution with her index finger and stroked the open pages of the Bible.

Then a call came out from the group, a command, and the girl turned and quickly ran back to the group, where the chief was concluding a discussion with Newport and his translator.

After half an hour more of formalities, Wahunsonacock and his tribal companions departed. Peter watched them go. The Indian girl was walking behind the chief and threw a quick glance over to him before the Indians entered the thick woods and could be seen no longer.

Peter rose to his feet, still feeling a little wobbly on his feet, and started walking over to his cabin. Mister Reed crossed paths with him and bid him good day.

"So do you feel like royalty today, lad?"

"Why do you ask?"

"I saw you talking down by the beach with that Indian girl."

"Yes. But not very successfully."

"Well, I heard she is an Indian princess. Daughter of Wahunsonacock, Powhatan chief. Goes by the name of Pocahontas, I hear. Strange bunch, they are..."

"Dress strange. Talk differently. But maybe not that different from us," Peter said, and then headed into his cabin carrying his Bible.

At the dock of the settlement, Newport and his crew were now loading the skiff to make a few final trips out to where the ship was moored in the bay.

Back in England, Andrew had been told that a ship might be setting sail from the New World. He hoped that it would bring news of the fate of his nephew and brother. But grim news of his own had also beset him.

Thomas Craig, his old mentor and friend from Scotland, had summoned him to his chambers at the Court of King James.

"You have done a great work with me and the others on the matter of the union of the crowns here," he said.

But Andrew could see in his face that he was bearing bad news.

"Sadly, I have just received a dispatch from the Crown."

Andrew braced himself for the news.

"You have been removed from any further work on this project with me."

"Who has signed it? Was it Cecil? Or one of the king's other counselors? The Privy Council?"

"No," Craig said slowly, trying to digest the importance of what he was about to share. "It has been signed by the king himself."

That struck Andrew like a dagger between his ribs.

"It further provides," Craig said, "that you are barred from any further government work, and prohibited from representing yourself as an agent of His Majesty, until further order from the Crown of England."

"This is worse than I had imagined," Andrew muttered. "Signed by the king himself. Cecil must have thoroughly poisoned His Majesty. Played on his suspicions that have been rampant since the gunpowder conspiracy first surfaced."

After a few moments reflection, he added, "I must away to Edinburgh with Kate. I must leave forthwith. I'll find work there. Teaching theology at the university perhaps. Or working with the staff of the Scottish Parliament. Something…"

"I'm afraid that will not be possible," Craig intoned sadly. "This edict also forbids you from leaving England."

With that he handed the large parchment, with the broken wax seal of the king of England on its edges, over to Andrew, who grabbed it and scanned it.

"There do not appear to be any loopholes, if that is what you are looking for," Craig said sympathetically.

"I should not expect to find any," Andrew said, "in a document drafted against me by Robert Cecil and placed before the king for signing."

"For what it is worth," Craig noted, "I have never found Cecil to be an evil or malevolent man. But I have found him to be excessively…*political*. He suffers from an abundance of suspicion, of everyone and everything. His chief aim appears to be one of manipulation—of those around him to further secure his position at Court—and to guard himself against betrayal and attack."

Then Craig concluded by reminding Andrew of Cecil's lavish land holdings and estates and palaces—so extensive that even the king himself had envied some of them.

"Cecil has established his own kingdom within the kingdom, so to speak. Which makes him vulnerable in a certain way—if caught between the two. That vulnerability, if there is any leverage at all, is where you may find a pivot point against him."

"Thank you," Andrew said, managing a strained smile. "Perhaps your wisdom will come to my aid yet."

"If I can be of any service to you," Craig said.

"Not to worry about that. Indeed, I am sure I will be asking you for goodly intelligence on the Earl of Salisbury, Mister Cecil, soon enough. Thank you, my good friend."

As Andrew was leaving, his mentor reminded him of one final thought.

"Just remember—kings may sit on four-legged thrones made of gold," he said with a smile, "but God holds the legs."

Chapter 53

Kate Mackenzie had taken Rose out that day in her own carriage. They had visited a shop in the mercantile district to buy some fabric so that Rose could mend some of her older garments. Over Rose's protestations, Kate paid for it. She had sent the carriage driver off to the livery while the two women shopped.

"First you pay for this month's rent for our family, and now this," Rose said. "It's too much. Your generosity is so bountiful, but you must not tend to us any further—"

"Nonsense," Kate replied. "The point of having money is to use it for good as long as you have it…because you may not always have it."

Rose studied Kate's face when she said that.

"I trust all is well with your family," Rose said, sensing a deeper meaning lying beneath Kate's comment.

"I just meant that we should enjoy God's blessings in season and out. He brings the rain. But he also brings the drought."

"Your husband, Mister Mackenzie—he is well?"

"Sound of body, yes. But there are many pressures coming to bear down on him. On us both, really. Just pray for us, will you?"

"I will. You will be in our prayers daily, I promise it. All I can do now is hope that someday I can repay your kindness."

Kate took one of Rose's hands in hers and clutched it to her chest.

"Perhaps some time you can," Kate said. "And when that time comes I will ask, have no fear of that!"

At the end of the day, Kate had her driver take them to Rose's family's apartment, where Kate paid a visit to Rose's ailing mother. She appeared to be a little better, at least for the time.

Then Kate said her goodbyes and got in the back of the carriage and was driven back home.

Andrew was there, waiting for her when she returned.

"I had such a lovely day with Rose," Kate said to her husband as he kissed her.

"I am glad you have struck up a friendship," he said.

Then something got Andrew thinking.

"Her age...Rose is a few years older, but just a few, than what Alice would be now."

Kate was standing in front of Andrew when he said that. She leaned against him and put her arms around him.

For a moment they simply held each other and said nothing.

But as they did, without words, they felt everything.

When Andrew finally loosed his embrace, his wife could read in his face the strain of some new burden.

"We need to talk," Andrew said. "*Privately.* Let's go into the library where the servants won't hear."

Kate followed Andrew into the wood-paneled library. He closed the double doors and sat down next to her on the small tufted couch.

"I have received news from the king," he said somberly.

Kate was fixed intently on his every word.

"I have been removed from all government service, until further notice."

Then he added a postscript.

"And I am forbidden from leaving England."

Kate's face immediately reflected her keen appreciation for this latest, devastating turn of events.

"The noose is tightening, my dear," Andrew said. "I must act now. Either the rope has to be cut quickly, or I will be hanging from it soon."

"What do we do now?"

"I have consulted Thomas Craig. God bless my old friend. I believe the key is to stop Cecil in his tracks. He must be made to reverse the king's decision."

"But how do we do that? I thought Cecil was your great opponent."

"He is. But we must find some way to put Cecil in the middle. Give him some great inducement to stop his campaign against me."

"What do you have in mind?" Kate asked, trying hard to mask her anxiety. "I'm sure you have some ideas…" She was trying to look hopeful as she explored Andrew's face.

"We must pray on it, good Kate. Ask the Lord to reveal something to us. Or else all is lost. And then the next step, for me, will be a heavy knock at the door—and a warrant for the Tower."

"How much time do we have…before that might happen?"

"Short—very short."

"Months?"

Andrew shook his head.

"Weeks?" Kate persisted, her voice strained with tension. "Days?"

"Some matter of days, I would suspect. Not weeks. I think they mean to act quickly before the Crown should suffer any further embarrassment—in the event that they come up with some evidence that I am involved in this spying ring Cecil alluded to."

"But you are no spy!" Kate exclaimed. "It's absurd."

"No, I am not. But Cecil has the information about Philip's encounter with Guy Fawkes. And now they have my statements in the Westminster Committee, which imply I may be disloyal to King James."

"There must be some way," Kate pleaded, "to prove your innocence. That these random events prove nothing against you."

"Nothing is random," Andrew said, "in God's design. We need to simply see the larger portrait from the perspective of the painter Himself. I believe...truly believe that He will reveal to us what needs to be done. Even though...there is so much we do not know."

Kate was studying her husband's face intently.

But Andrew was absorbed in thought, barely breathing. Just staring ahead in a fixed gaze.

After a while, his gaze broke and he looked at Kate. There was a glimmer of hope on his face.

"Yet," he said tentatively at first. But then more forcefully, "There is something we *do* know."

"What is that?"

"There must be enemy spies in the midst of the king's company." Then he added his resolution on the matter.

"So, dear Kate, it must be up to us to find them out."

Chapter 54

Some Weeks Later

Captain Newport's ship and the skeleton crew were blessed with fair winds and good weather. The trip back was considerably shorter—and less stressful—than the trip had been on the journey over to the New World.

When the ship made landfall at Blackwall, England, it was harbored. Besides the extra ballast in the bottom of its hold, the main freight it carried was a modest load of iron ore. The ore had been dug up from the hills near Jamestown. For years there had been many tales of gold and silver lying on the ground, ready to pick up; one of the reasons, among others, that nations like France and Spain had long had an interest in the coastal lands of greater Virginia.

But the initial search of the area surrounding Jamestown turned up no precious metals. The consensus among the mining explorers in the Jamestown settlement was that the bits of those gold and silver showing up in some Indian jewelry must have been the product of small, very limited veins.

Newport was under orders to give report to the Virginia Company in London of the progress of the settlement, and then oversee the stocking of a ship with provisions for return to Jamestown at the first fair weather.

But Newport was also bearing something else with him to London. An item lighter than any iron ore, admittedly; even feather-weight. But in another sense, what he carried with him was weightier than the tonnage of any freighter that sailed the seas under the English flag.

The ship's captain, after unloading at dockside and grabbing his ship's log, journal, and sea bag, checked into the Black Swan tavern and inn. He collapsed for a long sleep, but not before giving orders to the tavern keeper that if he were awakened for any reason, he would throw the man responsible into the harbor waters—with a ballast stone wrapped to his feet.

After sleeping most of the day, Newport awakened. He threw some water on his face from the porcelain basin, and then dressed in his captain's uniform. He opened his sea bag, took something out, and slipped it into his coat pocket. Then he went down for a mid-afternoon supper. On the way into the dining room, he stopped at the bar cage.

"I need to get a message sent. Immediately."

"Where to?"

"Ever heard of the mansion house Theobalds in Hertford-shire?"

"Aye—aye, I have...if you mean the great house of the good earl, Robert Cecil."

"It is the same. Do you have a trusted man to ride hard with my message?"

"My 'executive assistant,'" he replied with some measure of self-importance. "Rodney!"

In a minute, a short young man wearing an apron emerged from the storeroom.

"Message to be delivered to Theobalds, if you please," his master announced.

The assistant, wide-eyed, nodded silently. Newport looked him in the eye and then delivered his instructions.

"The note must be delivered today. Ride fast. Show it to no one except the earl, Robert Cecil, himself. Do you understand?"

The clerk nodded solemnly.

Then Newport reached in his pocket and retrieved several heavy coins and thrust them in the young man's hand.

"The rest will be paid you on your successful return."

"Excuse me," the young man said, "but the note, sir...where shall I obtain it?"

Newport snatched a piece of paper off the barkeep's table, dipped a pen in the inkwell, and began to write.

> To the Earl of Salisbury, the honourable Robert Cecil.
>
> I am at the Black Swan in Blackwall. It is urgent that you meet me here alone before the scheduled meeting with the Virginia Company tomorrow. It concerns matters of the greatest discretion.
>
> Your humble servant,
> Christopher Newport,
> Captain

Newport folded the letter in half, grabbed the burning candle on the desk, and dropped a large glob of wax on the edge of the letter, then impressed his captain's ring in the wax.

The young man snatched the letter and ran out to the livery stable. He grabbed the fastest horse, a black Arabian, saddled it quickly, and rode off.

Inside the tavern, Newport sat down at a wooden table and quickly polished off two bowls of the Black Swan specialty—the lamb stew, with plenty of fresh carrots and peas.

He downed two pints of the strongest ale, then ordered another. His table was in the corner of the crowded tavern, and he leaned back against the wall, with his feet propped up against the table. In the light of the oil lamp that burned on the wall over his head, Newport reached into his coat pocket and pulled out the piece of paper. He read it over again, and then a second time.

The letter that had been the subject of the George Kendall capital trial, which Mister Reed the blacksmith had purloined from Kendall's cabin, had now been safely transported from Virginia to London. And Newport had it in his hands.

But he found its contents just as puzzling, and as disturbing, as he had when he first set eyes on it in John Martin's cabin at Jamestown.

What will His Earlship think of this, I wonder, Newport muttered. Then he folded the letter and put it back in his coat. He leaned back against the wall and fell asleep.

Amidst the din of singing and drinking among the patrons at the Black Swan, Newport was relatively safe—safer than sleeping on the bed in his room. At least this way his back was protected, and there were witnesses about.

In the evening, the young messenger and his exhausted horse arrived at the gates of Theobalds. The gatekeepers inquired what his business was. He announced he was bearing an urgent message for Robert Cecil from ship's captain, Christopher Newport. One of the guards hopped on a horse and rode to the front door of the palatial mansion. A few minutes after he had entered the grand palace, he reappeared and rang a large bell outside the front door.

At the sound of the bell, the other guard signaled for the messenger to enter the grounds and opened wide the black metal gate.

It was then that the young man got his glimpse of Theobalds, the vast palace so grand that even King James himself had coveted it when he was first invited by Cecil to visit. Multiple tiered towers and spiral turrets beyond his ability to count. The palace was so wide and broad that it looked like it contained an entire city within its walls. Rows of stained-glass windows and arched entranceways boggled the mind. Robert Cecil was at home that night, and the whole place was ablaze with the flames of huge torches and brick firepits.

The young messenger rode up to the main entrance. His horse was taken by a groom in a red vest and broad hat with a large feather. The messenger dismounted and stepped up to the arched doorway.

But before he could grab the bronze lion-headed door knocker, the door swung open.

There, standing in the doorway in his usual slightly twisted stance, was Robert Cecil himself.

He said nothing, but thrust his hand toward the young man with his palm open.

The young man carefully placed the note from Newport in Cecil's hand, then bowed and stepped back.

Cecil slammed the door shut and then broke the seal and opened the note, reading it quickly.

"Hubert!" he cried out to his master of the house.

In an instant, his chief servant appeared and bowed.

"I will need to be awakened before dawn tomorrow. I will need an escort for my ride."

Hubert bowed again and disappeared.

Cecil walked into the empty great room, where tapestries hung on each wall. It was uncharacteristically cold and damp that evening, and a fire roared in the well of the fireplace, whose great stone mouth was taller than a man.

Crumpling up the note from Newport, Cecil tossed it into the fire. He waited until it was totally consumed before leaving the room and heading up the wide, winding staircase that led to his bedchamber.

Chapter 55

The following morning Robert Cecil and four armed escorts rode to Blackwall. When Cecil arrived at the Black Swan, he gave instructions to his guards to stand fast at the door, and that only he would enter.

Newport was still at his table in the far corner of the tavern. But he was awake. His hands were laid, one on another, on the table.

Cecil entered, spotted Newport, and limped over to the table and sat down.

"I trust this is of the utmost importance," Cecil said with a slight sneer.

"I do believe it is," Newport said. Then he produced the letter and explained that it had been found in George Kendall's cabin at Jamestown.

Quickly scanning the letter, then reading again more closely, the earl placed it down on the table and then looked around the room to make sure no one was within hearing.

"Who knows of this letter?" he asked.

"Only the members of the Jamestown Council," Newport answered. "We discussed it in closed session—with an agreement to keep it a secret, on the condition that I show it to you."

"And George Kendall?"

"Tried, found guilty, and executed by firing squad."

"On what charge?"

"Mutinous dissension...but he had also killed a man. And of course, there was the letter..."

"Which man did he kill?"

"Kensington. Though that was not his real name."

"How do you know that Kendall penned this letter?" Cecil asked pointedly.

"It was found in his cabin. And the council was unanimous in finding that the handwriting was his."

After mulling over what he had just heard, Cecil took the letter and slipped it inside his waistcoat.

"This must not be divulged to the Virginia Company," Cecil said. "This is now more than just an issue concerning the Jamestown expedition. Far more."

"It would appear so," Newport said, "though that would not be for me to decide...in that I am but a humble ship's captain."

Newport gave a revealing smile at that. Cecil continued to drive home the point.

"This goes to the security of the Crown and the welfare of England."

"Indeed," Newport said.

"What...what did you say that the name of the murdered man was?" Cecil asked.

"He went by *Kensington*. But that was an assumed identity. He was a Scotsman."

Cecil's head snapped upright, and his eyes were burning through the sea captain.

"His name?"

"Mackenzie. Philip Mackenzie. A true hero of the exploration,

I might add. And was murdered by Kendall, it seems, because Kendall feared that Mackenzie might reveal him as a traitor to England. And with good reason. Mackenzie probably harbored some thoughts about Kendall's…well…foreign sympathies. As several of us did also."

"Enough!" Cecil said emphatically, taking Newport back with his abruptness.

Cecil patted his coat to make sure the letter was still tucked there. Then he stood up to leave.

"Do I have your confidence and secrecy in this matter?" he asked Newport.

"The king," Newport replied, "and this kingdom have my utmost loyalty."

That was not the exact answer that Cecil desired, but he would have to settle for what Newport gave him. Cecil limped out of the Black Swan. Newport rose and headed over to the office of the Virginia Company where he would give a detailed—but redacted—version of the events at Jamestown.

While that meeting was going on, Kate Mackenzie, on the directive of her husband, was visiting the finest drapery, silk, and tapestry shop in London. She was a bit puzzled by her husband's instructions, but dutifully fulfilled them. It was a pleasing task, though, as it allowed her to browse through the finest imported fabrics in London.

After a few minutes the proprietor, a middle-aged man with a round figure and red cheeks and bald head, attended to her. They discussed the quality of the materials at length, and the proprietor was more than happy to expound on the exquisite nature of his fabrics.

"And you cater to the finest of England's homes?" she asked.

"More than that," the man said with a wink, and lowering his voice he added, "our fabrics are in use in several of the palaces of King James, Madam."

"You don't say?"

"Absolutely."

"And…in the homes of any of his counselors or confidants perhaps?"

"Quite so, yes," he said. "Now, as to the silks you were looking at—"

"And what counselors, pray tell, would that be?"

The proprietor bent over to Kate and whispered to her. "Theobalds," he said. "The palace of the earl Robert Cecil."

"My, how proud you must be!" Kate answered with a smile.

"Yes," he answered. And then he led her over to a collection of Persian fabrics.

Kate had been instructed to inquire of the extent of Robert Cecil's dealings with the finer shops—and to retrieve whatever intelligence she could about the source of his vast wealth. But Kate wondered what more she could possibly ask.

"So," she asked aimlessly, "you were of course very privileged in providing fabrics for Mister Cecil himself…"

"Yes, very," the man said smartly. "A most noteworthy method of payment too, I might add. Though I really shouldn't—"

"Noteworthy?" Kate asked. "Oh, you really must share that with me, good sir."

"Well, it is just that when the earl's—Robert Cecil's—house man arrived with payment, it was…rather surprising!"

"How so?"

"Why the coins, madam, the coins."

"Coins? He paid you in coins and not notes?"

"Yes, madam—coins."

Then after a pause, and relishing the ability to disclose intriguing secrets about one of his best customers, the proprietor explained. "They were *Spanish* coins. Imagine that!"

Chapter 56

Andrew had heard that the Virginia Company had convened a quick meeting to receive its report from the newly arriving Captain Christopher Newport. The next day, after gaining the benefit of Kate's conversation with the fabric shop proprietor, Andrew decided to boldly approach Newport himself and question him on the status of his brother and nephew. So he headed down to the harbor at Blackwall to search him out.

Newport was seated at a table at dockside next to his first mate, signing up crew for the next voyage back to Virginia. There was a large group of sailors waiting in line at the table.

Andrew interrupted Newport's business.

"I wanted to inquire, Captain," he began, "about someone at Jamestown."

"So do a great deal of others, good sir. But you'll have to wait till my business is finished here. I am busy, as you can see."

Then Andrew introduced himself.

"You said *Mackenzie?*" Newport exclaimed.

"Yes. I was inquiring about a fellow named *Kensington* and his son..."

Newport turned to his first mate, whispered for him to take

over the enlistment, and then rose, taking Andrew by the arm and leading him down the dock and away from the table.

The harbor was filled with ships loading and unloading, and sailors scampering up and down the ropes, repairing sail.

Newport paused a moment before explaining why he had taken Andrew aside.

"You have a brother, do you not...by the name of Philip Mackenzie?'

Andrew was taken aback. But he would not deny it.

"Yes, sir, I do—why do you ask?"

"I learned that he had gone by an assumed name—John Kensington—while he was with us at Jamestown."

"Please tell me," Andrew said intensely, interrupting him, "tell me any news you can share on his welfare."

"His welfare, yes," Newport began. "On that point...I am sorry to report sad news for you, sir."

He found a large wooden crate nearby and invited Andrew to sit down with him. Then he proceeded to tell Andrew everything—about the murder of Philip at the hands of George Kendall and the letter that became the subject of the trial. And about Kendall's execution.

"Your brother acquitted himself honorably, Mister Mackenzie," the captain said. "I am sorry about his passing and your loss."

Andrew leaned forward into his folded hands, numbed by the tragic news. Newport began to rise.

Then Andrew tried to clear his thoughts, and something he had just heard fixed itself in his mind.

"The letter...that you mentioned. Written by Kendall. You never...never told me what was in the letter that would have persuaded this Kendall fellow to kill my brother over it."

"There you have me in a bind, sir," Newport said. "Matters of state involved, I am afraid. I am not at liberty—"

"For many years now I have been a valued member of the Crown's group of counselors," Andrew said, rising. "This letter you spoke of not only tells me something more about the reason for my poor brother's cruel death…but it may have a far-reaching effect, beyond anything you have been privy to."

"Indeed, which is why Robert Cecil has ordered me to keep it close, I am afraid."

"Cecil?"

"Yes, none other."

"You consider yourself a loyal Englishman?"

"Quite so!" Newport said, a little shocked that such a question should be put to him by a Scotsman.

"Let me wager a guess," Andrew said, stepping up closer to the captain. "Let me speculate for a moment that the contents of the letter you speak of…finds its importance as a piece in a spying scheme. Am I getting close?"

"You tempt me, sir, to ignore the admonishment from the Earl of Salisbury."

"I tempt you only to protect king and country, Captain. Can there be any evil in that?"

"And how, pray tell, will my disclosing this letter to you accomplish that?" Newport asked him. There was a sincerity in his voice and a searching look to his eyes. As if Christopher Newport, a sea captain whose business required the skill to locate, and navigate, suitable harbors, was looking for a safe place to negotiate his competing interests. He must not defy the Crown of England, whose high counselor had made his position clear that the letter must be kept confidential. Yet at the same time, Newport wanted to honor his fellow adventurer, Philip Mackenzie, and to see justice done if it was in his ability to do so.

"God creates governments, Captain Newport," Andrew said. "And because He is the author of truth, how can that virtue not help but foster the safety and security of His government?"

Newport eyed Andrew closely.

There on the docks of Blackwall, that harbor smelling of fish and seawater, and crowded with ships that filled the horizon with a tangle of mainmasts, it would be a defining moment. Andrew knew it for sure, and in a way, Newport could sense it, though there was much he did not understand about Andrew's pressing need for information about Kendall.

"I will tell you but a little, Mister Mackenzie, as your brother's memory, and your loss, does compel me in that. But I cannot tell you all. Just remember that I risk much by speaking with you about this."

"And I, Captain Newport," Andrew replied, "shall risk everything, if you do not."

Chapter 57

Rose Heatherton was walking down the muddy streets of London, head down, exhausted, slowly working her way back to her family's apartment after several days of working as a tutor for the children of a wealthy widower.

The streets were crowded with carts and wagons bearing coal, wood, and vegetables to market. There were also the carriages that were carrying the more affluent Londoners who could avoid the muck and mire of the dirt roads, and the congested filth of the city that had grown into a maze of tall, multiple-storied commercial buildings and tenement houses, which were standing row upon row—places so dense with buildings that the sun seemed blocked from view.

It was late afternoon, and the taverns were starting to fill up, and the working people were filling the roads, scurrying home for supper.

Rose was feeling an overwhelming sense of loneliness. Why that particular day, she did not know. She had been waiting patiently for Kate Mackenzie to alert her to any news forthcoming from Jamestown on the fate of Peter. But it had been a week since she and Kate had met last, and still no word.

But her mind drifted, as it often did, back to Seacrest House on the Scottish borders. It was not just the appeal of that place, although she had always had a deep affection for the cliffs and the smell and sound of the ocean. And now, living in the crowded tenement district of London with her mother and brother, the memory of that great house by the sea pulled at her heart more than ever.

But there was also something else. Along that coast, on the high precipice overlooking the crashing waves far below, was where she had been with Peter that day, on the jutting hilltop which gently blended the cold gray stone and the soft, green moss that covered it. It was that moment with Peter at her side, when all of her feelings lined up like the constellations in the heavens. Her heart became fixed, like a star, with a devoted love for him.

Yet she wondered how she could be so certain about her love for Peter when the possibility of their being united now seemed so impossible.

Rose Heatherton remembered the pledge Peter had made to her. That even at the risk of his own life, he would make every effort to return to her. And that pledge was so like Peter—noble, loving, and brave, yet improbable when measured against the odds stacked against it.

In turn, she had made a kind of pledge herself, not to Peter, but rather to her own heart. Now she regretted that she had not had a chance to share with him, but it had not been possible, given the swirling turmoil of emotion that day when Peter first told her he was leaving England.

Her promise was a simple one. She would rather confine herself to the life a spinster, tutoring other people's children, than settle with marriage to another. Her employer had begun to hint at his affections for her. But Rose did not—could not—reciprocate. Rose had resigned herself to be one of those educated, well-thought-of-but-unenvied women who lived alone and would never marry or bear children of their own.

She heard none of the sounds of the street as she trudged on, consumed in her thoughts. Rose did not hear the call of the market vendors, or the clomping feet of the horses on the cobblestone pavement she had now reached in her walk.

Rose continued for another long block and then turned down a narrow, airless alleyway that led to a row of tenements where she stayed with her family on days she was not required to be in the home of her employer.

She knew she was late that day, and that she would disappoint her family. Rose had promised to pick up meat and vegetables and a loaf of bread in order to make dinner for her brother and mother. But her employer had been unexpectedly called out of town, she had been told by the children's house nurse. He left without paying her wages. She was penniless now. Her brother, William, had just lost his job the prior week. They would probably go hungry that night. It would not be the first time.

With God all things are possible, Rose thought to herself as she neared the steps to her apartment. It was something Peter had impressed on her before he shipped out. She hung onto that thought, even though the daylight she had felt confident would be at the end of the tunnel now seemed to be fading into empty shadows.

Somewhere inside, it was as if she had her hand on the knob of a great door and was preparing to close it—probably forever.

She took a deep breath, and then said again to herself, *With God all things are possible.*

She mounted the wooden stairway. From upstairs she could already hear the cries of babies and yelling. It sounded as if somewhere a man was drunk and was screaming out a string of profanities.

Then she thought she heard something else, but it was different.

The voice repeated itself. She stopped her climb up the stairs and then listened more carefully.

"I said," the voice called out, "that there are painted Indians there, and great rivers, and trees taller than all the buildings of London."

Rose gripped the wooden railing and slowly turned around; fearful of a disappointment so great that, if her ears tricked her, then her heart would most certainly stop beating from grief.

She looked down the alley. A figure was standing in the unlit passageway, standing still. The figure kept talking.

"And more terrors and wonders than I could ever explain, perhaps even in a lifetime."

Then the figure said something else.

"But all of the wonders of the New World just pale in comparison...to seeing you, dear Rose. Knowing you are safe."

"*Peter!*" she cried out and ran from the stairs and into the alley. Peter sprinted to her and picked up her up off the ground and kissed her and swirled her around in the air as he held her.

They embraced and wept and laughed and refused to let go of each other.

"How...when?" she stammered.

"I just pulled in aboard the ship from Jamestown."

"How did you find me?" she cried out.

"That was easy. It was journeying back here from Virginia that was the hard part."

"What do you mean?"

"Our captain had not been authorized to take returnees back on this voyage. But he took pity on me. After my father died—"

"Oh, Peter. No! I am so sorry," Rose said and wept even harder and took his rough, dirty hands and pressed them to her face.

"It was hard. But the Lord has been causing me to grow through all of this," he said.

Then as he held her tight again, Peter tilted his head back and admired her face.

"The same beautiful, gracious Rose," he said. "How blessed I am to have you in my arms!"

After several more minutes of quiet embrace, and as Rose finally collected herself from her weeping both for joy but also for the pain of Peter's loss, Peter brightened up.

"Let's eat. I am famished!"

Suddenly Rose's countenance fell.

"I am so sorry. I wasn't paid today. My family is going to be so distressed. And here you return all the way from the New World and I cannot so much as feed the man I love..."

Rose's lip trembled a bit. But Peter was laughing.

"What is so funny?" she asked in confusion.

"I have plenty of money," he said, jingling a coin bag.

"You do?" she said amazed.

"That's part of the amazing story. I will have to tell you all of it. But right now, let me take you to the butcher and buy the biggest ham they have for your family's dinner. And bread and vegetables. And cakes for dessert!"

Rose was momentarily speechless. She had Peter's arm wrapped in hers so tight that it actually started to get numb as they walked quickly to the market square.

But Peter didn't complain. He only smiled and stared at her as they walked on together. And in a torrent of stored-up experiences, Rose poured out everything that had happened since his departure.

Chapter 58

At the Palace of Whitehall, Robert Cecil had finished a personal meeting with the king. At issue, among His Majesty's various other requests—the purchase of a new batch of hunting dogs for his fox hunts and the tending to his favorite horse which had gone ill—there was also the matter of the opening of Parliament.

Although still nearly six months away, the event had arrested the attention of the king. As was his customary role, James was to give the opening speech and set forth his goals for the reign of the kingdom. And, as usual, the king would expect Parliament to go along with his scheme for the running of government.

But opposition within England against various of the king's policies had been fomenting. Cecil was the king's chief strategist. They had spent the better part of the day discussing how to trump their objectors.

After the meeting, Cecil made his way back in his personal chambers in the castle. He sat down at his desk. The task before him now was a much more focused one.

He sat at his expansive mahogany writing desk, fetched a long parchment sheet, and began jotting down a rough draft. The document was not going to come as a complete shock to the king, or at least Cecil surmised as much.

Arrest warrants for interrogation were fairly common in the kingdom, and even more so since that fateful night when Guy Fawkes was discovered lurking in the cellar underneath Parliament building at Westminster.

But this one would be particularly appropriate, Cecil had concluded, for two reasons. He jotted the two factors at the top of his notes. The king's advisor would have to remember the two points when he presented the warrant for His Majesty's signature. He would remind the king why he should execute the warrants without dispatch.

First, this was a warrant that dealt, at least in some remote way, with the gunpowder conspiracy. True, all of the known conspirators and traitors, including their confessors, had been tried and then publicly executed. Yet Cecil was convinced that Catholic sympathizers hostile to King James were still lurking within the chambers of the king's government. Cecil had increasing intelligence that information was being leaked from within the Court to foreign diplomats. James' natural fears of conspiracies against him would aid Cecil in obtaining his signature. Cecil would get to the bottom of it all, no matter how cruel the road that would be taken.

Then, there was the second reason.

The fact was, the king had already taken minor action against this individual. The arrest warrant—and the tortures of the rack in the Tower that would follow—was but a logical extension of the king's prior suspicions. King James would simply be reaffirming his own precedent against the suspect.

Cecil then pulled out a second sheaf of parchment. At the top he wrote—

UPON THESE PRESENTS, DOTH HIS MAJESTY,
KING JAMES OF ENGLAND, ORDER

THE SEIZURE FORTHWITH of a certain former member of His Majesty's government for interrogation on certain matters of subversion, treason, and other multiple offences against the good peace, and order and safety of the realm;

AND THAT THIS PERSON BE RESTRAINED AND INTERROGATED, INCLUDING ALL EXPEDIENT TORTURE, AT THE GOOD PLEASURE OF THE KING AND HIS LAWFUL AGENTS, the said person being known by the name of

Cecil paused. He weighed the name he was about to insert.

He was convinced this was no personal vendetta, no retaliation against the consistent chaffing he had received from this man. Yet, admittedly, the man whose name would be inserted in the arrest warrant had exhibited a certain arrogance. He had failed, continually, to acknowledge the king's supremacy over all matters, including matters of religion and faith. He had advocated an interpretation of Scripture that authorized, even though on vary narrow grounds and in few circumstances, defiance of kings when an issue of faith was directly implicated.

Cecil dipped his quill in the deep inkwell in the table. He would write the name, even though the evidence that linked the name in the arrest warrant to the gunpowder conspiracy was tenuous at best. Indeed, the link was not to the person himself, but to his brother.

But the fact that his brother, Philip Mackenzie, was now dead, did not make the matter moot in Cecil's thinking. The new intelligence of English government secrets being leaked to the foreign ambassadors of Spain meant that the presence of spies within

England was real. Andrew Mackenzie's brother had consorted with a Catholic anarchist; and Andrew had shown himself conspicuously disloyal to the king, though only in matters of theology. Wasn't that enough?

Besides, King James was privately reprimanding Cecil for failing to come up with suspects responsible for the treasonous communications to Spain. Some of the communiqués that had been intercepted dealt with internal discussions of the Bible translation committees. Advance information to Spain about that subject could give it ample time to further alienate the Pope against England, and perhaps even create Vatican support for a political coup against James. And Andrew Mackenzie's possible complicity in those treasonous communiqués was clear: He had been a high-ranking administrator on one of the translation committees and would had been privy to their discussions.

The intercepted letters to the Spanish Ambassador had also carried a promise that "further intelligence about the English exploration into Virginia would be forthcoming…" There also, Cecil could show a link between Andrew and the treasonous disclosures—his own brother had been part of the Jamestown settlement. Perhaps Philip disclosed confidential matters of the English exploration to Andrew, who in turn was in touch with the Spanish Ambassador.

Indeed, what more evidence did Cecil need to show than that?

Now his pen was ready to insert the name into the warrant for arrest…*Andrew Mackenzie.*

But before he could, there was a knock on the door.

"Come in," Cecil said.

The man who entered was a familiar face. He was Parliament's liaison to the king.

"Good day," Cecil said, greeting him with perfunctory courtesy.

"Lord Salisbury," the man began. "Our prior meeting was waylaid by interruptions. I trust you won't mind my taking the liberty today of entreating you now—"

"I am engaged in important business," Cecil said, glancing down at the unfinished arrest warrant.

"As is always the case with your many important duties for the king. And your various titles of authority, which seem to expand with regularity."

"Do you have some hidden meaning in that?"

"Only that with the demise of the Earl of Dorset as Lord Treasurer and your recent assumption of that title yourself, you have become the one with whom we must deal on matters of national finance."

"Do you have a quarrel with my financial dealings for the king?"

"Not I," the man said, "but the House of Commons most definitely does."

"Speak plainly," Cecil snapped.

"To make the point, the Commons is upset by your decision to execute tariff impositions on the merchants."

"The Crown needs money to run the business of the kingdom. Expanded debt requires new taxes."

"Perhaps so. But not taxes imposed by the king in excess of those authorized by Parliament."

"The king has the power to levy taxes, with or without Parliament's approval," Cecil shot back.

"And there is the rub, sir. It will require discussion between yourself and some of the leaders in the Commons. Negotiation.

Compromise. Those are matters in which you have also proved yourself most skilled."

"Thank you," Cecil said with a cautious smile. "Now, if I may return to my work..." he said, reaching for the parchments on his desk.

"One other issue," the man said. "The opening of Parliament."

"It is months off, man," Cecil said, attempting to sidetrack the discussion.

"Indeed. But Parliament desire ample opportunity to glean the king's thinking on his policies. For instance, where does the king stand on moving, albeit slowly, on the matter of royal succession?"

Cecil eyed the man. He had just touched on a nerve.

"The king," Cecil answered, "will likely ask that Prince Henry be made Prince of Wales and Earl of Chester. That, His Majesty believes, is a move in the right direction."

"Yes. Perhaps. But may I suggest that if the king desires that, then, in turn, perhaps the Crown should consider moving in concert with Parliament, rather than against it, in matters of the treasury?"

For a moment there was no further discussion. Cecil eyed the liaison. Then broke the silence.

"Do you have some pressing suggestion?"

"Yes, indeed I do. Several key members of Parliament are waiting, at this very moment, to meet with you. To start negotiating these very critical matters. They are, quite frankly, somewhat tired of waiting..."

"A meeting?'

"Yes."

"At this moment?"

"They are within but a short carriage ride away, sir."

Cecil glanced down at the warrant that still needed the name of Andrew Mackenzie to be inserted.

Then he looked at the liaison who was still standing in front of him, his hand folded behind his back. He was rocking back and forth on his heels.

Cecil took the warrant, covered it with several other papers, and stood up.

"Then we shall take my carriage, sir. And we shall talk on the way."

As they left his chambers, Cecil glanced back at his desk before locking the door behind him.

The arrest warrant, he mused to himself, would be the first order of business after his meeting with the House of Commons.

Chapter 59

Andrew Mackenzie was seated in his library across from his mentor, Thomas Craig. Andrew was reviewing the notes he had quickly taken after his meeting with Captain Newport, together with the information from Kate's visit with Cecil's fabric-shop keeper.

"On the matter of the Spanish coins," Andrew said. "You said you had some particular insight."

"Just this," Craig replied. "At the time of the negotiations surrounding the treaty with Spain several years ago, Cecil played a key role."

"I was aware of that. But not that he had been paid by Spain."

"Well, the pension paid in coinage that he received from Spain was deemed a gratuity, not a payment. It is not uncommon for the negotiating parties to receive gifts from the opposing nation, if that country is pleased with the resulting treaty."

"Though the *appearance* of such payments in the past," Andrew said, "might prove to be embarrassing to Cecil. Particularly given the fact that, from what you and I now know, Cecil is investigating improper disclosures from someone within the Crown to the ambassador of Spain."

"Perhaps," Craig noted. "But you will need something far more powerful than that to take Cecil off your scent and send him off in another direction. And, my friend, I fear that time is running short."

Andrew looked down at this notes.

"Then there is the information I received from Captain Newport," he said.

"What was the name on the letter?"

"According to Newport," Andrew replied, "the letter written by George Kendall was addressed to a certain man named 'Sir Panian Halfblood.'"

"Clearly a contrived name," Craig said. "It would hardly be thought that Kendall, a spy for Spain and an experienced soldier, would have been so naïve as to use the real name of the addressee."

"True enough. Which now presents the question—who is this Panian Halfblood fellow?" Andrew asked.

After considering it for a long while, Craig looked up at Andrew.

"Perhaps you are asking the wrong question."

"What do you mean?"

"Rather than asking *who* Panian Halfblood is, we should be asking, *why Panian Halfblood?*"

"I don't follow," Andrew said, wrinkling his brow.

"Just this. If the name is not the real name—and we both agree it is not—then why did George Kendall use that name?"

"Perhaps it was merely a code name."

"But," Craig said, "a code for what?"

"Or *who*," Andrew added.

"Exactly."

"There is something about the first name," Andrew muttered.

"Yes. *Panian*. What kind of given name is that? A nationality? A place of birth or residence?"

"Or something else altogether?" Andrew said.

Then, after looking down at the name in his notes, he shook his head.

"I keep getting the feeling," Andrew said, "that I have seen that name somewhere before."

"My mind is blank of that part," Craig said. "But on the *Halfblood* reference, I wonder if that is simply a factual description of the person's breeding."

"Yes, perhaps," Andrew said. Then he recalled something else.

"I do remember also," he said, "that Newport shared something else of great importance. About Kendall. That he had been a foreign spy for Robert Cecil at one time."

"An interesting fact," Craig replied. "But Cecil's network for spying is legendary. He has spies all over the Continent. Very effective ones I might add. The fact that Kendall was one of them but proved in the end to be disloyal to England and in the employ of Spain is simply another piece of the puzzle...but gives us no clear leverage, I am afraid."

After some period of silence, Craig rose and extended his hand to Andrew.

"I will learn all that I can, my friend, of the intentions of Cecil and the king regarding your fate," he said. "Though I fear that your assessments are correct. From everything I know, Cecil is under great pressure from the king to identify a conspirator behind this Spanish treason. And, most tragically for you, it appears that you are a likely target for his crafty arrows."

They shook hands warmly and Andrew showed him to the door.

After Thomas Craig had departed, Andrew returned to his library and sat down again, dejected that he seemed unable to decipher the unfolding Spanish conspiracy in time to avoid his own arrest and torture.

"*Panian,*" he muttered to himself. "Where have I seen that name before?"

Chapter 60

Andrew's intense contemplations were interrupted when he noticed his servant at the open door to his library.

"Pardon me," he announced, "but there is a Master Peter Mackenzie, your nephew, at the door. And a young lady, Mistress Rose Heatherton with him."

Springing to the doorway, Andrew rushed to Peter and embraced him.

"Captain Newport told me in confidence that he slipped you back to England. God bless the man!"

"He was my godsend," Peter exclaimed. Then he turned to Rose who was beaming in back of him. "And Rose you already know, as I have lately found out."

Andrew took Rose's hand and squeezed it warmly.

"We knew," Andrew said with a smile, "that if anything could bring young Peter all the way back from the New World it would be you!"

Just then Kate swept into the room. She hugged Peter, held on for a considerable period of time, and began to tear up.

"Pardon your old aunt," she said, "but you're like a son to us, Peter. We prayed for you and so longed to know you were safe. And now, at last, you are back in London."

Then Kate turned to Rose and invited her back to the parlor while the two men talked.

"When did you learn of Peter's return?" Kate asked, seating herself next to Rose on the embroidered settee.

"Not until he showed up at the alley outside our apartment building. Imagine my surprise and joy!"

Kate laughed and smiled at the bliss that was lighting up Rose's countenance.

"I am so sorry we had no notice of his arrival ourselves," she told Rose. "We have been...well, that is to say, Mister Mackenzie has been through a constant period of testing of late. Certain of the king's men have had my husband under suspicion on the most absurd allegations."

But Kate quickly refocused the discussion and then smiled broadly at Rose.

"But enough of that. Tell me, how has Peter fared these many months? It must have been so hard for him to shoulder the burden of being on foreign shores alone, and suffering the loss of his father."

"I can't imagine," Rose said. "But the Lord has been good. Protecting Peter. Providing a way back to England when all hope appeared to be lost regarding his early return. And Peter said that when he left, there was much sickness breaking out among the settlers. Peter himself only narrowly recovered himself in time to make the voyage."

"That poor dear," Kate said. But then brightened up and smiled, and added, "But now he is safe and home. And rejoined with you. I am so happy for you both."

"Oh, and I almost forgot to tell you about the double blessing!" Rose cried out.

"Do tell me, quickly."

"It seems his father was rewarded with a full share of investment in the Virginia Company for his faithful service at Jamestown—bestowed posthumously, of course. Because Peter was his only surviving heir, the Jamestown Council transferred the share to Peter."

"That is a blessing!"

"Even more than that. Peter said he had little desire to manage the investment share himself. He said he has no heart for commerce or business. In fact, he wants to study for the ministry. He wants to follow in the footsteps of his uncle and grandfather."

"Andrew will be so pleased...so deeply touched to learn that," Kate said. "So what will he do with his share?"

"Already done," Rose said, beaming. "Captain Newport offered him a wonderful price for the share. Paid him in cash, on the spot, upon their arrival back at Blackwall. Peter bought us enough food for a week and offered to keep us in the apartment until all of our fortunes return. So, between Peter's generosity and that of you and Uncle Andrew..."

Suddenly Rose blushed, realizing her misstatement.

"I am sorry, I meant you and Mister Mackenzie..."

"No, dear—you were right the first time. It would be his great honor for you to think of him as your uncle. As part of your family. And me as your aunt, if you will let me fulfill that role. And perhaps with the passing of time, you and I will grow even closer, my dear. Nothing could make me happier."

While Kate and Rose were talking, Andrew had led Peter into the library and closed the tall wooden doors.

"I am so sorry about the death of your father," he said to his nephew. "He was a remarkable man. I was fortunate to have him as my brother. But I am truly heartbroken that I did not treat him more kindly during our years together. I was amiss, terribly wrong in that..."

"There is no need, Uncle, for regrets. I am here, in a way, to bear a message from my father."

"A message?"

"Of sorts, yes. Before his murder, my father began to confide greatly in a good pastor at the settlement by the name of Reverend Robert Hunt. Amidst my sorrow at losing him, I can still praise God for two very encouraging things."

"I could use some encouraging news," Andrew said with some weariness in his voice.

"Reverend Hunt told me," Peter continued, "that my father had been restored to his faith in the Savior. He reaffirmed his commitment to Christ, repented of having wandered spiritually for years—"

"Praise God for that!"

"But there was also another turn of events. Concerning you."

"Me?"

"Yes. My father told Reverend Hunt that he truly repented of the wall he had allowed to develop between the two of you. He said he had long resented you because of your successes in government and in matters of the church. He said it led to a great bitterness. He also believed that Grandfather Ransom had somehow favored you over him, and that greatly dismayed him. But in the end, before his death, Father said that such feelings were not true, but were just the envy he bore for you."

"Envy?" Andrew exclaimed. "It was I who envied him. His bravery. His vision for new frontiers and uncharted horizons. If only I had told him..."

"In a way," Peter said, "I think he knew. He told Reverend Hunt he wanted to return to England one day, and for only one reason."

"What reason was that?"

"To address you face-to-face. And to express his love for you. And to make amends for all the years of strife between the two of you."

Andrew leaned his head forward. He covered his forehead with his hand as his eyes began to fill up with tears. He wanted to speak, but his throat was so filled with the overwhelming rush of emotion that he was speechless. He could only mutter three words in his weeping:

Thank You, God...

After a few moments, he collected himself and spoke.

"The news you have brought me is truly the most welcomed thing that has happened to me in a very long while. Forces have been arrayed against me here in London. It is a very dark time. But you have brought a ray of sunshine. Thank you for that."

Peter thought about what his uncle had just said and decided to probe.

"If it is not too much to ask," he said, "I knew of the false accusations that were surfacing against my father. You had shared those with me before I left for Virginia. But I was not aware of allegations against you."

"I shouldn't burden you with this," Andrew said.

"Please consider me not only your nephew but your friend as well," Peter said. "I would be honored to consider anything you share with me. At the very least I can pray for you more earnestly."

"It appears," Andrew said, summarizing as best as he could, "that the Crown has determined that there is a spy—or spies—within the government. Close to the king. Secretly sending communiqués to the ambassador from Spain about the most intimate details of the king's business and affairs of state. For some reason it has now become their obsession that I am one of those spies."

After a moment of reflection Peter nodded, beginning to understand the great risk his uncle faced because of the accusations of treason.

"Well," Andrew said rising and going over to Peter and embracing him by the shoulders, "at least you are safely returned to England. Come, let's celebrate with my wife and your delightful Rose!"

As they headed to the doors, Peter halted. Then he turned to his uncle.

"I don't know if this helps. Or if it even makes sense. But my father shared something with me at the Jamestown settlement."

"I would be interested to hear."

"He told me that George Kendall had sought every opportunity to block any search for survivors of the missing Roanoke settlement while in Virginia."

"Did he say why?"

"My father had the notion that the Spanish were involved. That they had bribed the Indians to keep secret the fate of certain English settlers who were taken into captivity. Had something to do with strengthening Spain's claim as the first occupier of the New World territories. Does any of that make sense?"

Andrew pursed his lips as he analyzed what his nephew had just disclosed.

"Yes. I think it does," he replied. "George Kendall was clearly a Spanish spy. Doing the bidding of Spain in the New World. And he was corresponding with a very powerful person within the government of King James."

Then he looked over at Peter.

"If you want something to pray about, here it is: that I discover who that person is before it is too late."

"Too late?"

"Yes. Before the boots of the Tower guards begin kicking down my door."

Chapter 61

The next day Andrew rose early in the morning. He needed to spend time in prayer. He knew that unless he was able to reveal compelling proof to Robert Cecil of the identity of the actual Spanish spy, then he would be persecuted as a convenient scapegoat.

His prayer was for wisdom and not only to receive it in abundance, but for wisdom posthaste. The hour was late. He knew that unless he acted quickly, the full force of the English government would soon be mounted against him.

So Andrew quietly slipped out of their canopy bed, walked down the spiral staircase, and then walked outside into the gardens in the back of their house. It was cool. Summer was now past. Autumn was upon them.

Some of the plantings were dying and colorless. But the ivy, as ever, was still lush and green. And the rosebushes were unusually hardy that year. As a result of Andrew losing his income, they had dismissed most of the house staff, including the groundskeeper. So Kate had taken to tending the garden herself. She had kept it trimmed and healthy.

As Andrew paced among the winding brick walks and hedges,

he stopped at their bronze sundial, which rested on a stone column to the side of the walkway.

The early morning sun was casting a sharp, thin shadow across the face of the dial, which had a greenish patina from the seasons of rain, and humidity, and time.

For a moment, and out of nowhere, Andrew was overwhelmed by the turn of events in his life. The loss of his daughter. The death of his brother, yet the miraculous healing of the breach between them even though they were in two different lands separated by an ocean. Then there was his marriage to Kate, the greatest earthly blessing he had ever known.

And what of his work? It seemed equally full of both blooms and thorns. Of course he had garnered great opportunities in the service of the king of England. Yet now it all seemed to be on the precipice—ending in a growing atmosphere of disgrace and accusation.

His end, he knew all too well, could be on the rack in the dank, filthy confines of the Tower of London. When arrested, he would be taken, according to custom, by boat. With guards on either side of him, he would be rowed on a small flatboat through the metal grated entrance that led to the Traitor's Gate.

But to Andrew, despite the obscurity of how he might escape that fate, his choice, his inner resolve, was very clear.

For me, it is either faith or fear, he said to himself as he stood before the sundial. *Therefore, I will choose faith. I must believe that God is sovereign. And that His compassion is everlasting.*

Then another blessing came to his mind. And he knew he had to praise God for it.

Thank You, Lord, he prayed, *that my brother renewed his commitment to Your Son, Jesus, before he was ushered into Your presence.*

As Andrew glanced down again at the sundial, he noticed a web that had been intricately spun by some tiny creature. The spider was gone with the passing summer. But left behind was the lacy fabric, almost invisible, that stretched from the edge of the sundial down to the stone column.

It had survived the rainstorms and winds of the summer. In the center of the pattern of the web was an almost perfectly round space.

Andrew studied it for a second or two. All the thin connecting lines. But there was a center part of the design. Leading to all the other strands.

Now his mind wandered back to his dilemma. And the Spanish spy.

"What lies at the center of my spider's web?" he asked out loud. "Or better yet," he added, "*WHO* lies at the center?"

Just then he heard the ringing sound of dishes being carried. He turned around and saw Kate approaching him with a cup in each hand.

"Are you praying, dear? Or just talking to yourself?"

"A little of both, Kate."

He took the cup of coffee she had prepared and kissed her tenderly on the cheek. Then the two of them sat down on a wooden bench that was situated in the center of the garden.

"Can I help?" she asked.

"You, precious wife, have helped me more than you will ever know."

"I want to help more," she said. "Anything."

Then, after just a moment of silence she spoke up again to her husband.

"I am sorry to burden you further, Andrew. But we received a letter yesterday from St. Andrews. It was from Jean."

"Is it about Father?"

"He is now confined to bed. And seems to be growing weaker every day."

"I have to go to him, Kate."

"You can't, my dear. There is an edict, signed by the king, prohibiting you from leaving England. If you deliberately defy that order and travel to Scotland, it would be the end of you. But Jean wrote that your father is asking for some of his papers to be brought to him...I think you have them at your old office in Edinburgh. But how you will fetch them, I don't know. Perhaps I can travel myself to Edinburgh on your behalf—"

"I must put an end to all of this!" Andrew exclaimed. "The rumors. The suspicions. The accusations. Living this way, I am no good to you...and heaven knows I am doing no good for the work I believe God had called me to. I have to end this."

"How?'

"I must arrange a meeting with Robert Cecil."

"But he means to charge you with treason. You've said so yourself."

"Yet he also holds the keys to this entire matter. The king would take no action against me without his approval. Likewise, His Majesty will only arrest me upon Cecil's instigation. I must face him."

"But if he meets with you, what will you tell him?"

"I need to convince him that I know who the Spanish spy really is."

"But do you know that? I thought that is the very center of this all."

Kate was right. Andrew was missing the center. He glanced over at the spider's web that was billowing gently in the breeze.

Andrew took a sip of the coffee and then took a deep breath and exhaled slowly.

Where do I start? he wondered.

Then he answered his own internal question.

I start with what I know.

"What do I know for sure?" Andrew asked out loud. "I know that George Kendall was a Spanish sympathizer who was committing treason with an unidentified member of the government, someone called *Mister Panian Halfblood.* And that, for some reason, the name *Panian* is familiar."

Kate was studying her husband in between sips from her cup.

"*Panian.*" He spoke the word out again.

Then for the longest time he said nothing. Then his face came alive and his eyes widened.

"How could I be so dull!" he exclaimed. "*Panian.* Of course. All that is missing in that name is the *sigma* at the beginning."

"What do you mean?" Kate asked, trying to follow her husband's ramblings.

"The Greek letter, the *sigma*, the equivalent of the English letter 's.' If you add that to the beginning of the word *Panian* you get the English spelling of the Greek word—"

"What word?"

"Book of Romans. Chapter fifteen, I believe. It is the Greek word for 'Spain.' The apostle Paul is writing that he intends to travel to Spain. *Panian* is nothing but a reference to the Greek word for Spain."

Then Andrew grew quiet again.

"But where does that leave us?" he asked. "A reference to Spain.

But we already knew that. We know that the person Kendall was writing to was a Spanish spy, correct?"

"Yes, dear. That is what you told me."

"So how does my knowing that *Panian* is a reference to Spain lead me any closer to the identity of the spy himself?"

Kate had no answers. And neither had Andrew. Until he looked over again at the spider's web and thought over the full name of the mystery man to whom Kendall had addressed his letter.

Then Andrew jumped up so quickly that Kate nearly dropped her cup to the ground.

"What is it?" she asked, taken aback by the look on Andrew's face.

"My dear," he cried out with an expression of astonishment. "I am demanding a meeting with Robert Cecil! Immediately!"

"Yes, but how...what will you tell him?"

By then Andrew had already set his cup down on the bench and was running back to the house. He paused only when he came to the sundial and then stopped abruptly and pointed to it.

"I plan to tell him, dear wife, that sometimes a spider can become tangled in its own web!"

Chapter 62

When Robert Cecil, Earl of Salisbury, received the written request by Andrew Mackenzie, through his courier, for a private meeting "at your very first opportunity, as haste is of utmost necessity," he could only chortle at the audacity of the note.

Was a man whose arrest and torture were so imminent in any position to make any demands on the second most powerful man in the realm?

But as Cecil considered it at length, he had to smile to himself. On his desk was the completed arrest warrant with Mackenzie's name inserted. All it lacked was the king's signature.

There might be a wonderful reason to invite Mackenzie to the Palace of Whitehall, to Cecil's private chambers for a meeting. After all, why should he have to send out the Crown's guards to scour the countryside looking for Mackenzie once the warrant was signed? Cecil had concluded that Mackenzie would probably contemplate flight to the Continent once he learned of the warrant in any event.

Cecil concluded that bringing him to the castle would close the trap most effectively. The Tower guards would seize him on Cecil's command and take him to one of the upper rooms of the

Tower of London and be held there until the ink from the king's signature was dry. And then it would be down to the rackmaster for the Scottish theologian and lawyer.

Cecil sent back a quick note commanding Andrew to arrive at Whitehall "with utmost dispatch pursuant to your intriguing request" and named the exact hour of the following day for the meeting time.

Then he sent word for a contingent of Tower guards to arrive at his chambers at slightly after the appointed time, and then and there to seize Andrew Mackenzie on suspicion of high treason.

After thus setting the machinery of the state in motion, all there was left for the king's highest counselor and now Secretary of the Royal Treasury to do, was wait. King James was out fox-hunting until the next day and couldn't sign the warrant until his return. And even though he preferred sleeping in the oriental silk sheets of his own beloved palace at Theobalds rather than the drafty Palace at Whitehall, Robert Cecil still slumbered well that night.

For nothing gave him more tranquility than knowing it was he who controlled the chess game.

The following day Andrew Mackenzie presented himself on the very hour and minute of the arranged meeting. Cecil smiled broadly and limped over to the comfortable couch next to his writing desk, and pointing to it, bid Andrew to "be seated and rest yourself."

Andrew obliged and sat down. Cecil studied his face. There was a sense of calm in Andrew's demeanor that Cecil found truly intriguing.

Perhaps it is just the bliss of ignorance, Cecil thought to himself, *not knowing the depth of his trouble nor the height from which he is about to fall.*

There was no attempt at pleasantries. No courtesies. No idle banter.

Cecil got right to the point.

"Why are you here?"

"To warn you."

"*Warn me?*" Cecil exclaimed. His voice was tinged with incredulity.

"Exactly."

"Of what?"

"That you are undoubtedly considering me to be a proper and most convenient prey...in effect the fox, sir, for your royal hunt. I mean you no ill will, and will honor your titles and authority as the Bible instructs me to do. But if you come after me, then know you full well that it will be you who will end up playing the fox skin, yourself, on the floor of the king's castle. Keeping his feet warm in the coming winter. Or catching the dirt of his hunting boots—"

"That's no warning you give!" Cecil snapped. "Merely impertinence!"

"Would it be impertinent for me, then, to say I have discovered who the Spanish spy is whom you seek?"

"You mean to say," Cecil smirked, "that the spy who sits before me says he knows the spy?"

"No," Andrew shot back. "I mean to say that you are a skillful spinner of webs and intrigues, whose craft benefited Queen Elizabeth and has now well served His Majesty, King James..."

"Your flattery is wasted."

"Not flattery. Merely prelude."

"Prelude to what?"

"To the meaning of *Mister Panian Halfblood.*"

"So you know of the letter. Well done. What of it?"

"Have you discovered who this Mister Halfblood is?"

"Not yet. But I wager that is exactly what you will be telling us—as soon as you are securely tied to the rack."

"Indeed. I am here to tell you exactly that. Not because I was part of any conspiracy…just as my poor departed brother, Philip, was innocent of such entanglements as well. To the contrary, the pieces of this puzzle have fallen out for me, I believe, as a grace from God."

"It is odd," Cecil said sarcastically, "how God's grace is summoned up to cover a multitude of treasons. In your case, a Spanish treason against England."

"Do you really believe that a Protestant Scot such as myself would advance the cause of Catholic Spain against a king who has, until of late, chosen me to help administrate the translation of the Word of God? Does that make sense?"

"Treason rarely does—"

"There you are wrong. I believe you realize, with your skills at foreign intelligence, that treason begins in the heart. So the question is this: Who has a heart to betray England and serve Spain? We know that George Kendall did."

"You have developed the high art of belaboring the obvious. You grow tedious…"

But Andrew would not be waylaid, and he plowed ahead with his revelation.

"But who else had a heart for such treason? Someone, perhaps, who is exceedingly brilliant. I have found, frankly, that exceedingly smart men are those who are also exceedingly arrogant. Thinking that their intelligence alone will keep them safe. That they can lay codes and ciphers as a joke to themselves, with themselves, for themselves and their own amusement, but never believing that anyone else can ever detect it."

"I have no time for riddles," Cecil snapped back. He was listening carefully for the sound of the boots of the Tower guard. Was that a noise he heard?

"Then let me solve the riddle for you," Andrew bulleted back. "*Panian* is the Greek word, if we add the required letter *sigma* at the front, for *Spain*. Interesting that the word for Spain appears only once in the New Testament. In the book of Romans. Interesting also that a member of one of the translation committees, a former professor of divinity at Leyden, was an author of a commentary on the book of Romans. And would have been familiar with that Greek word."

"So you would indict a cleric as a traitor on the basis of his knowledge of the Greek language! Your rambles are absurd!"

"Not indicting him on that basis alone," Andrew quipped. "But on the basis of the pretty little moniker he adopted for himself. *Panian Halfblood.* Or perhaps we could simply translate it *Spanish halfblood.*"

Cecil's smirk was now a scowl. He was sensing the endgame for Andrew's discourse. And it was making him increasingly uncomfortable.

"Who do you know, who would qualify as a *Spanish halfblood* who also has been serving on a translation committee? Remember that, according to my own sources, the treasonous letters you intercepted on their way to the London office of the Spanish Ambassador, Don Alonso de Velasco, contained, among other disclosures, confidential information about the private proceedings of the Bible translation effort."

Cecil pursed his lips and would not say the name. So Andrew spoke it for him.

"*Hadrian à Saravia.* Half-Flemish and half-Spanish. Has he not often spoken that himself? Obviously making light of his Spanish lineage to waylay concerns about his loyalty, as a disguise for his treachery. I made inquiries yesterday, just to make sure. Saravia was often seen in the private company of Don Alonso de Velasco. But since the capture of his lemon-juice letters, they no longer meet."

After a moment of silence, Cecil finally spoke with an icy cold detachment.

"Perhaps, then, he will be joining you in the Tower—"

"I believe not," Andrew rejoined.

"And why not?"

"Because Saravia may be a spider in this conspiracy, but the web is not his…for there is yet another spider loose in this dark adventure."

Cecil did not want to dignify Andrew's exposition with his own inquiry. But he could not help from doing so. For Cecil's own sense of strategy and skilled gamesmanship, together with another, greater motivation, compelled him.

"Another?"

"Yes. Another. I looked at this tangled web and wondered what—who—was at the very center of it. Perhaps even mistakenly. Or even innocently. But there in the center he was. Clearly to be seen."

Down the hall there were footsteps. Was it the guard?

"Who?" Cecil asked in a husky whisper.

Then Andrew stared back, directly into the eyes of the second most powerful man in England, and spoke it.

"Why it is you, Robert Cecil, Lord of Salisbury, Secretary of the Treasury—it is you!"

Cecil jerked back in his chair. His mind was racing. But his lips were clenched shut.

"I realized it as I looked at the web you had spun. Your use of George Kendall as a foreign spy, only to learn, ultimately, that he was a double agent for Spain and against England, giving them confidential status reports on England's ventures in the New World. Which raises an intriguing question also—when much of England was demanding the search for survivors of the Roanoke settlement, only two persons I know of openly opposed such rescue efforts. George Kendall was one. And you were the other."

"I had sound reasons…" Cecil said nervously.

"Perhaps. But avoiding the rescue of those settlers arguably played into the hand of Spain, a nation that has advocated for years its first surviving settlement and therefore ownership of the whole of the New World."

"We have a peace treaty with Spain," Cecil muttered.

"Which everyone in the government knows is merely a respite, not a cure, for the hatred and envy that Spain holds against us. And moreover, part of your fortune was paid to you from Spain, in Spanish coin, for your efforts in settling England's treaty with them. Just another part of the web with Spain you have been caught up in. And then we come to Hadrian à Saravia."

At that point, Cecil had given up hope that Andrew had not fully discovered his connection there too. He sank back in his chair, his eyes dull, his eyelids half closed.

"Mister Saravia is a longtime friend of yours, and a longer-standing client of your family's sponsorships. When it is learned that he is the Spanish traitor in our midst and you avoided publicly suspecting him, I am afraid you will have much to answer for. I wish you well in that endeavor. But if I am racked, then all of what

I have just told you will have to be told by me to Lord Chief Justice Popham, among others. If not, then I shall have no intention of any embarrassment against you, sir."

After a moment, Cecil summoned his mental resolve.

"What is it that you are asking?"

Suddenly there was a loud knock on the outer door. Both men jumped.

The Chief of the Tower Guard announced himself on the other side of the door.

"I am asking," Andrew said, lowering his voice and speaking quickly, "that the orders against my foreign travel be withdrawn. That I be restored to my prior government appointments. And that no further action be taken against me regarding this accusation of Spanish treason."

Cecil was still considering the matter, head down, eyes focused on the pattern on the woven rug on the floor, when another knock came on the door, this one even louder. Then Cecil glanced over at the arrest warrant on his table.

After what seemed like an interminable wait, he looked over at Andrew. He said only one word.

"Granted."

Then he turned to the door and bid the Tower guard in. Five guards with spears and swords rushed in. But Cecil's raised hand stopped them.

To Cecil's surprise, Andrew rose and stepped over to his chair, looking down at him, and then spoke in only the most subtle whisper.

"And one more thing," Andrew said as the guards shifted nervously in their places. "You will never speak ill against my dead brother again."

Looking up at Andrew's granite resolve and then glancing over at the guards, Cecil spoke his last word to Andrew Mackenzie on the matter.

"Done."

Andrew bowed and then left the room, breathing freely only when he had passed by the guards and was out in the echoing stone walls of the outer corridors.

Inside his chambers, Cecil looked at the captain of the guard and smiled.

"Well done, men," he said nonchalantly. "This was but a drill. And you all commended yourselves brilliantly. You may go."

Chapter 63

Andrew rushed home to Kate, brimming with good news.

"God has shown us favor," he said to her on their doorstep and embraced her for the longest time.

Kate, ever the pragmatist, wondered whether Andrew could trust the word of Robert Cecil.

"I trust his actions more," Andrew said. "He had the Tower guards right there in the room with us. He could have held me indefinitely in the Tower if he had the least inclination to do so. But in the presence of the guards as witnesses, he let me pass by them unmolested. He has to know that if he were to change his mind and try to arrest me now, that it would be wondered why he failed to do so when he had the guards surrounding me in his own private chambers."

Clinging to Andrew with her arms wrapped around him, Kate felt a great weight lifted.

"Peace," she whispered. "I sense that the Lord is granting us a season of peace."

"Now that I am restored to my prior positions in the government," he said, "we can rehire our old household staff again."

Then he took the fingers of her hands, which had grown red

and chapped from assuming the duties of the house herself, and he kissed them.

"Our groundskeeper can now take over the gardens again," Andrew said with a smile.

"Perhaps not," Kate said wistfully. "I should like to continue some of the gardening. Particularly the roses. I feel that I have mastered them…as they have mastered me."

Andrew gave her a quizzical look.

"They have made me endure the thorns," Kate said, "so I can much more admire the blossoms."

Andrew would have preferred to linger, but the ill health of Ransom Mackenzie, his aged father, who had continued to deteriorate, compelled him northward now that the king's edict had been lifted.

He traveled to Edinburgh first and stopped at his old office on the Royal Mile, just a block from John Knox's house by the Toll Gate; the second-floor office was less than a half mile from the spot where his father, a close confidant of Knox's, had a fateful encounter with a Highland lass named Margaret, during the turbulent rule of Marie de Guise and her French cohort.

Andrew snatched the pile of his father's papers; some of them were title documents for various properties, but most of them journals and diaries he had kept during the rise of the Reformation in Scotland. Andrew thrust them all in a leather satchel and then obtained the fastest horse he could muster and rode hard to the northeast, toward St. Andrews.

He hoped to arrive there with enough time to explain much to his father: about the fate of his brother, Philip; of his spiritual reawakening near the end. But most of all, that the pledge had been kept. That the breach between Philip and Andrew had been healed.

When he arrived in St. Andrews, there was a mild breeze blowing. He tied off his horse to the post. Down the street, the bells of Trinity Church were chiming.

But Jean Mcleod was standing at the door when he ran up to the front steps. And she was weeping.

"Oh Andrew, laddie," she said, and then reached out to hug him. "He's passed, dear laddie. He's gone."

Stunned, Andrew ran up the stairs to his bedroom. The lace curtains were gently billowing. Ransom Mackenzie was lying on his back in bed, eyes shut, in absolute stillness. Andrew bent down and kissed his cold forehead. Then he sat on the chair next to his bed and remained there.

When Andrew finally made his way downstairs, Jean and her sister gave him something to warm him after his long, cold ride.

Andrew could not summon the power to talk, so he simply sipped his drink, trying to understand how he had gone so quickly from tragedy to triumph in London—now to suffer the loss of his father, and without a final goodbye.

Jean could see it in his face. So she did the talking for him.

"He was at peace at the end," she said. "With himself, and with God."

Then Jean added, "And he spoke of you."

Andrew turned to Jean. His eyes were filled with tears.

"What...did he say?"

"He said that he was glad that you and Philip had reconciled."

Andrew put his cup down and looked up at Jean with a bewildered expression.

"I...don't understand," he said. "I never told him. How did he know?"

"He said that it had to do with the nature of God."

"What did he mean by that, I wonder? Do you know?"

"He told me," Jean explained, "that if God is able to reconcile sinners to Himself, then surely He can reconcile two brothers with each other. He said he had an inner peace that it was so. It was the last thing we spoke of. I went downstairs to fetch more pillows for him. And when I came back up and reached his bedroom, he was gone."

Andrew put his face into his hands and wept. It was not for his father, for he knew with certainty that Ransom Mackenzie was, that day, strolling the streets of heaven, looking up his beloved wife, Margaret, and his mentor, John Knox, and George Wishart and the other great martyrs of the faith—whose bodies had been burned as sacrificial incense in the bloody beginnings of the Reformation.

It was not for Ransom Mackenzie. Rather, he was crying for the miracles of grace.

After his father's funeral, Andrew returned to London. But his visit to Edinburgh and St. Andrews had stirred something in him.

And it was even more confirmed when he had his conversation with Peter.

"I have asked Rose Heatherton to marry me," he said. "She has consented!"

Andrew was overjoyed. And Kate, of course, even more so. Andrew asked Peter about his future plans.

"I will continue to work at the surveying shop until I have saved enough money," he said.

"Enough for what?" Andrew asked.

"For study in divinity. I believe the Lord is calling me into His service."

Andrew smiled at that. And then he suggested that they talk further about the matter.

Andrew had been granted back his old positions in the English government, on Thomas Craig's committee for the union of the crowns, and the translation committee for the king's new Bible. Money was now no longer an issue for him. And as circumstances would have it, the Scottish Parliament, looking to the eventual union with England, had enlisted his assistance and hired him as an advisor. He was also soon offered a preaching position at St. Gile's Kirk near the Parliament building in Edinburgh.

And so he was beginning to feel the pull between those two cities of two nations—Edinburgh and London.

But he was also sensing the coming religious and political earthquake that threatened to split England and Scotland once again. King James was looking to his sons, Henry and Charles, as his rightful heirs to the monarchy. But those close to the Crown knew that the king's wife, a secret Catholic, had raised them adverse to Protestantism.

It was only a matter of time before the battle for faith would begin once again.

"Have you considered the divinity school in Edinburgh?" Andrew asked Peter one day. "It is close to work I could give you, as my clerk, to assist me while I am advising the Scottish Parliament. What do you say to that? You could earn enough, I would suspect, to support yourself and Rose and pay for your schooling as well. What about it?"

Peter's expression brightened.

"In truth, Uncle," he replied, "I had given some thought to returning to Scotland with Rose. Let me pray on it!"

In the coming months, Peter took his uncle up on his offer. And more and more, Andrew and Kate began to slowly relocate their lives from London to Edinburgh.

Andrew finished his work on the translation committee. In later years, when asked what he felt was his most important contribution, he would always say the same thing.

He would point them to the Gospel of Luke. In the prior translations, the Gospel quoted Christ at the Last Supper as saying, "This cup is the new covenant in My blood, which *shall for you be shed…*." Andrew humbly said that at his urging, the committee adopted the version that more accurately translated the Greek text: "…My blood which *is shed for you.*"

By moving the tense from future to present, the verse could now carry the full theological truth of the sacrifice of Christ on the cross.

Andrew would often say the same thing about that verse when he spoke of it publicly. Most who heard him speak in his sermons or speeches thought they knew the depth of his comments. But few really did—only his wife and close family, and a minister of the gospel who had ventured into the wilderness of the New World and befriended his brother, Philip Mackenzie—only they could have known the whole meaning.

"Through Christ," he would say, with a sense of remembering in his eyes as he spoke it, "the healing power of forgiveness—of divine reconciliation between God and man, and between man and man—is always in the present—a new miracle in the making for those who are so reconciled. Now isn't that a remarkable thing?"

Chapter 64

Throughout those exhausting, trying years—during Andrew's work at the Court of King James, through the perils of the Gunpowder Plot, the flight of Philip and Peter to the wild shores of the New World in Virginia, and then finally as Sir Robert Cecil raised up deadly suspicions against Andrew himself—Kate Mackenzie had often found herself yearning for a "season of peace," as she had called it.

In the end, her hopes and prayers were answered. Though, as is wont to happen, they were answered in ways much different than she could have imagined.

Andrew and Kate, soon followed by Peter and his new bride, Rose, relocated from London to Edinburgh, Scotland. After all, the city of London, Kate would sometimes remark, "had never been home to us—not a fire-in-the-hearth kind of home."

Though Andrew and his wife had enjoyed multiple fireplaces in their London mansion in Blackfriars and had used them often, somehow it was never like home.

It could never be like the fires that were to warm them in their large, new country house near Edinburgh.

When Andrew began what would be his last great position—counselor-at-large to the Scottish Parliament—the members who sought his advice would urge him to take up residence in the city, in the fashionable district near the palace of Holyrood House and the Royal Mile, and close to the Parliament building itself. That way he could be close to his work and the constant, contentious debates that raged in Parliament concerning the future of Scotland, the dark turn of events on the throne of England, and the dismal prospects for the continuation of the Reformation that Andrew's father, Ransom, had helped guide.

But Andrew would have none of it. He and Kate had experienced their fill of big city life.

"I have found a farm," Andrew would tell the members of Parliament in the noisy halls of the Parliament Building. "It is nestled in a glen, in the country, with a wee glimpse of the mountains beyond. And it is a truly bonny farm at that."

"*In the country?*" they would exclaim. "Why would you ever do such a thing, man? Don't you want to be close to civilization? Close to the work here?"

But Andrew could only smile. And when he did, it was usually because he was visualizing his dear Kate at their farm north of town. Perhaps, at that moment, she would be tending the sheep, or cattle, or flocks of geese and chickens they were raising. Or perhaps she would be taking time to sit down for tea with Rose, who, with her husband Peter, had settled into the vine-covered guesthouse on the back stretch of the property. Or maybe Kate would be cheerfully directing her maids in their chores in the great stone estate house where they now lived.

But whenever a smile and that peaceful look would slowly break over Andrew's face like a sunrise on the craggy ridges of the Highlands, only his nephew Peter—his constant assistant in his work at Parliament—knew what he was thinking about. Peter, while he was pursuing his masters of divinity, was good to his pledge that he would act as Andrew's apprentice. He had learned to understand his uncle well, and knew the smile meant that Uncle Andrew was meditating on the blessings of their country home, a place of peace and beauty. It was a sanctuary that Andrew chose to name *New World Farm*—so titled in honor of Peter's father, Philip, whose final resting place lay on the other side of the Atlantic, in faraway Virginia.

And so Kate's prayer for a season of peace had been granted, at least in part.

But even so, for Kate and Andrew, and Peter and Rose for that matter, life would eventually bring about another change. The crushing weight of events of state that would soon bear down on all of them again.

In the years that followed Andrew Mackenzie's secret triumph over Robert Cecil, the king's most powerful advisor began a slow, but still surprising, descent. Cecil's attempts to manage the unruly and increasingly bitter English Parliament failed. King James, who till then had always been enamored of his counselor, began to seek advice elsewhere, and finally turned from Cecil all together.

In the ensuing years, Robert Cecil fell ill and died amidst such acrimony that it shocked even his strongest opponents. In the end, strangled by his own intricate and complex web, he departed this life isolated and abandoned. As for Hadrian à Saravia, Cecil, for as long as he lived and served the king, limited the appointments of his former friend and kept him under constant surveillance.

But Saravia's treason against England was a secret Cecil took to his grave. Andrew Mackenzie and his family were the only other ones who ever knew the truth.

King James increasingly turned his attention to his two sons as the heirs to the throne, with a particular eye on his favorite, Henry. But within a few years after Cecil's demise, Prince Henry died suddenly of a fever. The carefully constructed and cloistered political plans of King James were quickly unraveling.

Soon James himself lay abed, melancholy and desperately ill. When he died, his younger son, Charles, was elevated to King of England. And just as courtwatchers had predicted, he soon began to push back Protestantism not only in England but also in Scotland, gradually but methodically. From his throne in England, he began to dictate the worship in all the churches in Scotland, requiring them to forsake the Reformation principles of their faith.

In the end, little was left of the reign of King James, save one thing—the King James Bible, which Andrew had helped to shape, and which, ironically, remained a burr in the saddle of his son Charles' Catholic rule. Though not truly original—much of the translation relied on the earlier Tyndale version—nevertheless, the King James Bible stood for one important thing: that the Crown of England, arguably the most powerful political entity in the known world, had officially sided with the distinctly Reformation idea that the Bible was not only the Word of God, but that it needed to be printed in the common language, and be read and believed by the common folk for themselves.

Just as Andrew Mackenzie had predicted, with the rise of King Charles, Scotland and England again became embroiled in a deathly struggle over the spiritual identity of their people. Even in Andrew and Kate's waning years, which were long and full of love for each other, the fires of revolution still reached their quiet farm in the glen. Despite their desire in old age to escape the pressures of national emergencies and simply be left to tincker about with their animals and fix a broken fence here or plant some vegetables there, they would not be left alone.

The Scottish Parliament—indeed all of Protestant Scotland—was sensing the coming of a new revolution for religious freedom—perhaps even the specter of war. Riders came to and from New World Farm on almost a daily basis, carrying inquiries to Andrew from Parliament on the tenuous relationship between Catholic King Charles of England and Protestant Scotland—two kingdoms that, ironically, had been joined in the "Union of Crowns" aided by the work of Andrew at the Court of King James.

Andrew tried to answer them all, but as he became advanced in age, he began to say explicitly that his days were numbered. In his correspondence to the Parliament he would often write that he had been honored to have served both his church and his nation simultaneously, as had his father Ransom before him.

"But the time will come," he would write, *"when my age and infirmity will prevent me from any further service to those causes—those of God and country—for which I have labored these many years."*

Finally, in one of his last letters to the Protestant leaders in Edinburgh—written with, to be sure, a great measure of pride and satisfaction that was shared also by his wife Kate—he declared,

...when that time comes, you will receive a final good bye from this loyal Mackenzie. And yet, do not feel on such an occasion that you will need to conduct some far-flung search for my replacement—for by God's divine provision there is, close at hand, yet another...

Chapter 65

**Thirty years after the
Mackenzies' return to Scotland
February 28, 1638**

People from all over Edinburgh were pouring into the kirkyard of the Greyfriars Church just to catch a glimpse of the ceremony taking place within; the huge sanctuary of the church was already filled to overflowing. There was a palpable energy in the air. The older attendees knew what it was. Scotland had been there before. On the eve of spiritual revolution. Nearly a hundred years before, the sparks of the Reformation in Scotland had first begun to ignite. By the last decades of the sixteenth century, it was sweeping the land from St. Andrews to Edinburgh. Now, the battle for the Bible, and for freedom of worship, was about to commence yet again.

As the Reverend Alexander Henderson rose to the pulpit with a document in his hand, the place exploded with "God be praised!" and "Hosanna!" from the crowd.

Henderson lifted his hands and quieted them. Then he spoke.

"This document, which I hold in my hand, is the National Covenant that was promised to you as faithful followers of the Lord Jesus Christ by the preachers of the gospel in this land. It was made necessary, not by the ill will of the Scottish people, whose only desire is to worship God according to His Holy Scriptures. No! It was rendered necessary by the cruel attempts of our present monarch, King Charles of England, to slowly but surely subvert our worship and move us toward the religion of the Papacy!"

Again, the congregation rose to its feet and clapped and shouted. Again, the preacher quieted the crowd.

"In a moment we shall commence putting our names to this document. As for me," Reverend Henderson said, "I shall be signing in my own blood—to let the king of England know by what price I am willing to protect the true gospel of Christ in Scotland!"

More shouts and hosannas rose up from the crowd.

"But before we commence with the signing," Henderson continued, "I bid you all to listen carefully to someone who will address you next. He labored long and hard with me, and with my spiritual partner, Lord Johnston of Wariston, to help draft this National Covenant, and to give sage advice in both its language and its sentiment. Please give ear to Reverend Peter Mackenzie."

Peter Mackenzie rose to the pulpit and quickly quieted the crowd. The years had added a few sags to his handsome face, but his frame was still fit, and his eyes flashed with a clarity of purpose.

He began by reminding the congregation of thousands that he was convinced the occasion should be a sober time of prayerful reflection and spiritual commitment to the lordship of Christ—as Scotland, once again, faced a national crisis.

"First I give you news," he said. "The Reverend Samuel Rutherford, who many of you know has been languishing in prison in Aberdeen for the 'crime' of promoting the Protestant gospel, has now been released. I am told he is on his way to this kirk forthwith, to join with you in a national resolve to preserve the true gospel of Christ in this land. His letters from prison and his work *Lex*

Rex—on the biblical basis for supremacy of law over rulers—have been an inspiration to us all."

Then Peter smiled and pointed to the document being held up by Reverend Henderson.

"As you sign this document you will note two things. First, that this covenant is not written on fine, English linen paper," he said. "To the contrary—it was written on the humble skin of an honest Scottish deer!"

Laughter swept over the congregation.

Then Peter became more serious.

"But the second thing you must know is no laughing matter."

The congregation was now all but silent.

"Whether you sign in black ink or red blood, you must know this...that the Crown of England may well exact your blood from you for signing, whether you wish it or no. You venture out, my Christian friends, onto a frontier of faith. I have been to such places. The frontier...the wilderness...wild forests and foreign shores... where your life hangs in the balance, and where courage is needed as much as fresh water or meat. Where loved ones die at your feet. And where God shows you how the power of the gospel can reach anyone—the civilized and the savage alike."

As Peter stood in the pulpit before the massive crowd, for just an instant he was transported back to his days as an adventurer with his father, Philip, in the New World.

He thought back to that moment when he sat on the sandy beach of Virginia clutching his Bible, still overwhelmed at his father's death. When he was suddenly aware of the presence of another. As he had turned, he had seen a young Indian princess standing near, and had proceeded with great effort to try to engage her in conversation.

Years later, Peter learned that this same princess, Pocahontas, had successfully pleaded for the life of John Smith after the rough, intrepid explorer was captured by her tribe and was being readied for execution. And that she would marry an Englishman named John Rolfe, a devout Christian, having expressed a desire to become knowledgeable in the doctrines of Christianity. Her conversion to Christ, and her later voyage to England to meet King James, caused a sensation, and the news reached all the way to the Highlands of Scotland.

Peter's wife, Rose, would often beam with pride and tell folks that her husband "first planted the goodly seeds of the Bible in the heart of the Indian princess Pocahontas," though Peter, ever modest, would try to brush it aside.

Yet ever so often, Peter's heart would be caught up in the full force of the extraordinary events that had brought him hence.

As he now looked out over the vast crowd in the sanctuary of Greyfriars Church, it was one of those times. For a moment he had to pause—he swallowed hard so as not to choke up with amazement, and trembling, and awe.

After gaining his composure, he went on.

Knowing as he did the turbulent uncertainties of the future and the troubles that lay ahead for his fellow Scots, he smiled and then encouraged all who were listening.

"As you go," he continued, "go with God. He is no stranger to civil strife. His sovereign hand is sure. And His heart is compassionate. He may take you to the borders of new frontiers. Of lands and experiences you thought impossible. Of struggles seemingly unconquerable. But oceans...and kingdoms...and struggles—they are as nothing to Him. What He desires most, my beloved friends, is to rule the kingdoms of your heart. Yield to Him that kingdom, and the throne of it, and then see what great things He shall do!"

After the signings were over and the vast multitude had dispersed, Reverend Henderson invited Peter to stay with him and his family for the night before he departed to his home.

Peter kindly thanked him, but said he must ride through the night back to Seacrest. There in the Scottish borderlands, overlooking the rolling sea, in the grand house he had managed to ransom from creditors, someone was waiting for him.

And so, against the chill of the February night, Peter would ride until daybreak. As he rode, he thought—about all the lives that had been lived—his, and those of his father, and his father before him—and the lessons they had learned. How even men of immense power and wealth, indeed even kings, can be held captive in the steely grip of fear, suspicion, or sin. But also how God plants in the soul of mankind the yearnings to be free, imparting the truest and surest of all liberty through the person of his Son, Jesus, the King of kings. And then leaves the human race free to choose.

Between fear and faith.

Sin and salvation.

Captivity and freedom.

Peter, after his exhausting ride, would ride up the lane that led to the house. The crashing of the waves would be heard from just over the ridge. At the door, his wife, Rose, would be waiting. Their three sons and their daughter, all married with children of their own, were to visit the very next day. But on the day of his arrival, he and Rose would be at home alone.

"Have you seen fit to find a better realm," Rose asked, "now that your National Covenant is signed?"

Peter stepped even closer, until his face was nearly touching hers. It was such a short distance that now lay between them. Barely a hair's breadth. Peter never took it for granted. He could still remember being separated from Rose once, by the breadth of an ocean, and the distance of different lands, and of faraway continents.

"A better realm?" he asked—and then smiled. "Indeed I have."

Then he wrapped his arms around her and held her tight.

"For such a realm, dear Rose," he said tenderly, "is now within my embrace."

About the Authors

Besides *Captives and Kings* and *Crown of Fire*, the first book in the Thistle and the Cross series, **Craig and Janet Parshall** have authored three books together, including *Traveling a Pilgrim's Path*.

Craig is Senior Vice President and General Counsel of the National Religious Broadcasters Association. He speaks nationally on legal and Christian worldview issues, is a magazine columnist, and has authored six legal-suspense novels: the five books in the Chambers of Justice series, and the stand-alone novel *Trial by Ordeal*.

Janet is the host of *Janet Parshall's America*—a nationally syndicated radio talk show originating in Washington, DC. An author and a cultural commentator in the national media, she is also a much sought-after speaker on biblical issues that impact the family and the church.

CROWN OF FIRE
Craig and Janet Parshall
Book 1 of the Thistle and the Cross series

"There are words in this land as
dangerous as black gunpowder."
— *St. Andrews, Scotland, 1546* —

Ransom Mackenzie's life is changed forever when he witnesses one of the Scottish Reformers being burnt at the stake. Soon the young man throws in his lot with the Protestant revolutionaries and John Knox, their spiritual leader.

His dreams of heroism end abruptly when the rebellion is crushed. His father is arrested for printing the Scriptures in the common tongue, and Ransom is forced to hide in the Scottish Highlands. There he meets and starts to fall in love with wild, lovely Margaret.

But his time away from the turmoil is not to last. Knox, facing powerful opposition, summons him to London. Enticed by the glittering surroundings of the Court—and the allure of a young woman of the aristocracy—Ransom finds himself at a crossroads...where a man can burn for his beliefs, and silence is betrayal.

TRIAL BY ORDEAL
Craig Parshall

Kevin Hastings is ready to stake out his piece of the good life.
The last thing he has in mind is a spot under the Chicago River...
courtesy of the local Mafia.

Pursuing a good real-estate investment, the young professor stumbles onto a prime chunk of property in downtown Chicago. It just has an old church building to be cleared away. But the dream deal turns into an ordeal when Kevin discovers he's signed a contract with the Mob—one he can't deliver on.

With death threats coming from the Mob boss and lawsuits piling up, the one bright spot is his new love interest, Tess... until he finds out she's a rabid architectural preservationist.

What else can go wrong? Don't ask. Kevin hires an attorney to untangle the mess, and the guy turns out to be a master of legal intimidation and dirty tricks. When he starts dispensing pain and chaos, Kevin has to run for his life. He ends up finding sanctuary at a local rescue mission.

The lawyers keep ringing the cash register while the bell tolls for Kevin—and he begins to wonder if there's Somebody who can bring justice into all the torment...

"An enjoyable romp for legal thriller aficionados."
PUBLISHERS WEEKLY MAGAZINE

Also by Craig Parshall
THE CHAMBERS OF JUSTICE SERIES

The Resurrection File

When Reverend Angus MacCameron asks attorney Will Chambers to defend him against accusations that could discredit the Gospels, Will's unbelieving heart says "run." But conspiracy and intrigue—and the presence of MacCameron's lovely and successful daughter, Fiona—draw him deep into the case...toward a destination he could never have imagined.

Custody of the State

Attorney Will Chambers reluctantly agrees to defend a young mother from Georgia and her farmer husband, suspected of committing the unthinkable against their own child. Encountering small-town secrets, big-time corruption, and a government system that's destroying the little family, Chambers himself is thrown into the custody of the state.

The Accused

Enjoying a Cancún honeymoon with his wife, Fiona, attorney Will Chambers is ambushed by two unexpected events: a terrorist kidnapping of a U.S. official...and the news that a link has been found to the previously unidentified murderer of Will's first wife. The kidnapping pulls him into the case of Marine colonel Caleb Marlowe. When treachery drags both Will and his client toward vengeance, they must ask—*Is forgiveness real?*

Missing Witness

A relaxing North Carolina vacation for attorney Will Chambers? Not likely. When Will investigates a local inheritance case, the long arm of the law reaches out of the distant past to cast a shadow over his client's life...and the life of his own family. As the attorney's legal battle uncovers corruption, piracy, the deadly grip of greed, and the haunting sins of a man's past, the true question must be faced—*Can a person ever really run away from God?*

The Last Judgment

A mysterious religious cult plans to spark an "Armageddon" in the Middle East. Suddenly, a huge explosion blasts the top of the Jerusalem Temple Mount into rubble, with hundreds of Muslim casualties. And attorney Will Chambers' client, Gilead Amahn, a convert to Christianity from Islam, becomes the prime suspect. In his harrowing pursuit of the truth, Will must face the greatest threat yet to his marriage, his family, and his faith, while cataclysmic events plunge the world closer to the Last Judgment.